Kate —

Gun of the Preacher's Son

May God bless you!
Larry W. Davis

* Please read back cover & "Preface" 1st

For additional free copies of this
novel, or for prayer, questions,
additional materials (Bible, DVDs, etc.),
please call me (Larry Davis) at:
(912) 346-2197 (can also text this #)

* Also, please read the enclosed
article I wrote :)

Gun of the Preacher's Son

Larry W. Davis

VANTAGE PRESS
New York

This is a work of fiction. Any similarity between the names and characters in this book and any real persons, living or dead, is purely coincidental.

FIRST EDITION

Copyright © 2008 by Larry W. Davis

Published by Vantage Press, Inc.
419 Park Ave. South, New York, NY 10016

Manufactured in the United States of America
ISBN: 978-0-533-15963-5

Library of Congress Catalog Card No.: 2007909651

0 9 8 7 6 5 4 3 2 1

In Loving Memory of My Mother,

Rena M. Davis

Contents

Preface   ix

1. Chasing a Dream   1
2. A Snare Is Set   9
3. Gentle Is the Word   15
4. Trouble Comes to Town   20
5. Beginning of the End   29
6. Up in Flames   38
7. No Looking Back   44
8. Badge of Honor   51
9. Pit of Darkness   59
10. Angel of Light   67
11. New Folks   75
12. A Beautiful Dream   81
13. Mixed Emotions   89
14. The Horror Revealed   100
15. The Wrong Words   110
16. The Lazarus Effect   119
17. Danger on the Trail   127
18. The Nature of Man   133
19. Intervention   145
20. The Purity of Compassion   154
21. Love's Revelation   161
22. More Trouble and Prayer   169
23. The Race Begins   174
24. The Heart to Win   178

25. Rachel's Victory   185
26. Dancing and Reflecting   190
27. Disturbing News   195
28. The Lockets   199
29. A Prayer Brings Hope   203
30. On the Trail Again   209
31. The Dream   212
32. Remembrance and Gratitude   217
33. The Visitor   222
34. Off to Jail   228
35. Telegraphs and Trails   232
36. Thoughts and Scriptures   237
37. Back to Jail   242
38. Waiting   250
39. Takin' 'em Down   253
40. Going Home   263

Preface

This book has been written with *much* prayer, asking the Heavenly Father to guide the pen of the writer by His Spirit.

It is written in the form of a novel, to be more easily read and accepted by those who don't yet know Jesus as Master of their lives. However, its pages contain *many* verses from God's Holy Word and *many* meditative thoughts, thus it will also bless and edify the hearts of those who already endeavor to walk in His footsteps.

There is no foul language, "off-color" remarks or innuendos included in the novel, thus, along with its main *spiritual objectives* it is also an excellent, *clean* alternate form of entertainment for most all ages. Chapter 5 contains a fairly graphic description of the aftermath of a violent incident. Therefore parental guidance is suggested for younger children.

The novel contains *heartbreak, intrigue, suspense* and *romance*, in order to appeal to the general masses. The *romance* is depicted in a pure and Godly fashion, the way the "Lord of all Creation" originally intended for a premarital love relationship between a man and a woman to be.

Its *main purpose*, however, is that the Father's *love* will touch the hearts of those who are bowed under the weight of *bitterness* and *resentment*. It is intended to bring inner healing to those who lack the ability to *forgive* others who have brought hurt into their hearts, therefore freeing them to *live* a life *dedicated* to and *consecrated* by *love*.

It is intended to *bring to light* the Glorious Gospel of our Lord, Jesus Christ and *to deal with some of life's most difficult questions.*

It is also designed to be a tool in the hands of those who already know Him, to set the captives free: Luke 4:18 (KJV), "The Spirit of the Lord is upon me, because He hath anointed me to *preach the gospel* to the poor; He hath sent me to *heal the brokenhearted,* to *preach deliverance* to the captives, and *recovering of sight* to the blind, to *set at liberty* them that are *bruised. . . .*"

It is intended to bring healing to those in whom the Lord sees as having a broken and contrite spirit and who hunger and thirst after righteousness: Mat. 5:6 (KJV) "Blessed are they which do hunger and thirst after righteousness: for they shall be filled."

The writer has had to both *forgive* much *and be forgiven* for much over the years. *Love* and *forgiveness* are the very essence of living a Godly, Christ centered life. Matthew 6:14 (Amplified Version), "For if *you forgive* people *their* trespasses [their reckless and wilful sins, leaving them, letting them go, and giving up *resentment*], your heavenly Father will also *forgive you.*". . . Matthew 22:35–38 (Amplified vs.), "And one of their number, a lawyer, asked Him a question to test Him. Teacher, which kind of commandment is great and important (the principal kind) in the Law? [Some commandments are light—which are heavy?] And He replied to him, You shall *love* the Lord your God with all your heart and with all your soul and with all your mind (intellect)." This is the great (*most important,* principal) and first commandment.

Mal. 4:2 (KJV) "But unto you that fear my name shall the Sun of righteousness arise with *healing* in His wings."

Gun of the Preacher's Son

1
Chasing a Dream

Alexander Barrington was usually up before daylight helping his father Dan with chores. But he had busted a new bronco yesterday and his body still ached in every conceivable place. He decided to sleep in a while.

Alex had grown up around horses and had been riding since he could barely walk. In his twenty-one years he had learned to understand horses better than any wrangler, bronc buster, or thoroughbred rancher around. He could see a horse and read him like a book.

His natural instincts and years of wisdom were gained from his father and every horse man he encountered.

So uncanny was his eye for good horseflesh that his father consulted him before buying a new breeding stallion or mare. The local Spanish folk called Alex "el Amansador," which is Spanish for "horse tamer."

As a result of Alex's expert eye, the Barringtons owned one of the best horse herds in Texas.

The horse Alex had saddle broke yesterday was no run of the mill mustang and part of a dream come true. She was the best mare in a harem of mustangs that was led by a stallion he had seen running like the wind across the plains. Alex had long watched the stallion leading his mustang harem with his telescope.

The mare had birthed a foal a few days earlier.

As for the stallion himself, even at a distance Alex could see the magnificence of this great horse. He had already named him Storm for his lightning quick turns, tremendous speed and the apparent stamina he possessed. Alex had determined he would catch this horse if it took him a whole year to do so.

In fact, it *had* taken him nearly six months to accomplish this task.

He, his father and a neighboring rancher named Buck, had fenced in a small box canyon. They had put a gate on it and camouflaged it with brush. Several times they had tried to herd Storm and his harem of six mares into the trap, but it seemed like Storm was reading their minds and would, at the last moment, abruptly change course and head off into the foothills. A couple of times they got close enough to have roped one of his mares.

Then, one evening as Alex sat on the front porch and pondered the situation, an idea came to him. He didn't know why he hadn't thought of it before.

The next morning he explained his plan to his father. They rode to Buck's ranch and informed him of the new strategy. Buck scratched his head and looked at the ground for a moment, then looked up with a grin on his face and said, "By Jiminy, Ah thinks it jus' might work!"

That afternoon they rode out to the box canyon with Buck, who drove a wagon loaded with hay, a water trough and a barrel of water. They put the hay and trough inside the enclosure, toward the back. They then filled the trough from the water barrel. The next day they rode out on the plains in the area of the canyon, to look for sign of Storm and his harem, but couldn't find hide nor hair of them. For the next week they rode out every couple of days, with no success. On their fourth trip out they finally saw the horses. They rode as quietly as possible, trying to get as close to the herd as they could before being noticed.

Fortunately they were upwind of the horses which meant Storm wouldn't smell them coming. Also, it just so happened that they came to a shallow arroyo that was running in that general direction and just deep enough to keep the mustangs from seeing them. When they got to the area closest to the horses, they quickly guided their mounts up the side of the escarpment and came up about fifty yards from Storm and his mares.

The chase was on! All three men were ready with lariats in hand. After about five minutes of riding all-out, they came within roping range of the closest mare. Alex, with deft precision, tossed his lariat over the head of the mare and Buck also found his mark.

With the lariats attached to their saddle horns, they slowly pulled the mare to a stop. They could see she was with foal, so they handled her as gently as possible. She was too winded to struggle much as they led her back to the box canyon. Once inside and with the gate closed, they took the ropes off her. She pranced around nervously, trying to find a way to escape.

Dan and Buck returned to the ranch and would no doubt talk about the day's adventure over one of his mother's fine meals. Lorena Barrington had a knack for cooking that was similar to Alex's ability with horses. He became hungry thinking of the delicious food he would miss tonight.

Alex took the saddle and bridle off of his own horse. After grooming her and allowing her time to eat hay and drink her fill, he put the saddle and bridle back on her and put her in with the mustang mare. He then tied a rope to the front of the gate and ran a second rope around a limb on the wall of the canyon, securing it to the back of the gate. The first rope would open the gate and the second would close it.

Taking the ends of these two ropes, he took his bed roll, canteen and hardtack, climbing to a ledge about twenty feet up the canyon wall to give him a visual vantage point. He had chosen the side of the canyon that was currently upwind of the direction Storm would probably approach from, looking for his lost mare. Alex hoped that two things would go in his favor; that the wind wouldn't shift directions and that clouds wouldn't come in and cover the moon, disabling him from seeing Storm and his harem coming. He had hobbled Storm's mare toward the back of the enclosure so she wouldn't be able to run out when he opened the gate for Storm. Alex felt something inside making him sense he was destined to catch Storm. He had feelings like that sometimes but didn't understand them.

Alex's father, besides being a rancher, was also a preacher. The whole family including his younger sister, Rebecca, now seventeen, rode to El Paso every Sunday. His father was the pastor of a church there. Its members consisted of about thirty adults and their children.

His father was not a loud and boisterous preacher. Instead, he spoke with a calmness and deliberation that somehow captured peoples' attention. Alex would often look around the congregation and notice that every person's eyes were fixed on Dan Barrington. He could see that they were absorbing every word as if they were listening to Moses or the great apostle Paul. His father was a soft-spoken, yet persuasive man, who engendered trust and respect.

He didn't dwell on hell-fire and damnation like many other preachers, but focused more on Jesus' words to, "Love God with all your heart and to love your neighbor as yourself." He said the Bible taught that this enabled a person to obey *all* the commandments. He spoke with the authority of a man who had lived through many trials, tribulations and temptations and had found victory in the face of these difficulties.

Alex knew that if he told his father about his intuitions, like the one he felt now about Storm, he would say something like, "Son, ya've got ta respect these inner feelins' an' allow tha possibility that they're from tha Lord, 'cause tha Good Book says that tha Spirit o' God speaks in a still, small voice on tha inside of us." Alex respected his father immensely, but he had a hard time believing that the Almighty would speak to him personally. And if He did, why would He speak to him about a horse? Would Storm someday save his life or something of that nature?

Alex looked up at the stars pondering these things. He didn't know much about his father's past. He'd assumed his father had always been a rancher, although it had seemed odd to Alex that the man he knew as a rancher and preacher never spoke of his life as a young man. It wasn't until about a year ago that he had, by chance, learned something about his father's past. He had just come out of the barber shop when he saw two strangers staring down the street in apparent amazement. He followed their gaze and saw his father entering a local mercantile.

One of the men said to the other, "Isn't that Dan Barrington who was a deputy sheriff in Tombstone?"

The other man said, "Why, Ah'm sure it's him, but Ah can't believe he's walkin' 'round town without a gun on his hip."

The first man said, "Yea, Ah remember seein' 'em in Tombstone go up ag'in four men. You'd a' thought his two Colts was a Gatlin' gun, tha way he sprayed lead inta those hombres."

The other replied, "Yea, Ah wonder what he's doin' here in El Paso?"

The first man then said with a tone of disbelief, "Wall, Ah heard he got religion or somethin' an' decided ta try an' send folks ta heaven 'stead o' hell."

After that encounter, Alex had often thought of the words of those strangers. He'd wanted to ask his father what had turned him around and put him on the "straight and narrow," but he figured if his father wanted him to know, he'd tell him in his own time. Alex wasn't the sort of man to pry into other's business. Not even his father's.

Once, just a few months ago, Alex and Dan had ridden from their ranch near El Paso to San Antonio to buy a prize Angus breeding bull. His father had wanted to increase the quality and quantity of their cattle herd. They not only bred horses on the ranch, but also were trying to build up a respectable herd of cattle. Most of their herd, until then, consisted of native long horn cattle which had been feral and unbranded mavericks that were rounded up from the chaparral.

On the trip back to the ranch, his father had shared some things about his past with him. They had been sitting around the campfire on their last night before arriving home. All that day Alex had noticed his father had been in a somber, almost brooding mood. It was as if he were wrestling with some tough decision.

That night around the campfire Dan Barrington had pulled out his harmonica and played a few lonesome type melodies that seemed to match the unusual mood from that day. Finally, he had put the harmonica back into the saddlebag which lay beside him. He still seemed to be wrestling with some important decision. He looked at Alex with a sort of sadness in his eyes. It seemed to Alex that he was seeing the ghosts of terrible times past in his father's eyes.

There was a painful sort of melancholy also distinguishable in his look.

He remembered his father had then said, "Ya know, Alex, if a man lives long enough . . . in constant company o' other men . . . who have mostly . . . evil on their brain, if yu're not careful, some o' tha . . . meanness can creep . . . inta yor own soul . . . ya can wind up doin' some things . . . that pains ya for tha rest o' your life. But if ya've got any good left in yor heart . . . after those things are said an' done . . . then ya start thinkin' how different . . . ya should o' acted at times. How, maybe it's possible . . . for ya ta turn some o' that bad aroun' an' even try ta make some restitution . . . for those dark moments in your life. Well, Ah've done plenty things tha wrong way . . . when Ah was younger. There's no need in me describin' all those things ta ya in detail. But, Ah've been thinkin' . . . maybe Ah can help . . . spare ya from makin' some o' tha same mistakes."

Alex had never seen his father struggle for words, like that night. Alex had wanted to tell his father that it would be okay to tell him some other time, to spare him from the obvious difficulty and pain he was enduring from remembering the un-named horrors from his past. But he sensed his father needed to speak some of it, to regain some semblance of peace in his soul.

Dan Barrington painfully continued saying, "Before ya were born . . . Ah was a violent man. Ah committed most o' this violence while upholdin' tha law . . . but killin' . . . no matter for what reason . . . takes somethin' outta ya' that ya jus' can't put back in. After each gunfight, yo're glad yo're still alive . . . but at tha same time, a piece o' somethin' inside ya dies, along with tha last bullet . . . ya sent through tha other man's body . . ." He held out both hands slightly trembling with emotion and said, "In these hands, Alex, lies tha power o' life an' death."

His father had reached behind him and pulled out his worn Bible saying, "In this book, also lies tha power o' life . . . an' death. Tha difference is that when ya use yor hands ta play judge an' jury, ya only spill tha blood o' one vile, corrupt an' perverted human. But when ya use God's weapon . . . tha Sword o' His Word, then tha only blood . . . necessary ta be shed, has already been shed centuries ago, by God's Son. It's much better ta use tha Sword o' tha Lord than tha gun o' man, ta do yor part . . . in stoppin' some o' tha evil in this world. Ah know Ah've taught ya how ta use a gun, 'cause Ah believe God allows us ta protect our loved ones . . . an' ya need ta carry a gun ta shoot snakes or any predator attackin' yor livestock. The reason Ah'm tellin' ya this, is so . . . ya'll have more understandin' . . . an' more wis-dom, than Ah did, when it . . . comes time for ya ta make im-portant decisions . . . in yor life, concernin' which o' these . . . two weapons ya have ta chose between, when tha time arises. Well, Ah think Ah've said all Ah need ta say . . . tonight son. Ah know ya don' fully understan' an' . . . fully comprehen' . . . some o' tha things Ah've told ya tonight. But, Ah believe Ah've given ya some food for thought, that may be . . . very important ta ya . . . sometime in tha future."

His father had then rolled over with his back to the fire, pulling his blanket around him. It had seemed as if he had sensed something foreboding in the near future. He didn't fully comprehend all of what he had just heard. He understood the *words*, but he didn't understand the *emotions* connected to them. Especially, what it was like to take another human being's life. He felt the same sense of destiny about capturing Storm that night.

His thoughts were interrupted when he suddenly heard a noise. At first he couldn't distinguish its source.

It continued to draw closer. Now Alex recognized the approaching sound of unshod horse's hooves.

2
A Snare Is Set

The moment Alex had waited for so long was finally very near. He pulled slowly on the rope that would open the gate. He desperately hoped it wouldn't make a noise that would alert Storm. Inch by inch, the gate swung until it was about half open, enough space to allow Storm to pass through it. By that time, sweat was dripping down Alex's forehead into his eyes from the nervous tension.

The sound of the approaching horses drew nearer. Alex was finally able to see the pale form of Storm approaching. Storm suddenly stopped and appeared to be listening more intensely. Then he whinnied. The mustang in the enclosure answered that call and Alex held his breath, hoping that his own mare would not answer as well, for that would alert Storm that something wasn't right. Thankfully, his mare was silent.

Storm continued to advance toward the gate, his ears perked and rotating to hear any sound that was out of place. Storm sniffed at the gate and Alex thought for a moment he wasn't going to enter. But after a few moments, he went through the gate and began to trot into the small box canyon. He seemed in a hurry to get his mare and leave. Now, Alex pulled the second rope quickly closing the gate. The other five mares, startled by the sudden movement and noise, began to panic. They were used to Storm always protecting and leading them.

Alex climbed down from the ledge and ran to quickly lean a log against the gate. This really unnerved Storm's other mares and they bolted into the darkness.

The log Alex had prepared was slanted on the end and designed to fit snugly into a notch on the top rail of the gate. He had also dug a shallow hole precisely where the back end of the pole would be, thus wedging the pole against the gate. Alex had made further preparation to secure the gate by placing another pole horizontally in front of it upon posts which were forked on the top. His father and Buck had dug deep holes and had tightly packed dirt around these making them as sturdy as any fence post could be. They had placed these extra posts for the support pole to make sure the gate was as strong as possible. They figured once Storm realized the fence and gate were too high to jump, he might try kicking his way out.

He did exactly that. He kicked three or four times. Again Alex waited anxiously, hoping the fence and gate would hold. Since they did indeed hold, Alex went into action with the next part of his plan. He climbed back up onto the ledge where he had previously been waiting, carrying two more lariats up with him. The ledge was right in line with the fence, and Alex could see both sides of it.

Once Alex was on the ledge, he readied the two lariats. He tied one end of each lariat securely around two different gnarly trees which protruded from the nearby rocks. He had previously checked each tree to make sure they were both strongly rooted and would support a lot of weight.

He watched Storm prancing in the moonlight around all sides of the enclosure, trying to find a way out. When Storm came within throwing distance, Alex tossed the looped end of one of the lariats over the stallion's head. Storm immediately began to rear up and pull against the rope. Now Alex picked up the business end of the second lariat. Again, he waited for the right moment and dropped the second lariat over Storm's head.

Storm reared twice after that, but began to settle down some and realized he had lost the battle at least for now.

Alex began talking softly to Storm, to let him get used to the sound of his voice. He pawed at the ground and snorted, but after half an hour or so, he stood still and perked up his ears, as if trying to figure out if Alex was friend or foe. Whatever his former encounters with man were, he seemed to sense that Alex was somehow different from the others. Alex continued to talk in his soothing manner.

It was still several hours until dawn, so Alex ate some of the hard tack and quenched his thirst from his canteen. He spread out his bedroll, having to move some rocks and pebbles out of the way. His bed would certainly be hard, but Alex was so exhausted that he soon fell asleep.

He awakened as the sun began its daily ascent into the sky. He glanced down at Storm, who he discovered was placidly nibbling at a bush. He looked up at Alex and snorted. This was Alex's first up-close look at the stallion in daylight. He looked even more magnificent up close and Alex had never seen a horse quite like him.

He appeared to be a cross between a quarter horse and a thoroughbred. He surely didn't fit the standard for a wild mustang. He was definitely a hot-blooded horse. He was taller and longer legged than a mustang or quarter horse. He appeared to be about seventeen hands high at the withers and was perfectly proportioned. He was well-muscled with a broad chest showing that he had large lungs made for endurance. He had a deep girth, sloping croup and extremely muscular haunches which would give him jumping and running power and a quick start. His forelegs were also heavily muscled above the knees. He had a heavy crested neck, wide set eyes and a very handsome, intelligent-looking head. He was all gray with black mane and tail. He had a black star on his forehead.

How could such a fine horse end up running wild? Without checking the number or the wear on his teeth, Alex estimated he was about five or six years old. A horse is fully grown at five years old, but isn't fully mature until seven. There was no visible brand on him. Had he somehow strayed as a yearling or colt? Maybe he'd had a cruel owner or trainer and ran to answer the "call of the wild," putting distance between himself and humans. Alex was perplexed and couldn't think of a proper scenario.

He began talking to Storm in a soothing tone. He'd always had an innate ability to gain a horse's trust. He hoped this ability would work with Storm also.

About an hour later, Alex could see Buck and his father riding up. He could spot his father's riding posture from a good distance. He knew they were anxious to find out if the plan had worked. Alex would be very pleased to see the expression on their faces when they arrived and found out the plan had indeed worked. Dan Barrington would be glad that Alex had captured a superb mount and he also knew Storm would probably be the best breeding stallion in the whole territory.

When Dan and Buck saw that the gate was closed with support poles in place, Alex saw the grin of excitement light up their faces. He motioned for them to climb up to the ledge where he was. When they got up to the ledge and had their first close view of Storm, the expression of excitement on their faces was joined by a look of amazement and awe.

No one spoke for about a minute, then Dan clapped Alex on the shoulder and said, "Great job son." Alex felt very proud at that moment and said, "It was sure worth all tha work. He's such a great specimen o' tha Lord's handiwork that Ah feel like he should belong ta a King 'stead of a common person like me."

His father said, "Nonsense. Tha Good Book says that a laborer is worthy of his efforts. Ya've earned yor right ta this horse, Alex."

12

Dan and Buck climbed down from the ledge to get their lariats. Alex waited until they were positioned in front of the gate before he loosened the lariats from the trees. He then told his father he was going to climb down the ledge to the inside of the enclosure.

Dan said, "Ya be real careful, son. Ya don't know what this horse is goin' ta do when he finds out tha lariats are loose. Buck, stay here at tha gate. Ah'm goin' ta get on my horse in case Ah need ta charge in there ta protect Alex."

Buck said, "Sure," and then called to Alex asking him to let him know when he had the lariats in hand again and was ready for him to open the gate.

A few moments later Alex said, "Okay. Open 'er up." Buck removed the poles and pulled the gate open. He entered on foot, while Dan rode his horse into the enclosure. When they got inside they saw Alex holding both lariats and heard him speaking to Storm in his calm, gentle manner.

When Storm saw the other men, he shied away from the direction of their approach. He snorted and pawed at the ground a few times. Alex continued to calm the stallion with his voice. When Dan got close enough, he tossed his lariat over Storm's head. Storm then reared once and began to pull against this new and unwelcome obstacle. He pulled against Dan's lariat but it was secured to his saddle horn. Alex continued to ease Storm gently. After a few more moments of struggle, Storm began to calm down.

Buck went back into the canyon and got Alex's mare. Slowly, Buck led her to Alex. Alex then mounted her and secured one of his lariats to the saddle horn. While Alex and Dan waited, Buck went out and mounted his own horse and rode slowly back inside. He rode to the back and took the hobble off the other mustang and she immediately trotted nervously to the opposite side of the canyon about forty feet away. Buck then rode back to Alex and took the third lariat, securing it to his own saddle horn.

Buck asked, "What ya' think we ought ta' do with tha broomtail there?" He was referring to the mustang mare.

Alex said, "Ah think we ought ta let *her* figure that one out on her own. She might even follow a distance behind Storm an' come right on ta tha ranch with us."

So, once they were outside the gate, the three started toward the ranch. Alex was in the front leading Storm, while Dan and Buck flanked the left and right. Alex only allowed Storm about fifteen feet of slack. He continued to talk soothingly to the stallion.

After a few minutes Alex looked back and sure enough, the mustang mare was following about seventy-five to a hundred feet behind them.

He'd thought to himself, "Looks like we got three for tha price o' one. Storm, tha mare an' tha unborn foal she's carryin'. With Storm as sire, tha foal is sure ta be a fine horse as well."

It was this mare, the strongest and finest of Storm's harem, that Alex had saddle broke the previous day.

3
Gentle Is the Word

Once back at the ranch, Storm was placed in a corral with his mare that *had*, in fact, followed them back to the ranch. For the next several days, Alex spent three to four hours a day at the corral to allow Storm to become familiar with him so he would gain the stallion's trust.

Alex knew some horses needed the bronc busting approach but he intuitively understood that Storm should be "gentle" broke. He knew that sometimes, when a horse is ridden to submission, he could be a good standard saddle horse and good for a remuda, but his spirit is often broken in the process. Alex certainly wanted Storm to remain spirited. A spirited horse is only able to be ridden and controlled by one person, but their loyalty and devotion to that one person far exceeds that of a common saddle horse. To bronc bust Storm would also almost certainly lead to sprains and possible broken bones for Alex. Storm was far from the ordinary broomtail stallion.

He possessed tremendous strength, both of muscle and of self-will.

After three days of Alex calming Storm in his soothing, placid manner, the stallion began to approach closer and closer to the corral fence. By the fourth day, Alex was able to get Storm to eat sweet feed right out of his hand.

By the end of the week, Alex felt it was time for him to enter the corral to give Storm his now routine hand feeding. Even though Alex had a special way with horses, he was amazed at how quickly a horse such as Storm had adjusted to his presence. The rapport between him and Storm was growing into genuine affection. Alex could sense a bond forming between them. A stronger bond than he had with any other horse. He continued to believe that for some reason, destiny had brought the two of them together.

Alex's father had been handling most of the ranch chores by himself this week, knowing how important it was for Alex to spend time with Storm. Now that the bond was established, Alex knew that he needed to get back to handling his share of the ranch work. He could still spend time with Storm in the evenings.

It was almost time for supper when Alex finished mucking the stalls and pitching fresh hay down from the barn loft into the feeding troughs. He headed for the back porch, where the wash stand was, so he could clean up. He could smell the mouth-watering odor of fried chicken and fresh baked biscuits through the kitchen window. This made him eager to sit down at the table to dig in.

Alex was really hungry and nobody he knew could fry chicken like his mom. Alex and Dan always kept a clean shirt, hanging on a peg by the wash stand. Lorena Barrington could never cotton to anyone sitting down at her table wearing a shirt that had been near horse or cow manure.

In a crowd, you'd hardly notice Alex. At first glance there was nothing striking about his appearance. Only when you watched him, were you aware of the smooth way he moved like a mountain lion. There was nothing out of the ordinary about his physical stature that the casual observer would notice. But, to see him now at the wash basin with his shirt off, you would certainly notice that the good Lord took special care when putting Alex together.

Every part of his body was harmoniously synchronized, much like a finely crafted Swiss watch. To see him bare from the waist up was amazing, for he looked ordinary with shirt on. *Beneath* the garment were ripples and hard bulges of muscle that were joined by sinewy cords. One could sense the tremendous strength and agility packaged neatly on his torso. Part of his physical prowess was inherited, but much of it he had earned by hard physical labor on the ranch. He never shunned work, but seemed to revel in it.

His family hired line riders annually who drifted from ranch to ranch seeking jobs. A while ago, a former professional prizefighter turned cowpoke, who everyone knew only as Julius, had spent a whole year on the ranch. Alex was fascinated when the ranch hands had asked Julius about prizefighting. Alex wanted to know about the techniques and training a pugilist practiced. When he expressed his interest in this sport, Julius was pleased and began to work with Alex in his spare time.

Julius was amazed with the enormous speed, agility, power and reflexes Alex displayed. Julius had made a heavy bag from a burlap sack filled with a mixture of hay and sand. This was hung in the barn from support beams. He had covered the bag with softer material, to protect Alex's hands from abrasion by the coarse burlap. Alex also wrapped his hands with cloth before working out with the bag.

Julius taught Alex the various aspects of prizefighting in stages. First he showed Alex that learning his center of balance was of utmost importance. That if you are not always balanced and did not keep solid footing, an opponent could easily take advantage and close with an attack. This would be very difficult to defend against or to counterattack.

Julius then taught Alex the essentials of footwork. That to keep moving while he maintained his center of balance made him a very difficult target. Alex also learned various kinds of punches. The jab, the upper cut, the left and right hook, etc. He learned how to block and counterpunch, how to set up combination punches and how to feign with one hand, while throwing a punch with the other. He learned how to put his weight into a punch and that the most effective punch was short and straight.

He learned things to avoid, like haymakers or roundhouse punches, which take far too long to reach the target and leave you off-balance. They also lack the added advantage of your body weight behind the punch. Without the body weight, a punch lacks most of its potential power.

Julius had spent a couple of years in Québec, Canada, where he had learned Savate, the art of French foot fighting. He shared his knowledge of this with Alex also. Julius taught Alex how to street fight as well, since most fights were not fought in a ring with a set of rules to go by.

Alex learned how to use his elbows, knees, forearms and head for close-in fighting. He learned the most vulnerable areas of the body: the solar plexus, kidneys, groin, throat and the ribs. Julius stressed to Alex many times that this kind of fighting should only be used if he was forced into a street fight with a huge, powerful opponent or outnumbered by more than one attacker.

Alex didn't desire to use his skills with a gun, learned from his father, or with his fists, learned from Julius, to hurt anyone. He enjoyed the challenge of learning and becoming proficient at things he set his mind to do, whether it was roping cattle, training horses, nurturing a herd of livestock or plowing a field. Alex was the type of man that put all his effort into whatever he did. He wasn't satisfied with anything else. He loved the feeling of satisfaction when he mastered things that were challenging and difficult to accomplish.

Vain pride was not his motivation. What he did, he did with the motivation to learn practical things that he may need to know in the future. Alex realized, however, that some of life's lessons can only be learned by working through situations as they arose in the day-to-day, unpredictable events of life. Some things can't be foreseen and have to be dealt with as they occur. Alex was soon to face one of those unexpected events that would change his entire life.

The kind of thing that no one can ever be fully prepared for.

4

Trouble Comes to Town

Today began like most other Sunday mornings for the Barrington family. Alex awoke just before dawn, when the first rooster crowed. He got up and lit the lantern, which shared space on the small table with his washbasin and pitcher of water.

He could hear his mother and seventeen-year-old sister, Rebecca, rustling around in the kitchen. The smell of Mesquite wood burning in the stove mingled with the inviting aroma of biscuits, bacon, eggs and coffee, all blended together to extend a warm, beckoning call to Alex. He loved the close ties that his family shared.

Sunday morning was Alex's favorite day of the week. He never figured out how his mother and sister were always able to wake up *before* the first rooster crowed. He figured it must be something the good Lord had just gifted women with. There was somewhat of a ritual the Barringtons followed on Sunday mornings which was a bit different than the other days of the week.

Alex and his family always made sure that the major chores were complete by dusk on Saturday, so there would only be the most essential chores left to be done on Sunday morning. Things like milking their two jersey cows and gathering any remaining eggs from the chicken coop.

He and his father would take care of these minor chores, while his mother and Rebecca finished getting breakfast ready. After breakfast, they would hitch up the wagon and ride into town for church services, about a three mile ride each way. Lorena and Rebecca always packed a basket of food to take to town on Sundays.

There was usually chicken or smoked ham which they had cured themselves in their smokehouse. Also there were biscuits and sometimes a pie, when they were able to buy tins of cherries, peaches or apples to make one with. When in season, they would take freshly grown vegetables from their garden.

About once a month or so, each family coming to church would *also* bring a basket lunch. After the service, weather permitting, they would have a potluck dinner outside. This happened to be one of those Sundays, when a potluck dinner had been planned. Alex always enjoyed those dinners, after which the younger children would play together until mid-afternoon.

The women would get together in a group to chat. If it wasn't raining, the men and older boys would congregate under an old cottonwood tree and talk about the Bible, politics, farming and ranching. Alex was pretty much the quiet type and would rarely join in the conversation, but would listen instead, soaking up the information shared. He learned a lot about the world, Bible doctrine, politics and the like, from these discussions.

There were several families who had moved to America from Germany, Ireland and Scotland, so Alex was able to learn something about these places from the vivid descriptions of them. They'd tell of the good and bad of things of their motherland. Now, they all considered themselves to be Americans, but you could hear in their voices, at times, a bit of homesickness.

All had come with a bit higher expectation about North America than reality could actually offer them. Nevertheless, each one would make it known that though conditions of life on the frontier were harsher than they had anticipated, the freedom they had to go where they wanted and claim a section of land as homesteaders outweighted the hardships. Alex learned that the progress, growth and enhancement of a nation could not be realized without those who are willing to take risks.

Many a pioneer and homestead family had suffered the loss of a family member. At times a whole family would succumb to an Indian attack, flu epidemic or one of the many other hazards of settling a frontier. The way this was described by some, though, made it seem worthwhile. Alex sometimes thought to himself, that each *headstone* could be looked at as a *milestone* of civilization.

This thought returned to him during the dinner which followed today's service. Little did he realize, however, how deeply this sentiment would be challenged before the week was over.

The sermon Dan Barrington had given this morning was a masterpiece on forgiveness. He used two passages in the New Testament which are the epitome of forgiveness. He spoke of Jesus, who after being tortured, beaten, crowned with thorns and finally nailed to the cross, had asked the Father to forgive his assailants, for as He'd put it, "They know not what they do."

He also spoke of Stephen, who, while being stoned to death, had uttered the same words because the same Holy Spirit that dwelt in Jesus, can and will also dwell in anyone who would repent of sin and ask Him into their hearts. Dan Barrington had spoken on several occasions about this topic, but this morning's message seemed to bear some special significance to Alex. He felt that the revelation it held was written indelibly upon his heart, as if the finger of God himself had inscribed it there.

Once again, Alex felt that peculiar sense of destiny, like he'd felt only a few times in his life. The last time being when he had captured Storm and here again with words quoted directly from the Scriptures.

Today, the men's gathering after the worship service was dominated by deep discussions regarding the morning message. Alex had passed by the group of women on his way to get more coffee. He noticed that they, too, seemed unusually captivated and moved by this truth from the Holy Scriptures. They were in a deep contemplative conversation about it also.

For some reason, when Alex heard parts of this discussion, the hairs on the back of his neck stood up on several occasions. He pondered whether or not God was behind this strongest sense of destiny Alex had ever felt. Surely that was possible. Alex just didn't understand the reason for this deep, unusual stirring of his heart and soul.

Alex knew well that the heart, a person's spirit, is a specific part of man that has the ability to speak to and hear from God's Spirit. The soul, on the other hand, is the center of man's emotions and reasoning. The Bible says that the carnal, unregenerate *soul* is the natural mind. It is the enemy of God and indeed, *cannot* understand the things of God. Man's *spirit*, however, *can* understand and accept, by faith, things that our minds would *naturally* reject. Alex knew this truth was set forth in John 8:1–8.

Although unaware of it at the time, the words of this message would have great reason to return frequently to Alex's mind and spirit in the coming weeks and months.

Today's dinner ended with a rather solemn, thoughtful expression evident on the faces of each adult who had been in the church service this morning. Only the younger children seemed oblivious to the preoccupied thoughts of their parents. It was late afternoon when the social visiting came to an end.

A portion of the church families' homes was a good distance from town. Many folk lived much farther out than the Barringtons. Some had what were called "Sunday Houses" in or near town. These were usually small, two room dwellings. Families living too remotely to make the commute to and from town in one day would leave their farms or ranches on Saturday morning. They would journey to town, taking care of shopping and business, spending Saturday night in their "Sunday House."

They would then attend church on Sunday morning before returning home. Being now late afternoon, it was time for folks not living in town to begin their journey home.

Today Alex's family followed Randall Blake, a member of the church who also owned a local mercantile store, which he opened especially for them since the store was closed on Sundays.

After retrieving packages Randle had ready for the Barringtons, Alex and Rebecca walked behind their parents, lagging a bit to look in the windows of some of the other shops.

Although many businesses closed on Sunday, unfortunately, this was not true of a couple of saloons in town. As they were walking back toward the church, where their horse and buggy awaited, Alex noticed two rough-looking hombres who were obviously under the influence of drinks recently poured down their gullet.

Alex had seen men in this condition numerous times, but had never encountered any real problems with them. This time, however, it seemed that one of the men had fixed his gaze on Lorena Barrington.

Alex noticed the man seemed to be intentionally blocking his mother from proceeding down the wooden sidewalk. He saw the half-drunk man speak words to his mother. He then noticed his father, whose face had suddenly taken on a stern and angry look. This was a degree of anger he had never witnessed in his father before.

Alex and Rebecca stood there kind of dumbfounded, watching, not understanding exactly what was going on. They were just far enough from the exchange of words to catch only a part of the conversation. Alex saw with horror the man reach for the gun strapped low on his right hip. Of course Dan Barrington was unarmed, so he did the only thing he *could* do. His left hand moved with great speed as he took a quick step, closing the gap between himself and his would-be assailant.

His left hand trapped the right gun hand of the other man before the attacker could clear leather. By this time, Alex was running up with the intention to assist his father, because he didn't know what this skunk's partner might do.

As he approached he saw Dan Barrington's right hand move up, grabbing the aggressor's throat. Dan, with his great strength, lifted the man up against the wall of one of the shops, until the man was barely able to stand on his tiptoes. His face first turned bright red and then began to take on an ashen, pale look. Alex was sure his father would either snap the man's neck or strangle him to death. Alex couldn't really intervene in his father's situation. He was keeping an eye on the other man, who was watching with a stare that expressed equal parts of disbelief and a look of enjoyment.

Alex kept one of his hands behind his back, to give the second man the idea that he may, in fact, have his hand on a gun stuck in the back of his belt.

If the second man had any intention of joining in the fracas he was evidently wary of Alex, so he just stood his ground. About the time when Alex was sure the eyeballs of the man his father had against the wall would pop out of his head, Dan suddenly released his grip on the man's throat. He pulled the gun out of his holster and tossed it far out into the dusty street.

He then grabbed the man by his belt and shirt collar and slung him, what seemed to Alex to be a full ten to fifteen feet into the street. He landed on his back and appeared to have the breath knocked out of him. As he struggled to distance himself from Dan, he began to crawl quickly backward. He was facing upward, but crawling backward on his hands and feet. Had the circumstances been different, the man's look and his actions would have been humorous.

It was about this time that Justin Martin, the town marshal, came trotting toward the scene. Evidently, someone witnessing the conflict had hurried to the marshal's house to inform him what was happening.

When the marshal arrived, the perpetrator was being helped to his feet by his compadre. After hearing a very brief account of what had occurred, marshal Martin took the attacker by the arm and began leading him to the calaboose. Dan Barrington, by this time, had retrieved the man's gun from the dusty street and had tucked it into his waistband. Dan was keeping a wary eye on the assailant's partner.

Now, the man's demeanor had changed. He no longer had an amused look on his face, but instead, a look of malice with a hint of what appeared to be embarrassment. He seemed to be conflicted as to what he should do.

Alex knew that both men were gunfighters by the way they strapped their irons low on their legs, common among those who live by the gun. They were probably either hired gunmen or outlaws. Marshal Martin motioned for the Barringtons to follow him to the jail.

Dan Barrington had already started in that direction, but had paused to make sure the rest of the family was following. He had no intentions of leaving them in harm's way with the other man still standing there with mounting anger in his eyes. His fingers were twitching, as if he were contemplating whether or not to go for his gun. The marshal and Dan were keeping an eye on the second man as Alex, his mother and Rebecca joined them. Then they proceeded to the jail.

After locking the offender in one of three jail cells, the marshal closed the door which led to the cell area and returned to the outer office area. He asked Dan and Alex to step outside with him so he could have a word with them.

Once outside, Justin hitched up his gun belt a bit and spat tobacco juice into the street. Justin Martin, usually a jovial and pleasant fellow until someone got his dander up, looked at Dan and Alex with a dead serious look.

His eyes wandered down the street to where the arrested man's friend had been standing. He was no longer anywhere in sight. Justin fixed his gaze on his friends. He hesitated a moment before speaking and you could tell that it wasn't exactly good news he had on his mind.

"Dan . . . Alex . . ." he began uneasily. "Ah won't ya ta be on guard at all times for a while. Ya need ta carry a weapon wherever ya go. This here hombre we jus' threw in tha clinker seems a pretty good match for tha description o' Sanchez. No one knows his firs' name, o' for sure that Sanchez is his birth name either. He heads a gang o' real bad hombres. S'posedly, he an' his cronies are responsible for several bank robberies, tha las' one bein' in Tucson."

He took some more thought and then said, "Ah'll have ta send a wire ta tha sheriff there an' see if he has a drawin' o' this here feller. Ah do know that Sanchez is s'posed ta have a scar runnin' from his left ear, up to'ard tha corner o' his left eye, jus' like this here feller has."

Martin looked around for a moment with concern evident on his face and then continued, "He's s'posed ta have 'bout five or six men that ride with 'em. What we've got on 'em here, won't allow me ta hold 'em long. 'Less Ah kin get some proof o' who he is a 'forehand, Ah'll have ta cut 'em loose, like it or not. Sanchez is a cold-blooded killer an' tha 'sorted bunch he has with 'em seem ta be pretty much like 'em."

The marshal spat again into the dusty street and continued, "He's 'sposed ta be a half breed an' hates all full blood North 'Mericans for some reason. Rumor has it that his Pa was a North 'Merican an' mean as a snake. S'posedly he beat Sanchez an' his ma on a regular basis an' wound up killin' Sanchez's ma. Guess that's probably why he hates North 'Mericans so much. They say he wasn't 'cepted by his Mexican kin folk either, 'cause they figured he'd be jus' like his Pa. Anyways, whatever made 'em mean, made 'em real dangerous an' he's s'posed ta be fast, accurate an' deadly with a gun." Marshal Martin scratched his chin contemplatively before continuing.

"Wul, that's 'bout all Ah kin tell ya for now, but jus' 'member ta watch yor back. Ah'll let ya know anythin' Ah find out."

Dan said, in return, "Justin, ya know Ah swore off tha violence an' don't carry a gun anymore, but Ah'll keep my eyes open, best Ah can. Ah'll try ta ride back ta town an' check ta see what ya've found out 'bout these men, in a couple o' days or so. How long can ya hold 'em in that cell?"

Justin responded, "Only a day o' two, for disturbin' tha peace. If he'd o' been able ta clear leather an' get off a shot at ya, Ah could'a held 'em 'till that circuit judge gets here. 'Course, if he *had* been able ta get off a shot, he jus' might o' put a hole in ya. Ah shor wouldn't a wanted that! Ah'm 'fraid my hands are pretty much tied 'less Ah kin git some proof o' who he is by tomorra'. Ah, don't see any possible way Ah kin get a picture of 'em that quickly. One thing Ah kin do is ta wire some other towns 'tween here an' Tucson." He paused, then continued.

"We might git lucky an' find a town close 'nough by that might have a picture of 'em. If Ah do happen ta get word some town close by has a picture or drawin' of 'm, Ah kin hold 'em on suspicion long enough ta get a rider ta bring tha picture over here. That's the best Ah kin do."

Alex's dad thanked Justin. They went back inside the jail office to get Lorena and Rebecca.

The trip back to the ranch was pretty much silent. Dan didn't explain the whole situation to Lorena and Rebecca. Alex figured he didn't want to alarm them and make them subject to even more trauma and fear than they already were experiencing from the ordeal.

When they got near enough to the ranch to see its outline in the fading daylight, Alex felt deep inside that there was some impending trouble in the air.

5
Beginning of the End

The next day Alex saddled Storm. He had been getting Storm prepared for a saddle by first putting a saddle blanket on him. Storm shied away for a bit and then had accepted the blanket. Then Alex had brought out a saddle and let Storm smell it. When Alex put the blanket on and then added the weight of the saddle, Storm stayed remarkably calm. He turned his head and rolled an eye back at the saddle. His trust in Alex had grown quickly. Alex removed and then replaced the blanket and saddle several times that day. Alex also put a bridle on Storm, which he also accepted quite well.

On Tuesday, Alex put the saddle and a simple hackamore on Storm. He spoke to the stallion in his gentle, assuring manner, for about half an hour. Then Alex slowly placed his left foot into the stirrup and began to put more weight on that foot, still speaking gently to Storm. Finally, he mounted the saddle completely. Storm looked back at Alex and lowered his ears for a few seconds. When a horse flattens his ears on his head, it means he is angry. Alex half expected Storm to let loose and start bucking, but as Alex continued to talk softly to Storm, he lifted his ears again. Alex rubbed the horse's neck and leaned forward in the saddle so he could scratch Storm between his ears.

All the hours Alex had spent with Storm had paid off. The bond that formed between them was stronger than the mustang's natural instinct to throw Alex off his back.

Now, Alex only needed to train Storm to respond to riding commands. Things such as understanding the slight pressure of the reins on his neck or a leg pressing against either side of the horse's ribs to turn him right or left. Also, a tap with a heel on the stallion's flanks to signal him to move forward or to pick up the pace. He would also teach Storm voice commands.

On Wednesday, Alex's mom called for him to come into the house. She wanted him to ride into town to pick up some tins of cherries, peaches and assorted vegetables which Randall Blake had told her would be in stock by then.

Lorena Barrington was a very beautiful woman. Even now that she was in her forties, she still caught the eye of most men. She had long brown hair, blue eyes and a smooth olive complexion. Alex knew that she didn't like to go to to town by herself and the incident on Sunday certainly hadn't increased her desire to go alone. His mother and Rebecca were canning the tomatoes they had grown in their small garden.

Rebecca had also grown into a beautiful young woman. She looked very much like her mother, except her hair was blonde instead of brown. Every young, single man for miles around began to notice her over the past year or two. During that time, she had grown into a fully developed and attractive young lady.

Alex was proud of his mother and sister, not because of their looks, but more because of their high moral standards and affable personalities. It seemed they were both always cheerful and consistently had a kind word for anyone they met. Alex was always glad to do anything he could to help either of them. His family meant everything to him so of course he was willing to make the trip to town.

Alex had been riding Storm around the ranch and the stallion was quickly learning the gentle pressures and verbal direction of his master. He decided that riding Storm into town would be a good learning experience for the horse.

On the way into town, Alex marveled at Storm's smooth, rocking chair gait as he cantered along the road. Alex was not a vain young man but he couldn't help feeling proud of Storm. He knew that Storm would attract a lot of attention in town and that many would admire the beauty, gracefulness and apparent power of the stallion.

When he and Storm rode into town that was, indeed, the reaction of every man, woman and child who had an appreciation for a magnificent horse. Most who saw him stopped in their tracks and gaped in awe as the two rode by

Alex stopped by the barber shop before going to the mercantile to pick up the tins of food for his mother. He wanted to get a haircut and a shave. Today seemed like such a special day and Alex was even more talkative than befitted his normal, quiet reserved manner. When Al, the barber, and a couple other men in the shop asked Alex how he had come by such a fine horse, Alex explained in detail about the pursuit, capture, gentling and training of Storm.

All three men were amazed and they were looking at Alex with a new kind of respect. Alex was embarrassed by this. He wasn't used to having much attention and it made him feel a bit uncomfortable. So, he intended to go straight to Randall's to pick up the tins and head home soon.

When he stepped out of the barber shop, he had begun to walk across the street when he heard a familiar voice calling him. He turned to see marshal Martin walking toward him. They shook hands and greeted each other but Alex could tell that Justin had something troubling on his mind. Justin looked at Alex and spoke in a somber tone.

He said, "Alex, 'fraid Ah got some bad news. Ah had ta let Sanchez go yesterday. He left town with his gang in a real hurry. Sorta like tha devil hiself was after 'em. 'Bout two hours after he left, Ah got mail from Tucson. Shor 'nough they had a picture of 'em an' it's a picture o' the same hombre all right. Ah was jest 'bout ta ride out ta yor place an' warn y'all. Might be Ah've been worry'n 'bout nothin', but Ah jus' got a bad feelin' 'bout all this."

Alex's heart dropped to his stomach and his pulse raced. He also had a bad feeling about this news. As such, he forgot all about the tins of food.

Marshal Martin said, "It's outa my jurisdiction, but Ah kin saddle up real quick an' go back ta tha ranch with ya, Alex."

Alex replied, "Thanks, but no time for that, marshal. Ah've got ta get back there pronto!"

Alex left Justin standing there and jogged quickly back to where he had left Storm tethered and grabbing the reins he leaped into the saddle with one graceful bound. It seemed that Storm realized the urgency and immediately sprang into a gallop back toward the ranch. Under normal circumstances and on any other horse, Alex wouldn't have allowed him to keep that pace. The situation was critical, however, and Storm was all heart, muscle and lungs.

Storm covered the distance back to the ranch in record-breaking time.

Alex's imagination was first running wild during that breakneck ride, but toward the end his mind steadied like a steel trap. He focused his thoughts on possible scenarios and what action he would need to take, if indeed, Sanchez and his men had headed toward the ranch.

Though Alex didn't have the habit of carrying a six shooter on his hip, he had a rifle strapped to the saddle. If the outlaws were there, Alex planned to ride in shooting to put them on the run.

When Alex got within visual range of the ranch, he detected no movement. Maybe this was just a false alarm. Maybe his mom and Rebecca were in the house and his father was in the barn or out checking the livestock. But, Alex, sensed that something was very wrong. He just couldn't shake that feeling inside. Storm was acting nervous also, like he could smell trouble.

Nothing could have prepared him for the horrible scene he encountered when he rode into the area of the front yard of the house. Not far from the front porch, face down in the dust, was Alex's father. His hat was lying nearby. Alex could see the crimson stain on the back of Dan Barrington's shirt. Alex felt overwhelming nausea as tears began to run down his cheeks and he started to tremble. He dismounted with rifle in hand and carefully bent down to check his father. He kept an eye on his surroundings in case the outlaws might still be around.

As Alex grabbed his father's shoulder and turned him over, Dan Barrington groaned slightly.

With his father now on his back, Alex could see the red stains at the corners of his mouth. Alex knew from this that he had probably been shot through a lung. Dan Barrington weakly opened his eyes and they appeared to be glazing over. But his father recognized him and tried to speak. Instead of words, there was only a gurgling sound. Alex sat down cross-legged on the ground and pulled his father up into his lap and into a partial sitting position. This seemed to help his father to breathe a bit easier.

Dan then began to whisper words that were barely audible, but Alex was able to understand the words he agonizingly spoke in broken syllables.

Alex heard him say, "Promise me that yu'll forgive . . . these men . . . remember what . . . Ah told ya 'bout . . . not . . . lettin' evil men . . . pull . . . ya down ta their level . . . Ya've got ta learn ta forgive . . . Jus' like . . . Jesus said . . . while hangin' on the cross . . . "Father, forgive 'em . . . for . . . they know not what . . . they are . . . doin' . . ." Dan's voice trailed off so faint that Alex could not understand anymore. Then he took one last rattling breath and stopped breathing.

Alex laid his father's body back down in the dust. An overpowering sadness gripped his heart. He realized that Sanchez and his men had dry-gulched his father. They had shot him in the back before he had any warning.

Alex knew he had to go to the house now to see if his mother and Rebecca were still alive. He walked like a man in a dream. He cringed at the thought of what may have happened to them.

He entered the house. Lorena Barrington was lying across the kitchen table, her clothes ripped and torn. Her face was bruised and her eyes were open, glazed and staring up at the ceiling, yet not seeing anything. Alex lifted her upper torso a bit off the table. Her head hung in an awkward position and Alex knew her neck had been broken. He laid her down, tears still streaming down his face.

He then looked through the rest of the house and found Rebecca in his father and mother's room sprawled upon their parents' bed. Her hands and feet were bound with strips of her own dress. Her face was set in an expression of horror. There was a single gunshot wound to her heart. Those beasts who called themselves men didn't want to leave any witnesses behind.

Now weeping agonizingly, Alex took one of Rebecca's hands in his own vowing out loud, "Ah'll kill ever' last one of 'em, Sis!" As he gently held Rebecca's hand, he noticed that four of her fingernails were bloodstained and upon closer inspection, he saw that there was skin gathered under the nails of those four fingers. He said, "Good for you, Sis. Ya caused some pain for *one* of 'em."

Alex realized from the amount of skin that the man she clawed would certainly have permanent scars. The scars would most likely be on his face or neck.

Alex suddenly felt numb all over. It was a strange feeling. Moments earlier, he had been weeping uncontrollably. Now it was as if all emotion had suddenly left him. That is, all emotion except the burning hatred for Sanchez and his pack of human wolves. Alex had never hated anyone. This was a new emotion for him. It seemed to consume his very soul.

Neither had Alex ever lost a family member. Now *all* were lost. Earlier, he had felt that he would never stop crying. Now he wondered if he would ever cry again. An inexplicable loneliness permeated the core of his being. His family had been murdered. It was as though his heart had been ripped out of his chest and he was left with a cold void. A vacuum which seemed totally empty, except for the unfathomable darkness that now filled it.

Alex closed his eyes and buried his face in his hands. It seemed that there was nothing in his mind that moment, except a vision of the faces of his father, mother, sister, and the appalling faces of Sanchez and the man who had been with him that afternoon in town.

Alex sat in that manner for what seemed like a long time. Finally he got up, lifted his sister gently in his arms and carried her outside. He walked to a low hill just behind the house and laid her on the ground. He then returned for his father and mother, carrying each one to the same hill and laying them side-by-side. It seemed that he was in a dream. It was like the worse possible nightmare.

He kept thinking to himself, "Maybe Ah'll jus' wake up in my bedroon an' this will all be jus' a dream." Yet he knew this was no dream.

He walked numbly to the barn, where he picked up a shovel and headed back to the hill behind the house. He was vaguely aware that the position of the sun showed that only about an hour had passed since his arrival at the ranch.

He dug the graves deep. After burying his family, he placed stones over the fresh mounds of dirt to keep the wild critters from digging them up.

Alex said a prayer after he'd finished the burial, but the words sounded empty and meaningless.

He couldn't keep his thoughts from returning to the men who had taken his loved ones from him. When he had finished the brief and lonesome ceremony, he began walking through the area surrounding the house, looking for signs of Sanchez and his men. He had learned at an early age from a Yaqui Indian how to read signs. He could tell tracks of one horse from another by subtle differences which go unnoticed by the untrained eye. He could spot the slight impressions of a crack on a horseshoe.

He could tell the size and approximate weight of a horse or man, by the depth of the prints in the ground. There is always something different about each track. A man walks with his weight placed either on his heels, toes, or the sides of his feet. He could also tell the height of a person by the distance between their footprints.

He collected all this information in his mind before dusk. He then went into the house and packed food and other supplies needed for the trail, along with cash and gold coins from a box his father had hidden behind the clothes in their closet.

He walked over to his father's set of Colt .45 Peacemakers that hung on a wall peg. He stared at them a few moments, his eyes fixated on the guns and holster. Thoughts and visages paraded through his mind and he wondered if these six shooters could talk, what kind of gruesome tales of the past would they have? Finally, Alex took them down from their resting place. He slowly buckled them around his hip and tied the leather thongs to his thighs.

It was now dark outside and he went on the front porch and sat there looking at the stars, wondering if his family could see him. His mind began reminiscing of various events he and his family had lived through together. As he looked at the stars and moon, he also wondered about God.

Alex had always believed in God, but he now struggled with conflicting thoughts and emotions. If God did exist and if He *is* a God of love as Dan Barrington described Him, then how could He allow the evil that is present in the world? How and why did He allow Alex's family to be slaughtered in this way?

After a while, Alex slouched down in the rocking chair and slowly drifted off to sleep.

It was daylight when Alex awoke to the sound of approaching horses. He instinctively placed his hand on the butt of one of the Colt .45s.

6
Up in Flames

As the riders drew nearer, Alex saw that it was Buck and marshal Martin. He eased his hand from the Colt .45 and stood up. The two men trotted their mounts up to the porch, dismounted and looped the reins of their horses over the hitching post in front of the porch.

Buck spoke first, "Howdy, Alex." There was a strained note in Buck's voice and Alex noticed they were both looking around the ranch with an uneasy appearance. They knew something was seriously wrong here. Justin's gaze rested on the large stain on the ground a short distance from the house. The stain of Dan Barrington's blood, which was crimson when Alex arrived yesterday, was now a dark brown.

Buck saw Justin's fixed gaze and his eyes followed the marshal's to the stain. His face became pale and the corner of his mouth twitched as he tried to hide a grimace. Buck had long been a loyal friend of the family and the realization of what had happened hit him almost as hard as it did Alex.

Buck's gaze shifted back to Alex and he saw that Buck had noticed the Colt .45s strapped to his legs. Buck's eyes met the hollow, near emotionless, stare from Alex's. Buck returned that gaze with a look of compassion and understanding.

After few moments Alex said, "Buck . . . marshal . . . have a seat," motioning toward the four rocking chairs on the porch. They both sat down and marshal Martin pulled his chair out and around to face Alex.

The marshal began, "Alex, Ah need fur ya' ta describe what ya saw here yesterdee when ya got back here at tha ranch."

Alex just sat for a few moments, preparing his mind to relate the grissly scene. He knew that the marshal needed the information to make a report and notify Sheriff Barkley. Also, other town marshals and sheriffs in neighboring counties would need the details. Finally, the lump in Alex's throat eased enough to tell the story to marshal Martin. The marshal and Buck both knew of Alex's skills at reading sign and asked him to tell them what he'd found.

Alex told them that he had been able to distinguish tracks of six different horses and men who had never been to the ranch. He also told them he'd seen evidence in the chaparral by the ranch house which showed that the men had waited in the bushes. They had evidently been watching, waiting for the right time to strike.

He told them that there were cigarette butts and other signs which meant they may have been there most of the night and had probably watched Alex leave the ranch for town. That the tracks in the ranch yard were fresh and had been made only an hour or so before he had arrived back at the ranch. Alex then asked marshal Martin to describe the type and the size of the horses Sanchez and his men were riding when they had left town two days ago. He also asked the marshal to describe, as best he could, the men that he had seen riding with Sanchez.

Alex then said, "All adds up, marshal. Tha same number o' horses an' men . . . tha tracks of tha men an' tha horses all match tha sign left here. It was Sanchez an' his gang alright."

The marshal said, "Ah'll also get tha infurmation out 'bout one of these here fellers havin' four claw marks on 'em that Rebecca saddled 'em with. If she tagged 'em on tha face, that'll help a lot."

After a few moments of silence, the marshal got up and said, "Wul son, Ah shore am turrible sorry 'bout all this. Jus' wish Ah could o' kept Sanchez locked up long 'nough ta get that infurmation Ah needed. Ah'd o' been able ta keep 'em locked up an' Ah'm sure he'd 'o dangled at tha end o' a rope. None o' of this here would o' happened if Ah jes' could o' got positive identification on 'em quick enough."

Alex said, "Ah know, marshal. Wasn't yor fault. Ya did all ya could. But Ah swear ta ya, marshal . . . every last one o' those hombres are marked men . . . they'll pay for all their wrongdoings. They've all jus' signed their own death certificates."

Marshal Martin said, "Ah understan' yor feelings, Alex. Jus' be careful they don't finish tha work o' wipin' out tha whole Barrington family. Ya gonna have ta be slippery as a greased snake ta get done what's on yor mind an' still come out in one piece. Ah got a friend in Las Cruces who's a purtty high-rankin' U.S. marshall, by tha name o' Tihlman. Ah'll send 'em a wire 'splainin' things ta 'em. From tha direction ya said they're a headin', Ah'd say these here devils is headin' up tha Outlaw Trail, which'll take 'em right through tha Las Cruces area. This here friend Ah got there Ah believe'll swear ya in as a deputy United States marshal ta keep ya on tha right side o' tha Law. He knew yor Pa too. Anybody in Las Cruces kin tell ya where ta find 'em. Good Lord be with ya, son."

The marshal shook Alex's hand firmly with deep emotion in his eyes. After that he mounted his horse and trotted off toward town.

While Alex remained seated on the porch in deep contemplative thought, Buck walked back to the graves, on the hill to pay his respects. After a short while, he returned to the porch, looking sad and haggard.

"Alex," he began, "Ah know yur anxious ta get on tha trail, but ya know that one man travelin' alone, kin get ta where he's goin' faster than six men travelin' together. 'Specially men like these here rascals, who'll be takin' their time ta do more mischief 'long tha way. Ah think ya ought'a come over ta my place this evenin' an' have supper with me an' tha wife. Ah know Anna will want ta feed ya a good supper 'fore ya leave. Ya kin hit tha trail tamorrow."

Alex agreed to go by Buck's and then said, "Buck, Ah got a couple o' things Ah've got ta do before leavin' the ranch here. Ah need ta be alone for jus' a bit longer. Ah'll come on over shortly after dark."

Buck said, "Sure, Alex. Ah understand." He then rode off at a slow pace. Even Buck's horse, Prince, seemed to pick up on Buck's gloomy mood and walked with his head down a bit lower than usual.

Alex remained sitting on the porch for hours with thoughts rushing through his mind like a downhill train. He finally got up and walked out to the barn. There, he picked up one of three cans of kerosene. He walked back to the house and started pouring the smelly liquid throughout.

Alex could barely stand to be inside the house. Even though he'd already buried his family, the visible bloodstains and the horrible thoughts of his mom and Rebecca and the torturous, barbaric acts they had been forced to endure before their death, plagued his mind. Neither could he shake the picture of his father from his thoughts, lying in the dust just a few yards from the house.

Since he was still alive when Alex had arrived, Alex knew that his father was aware of the plight his wife and daughter were in. Dan was probably able to hear their screams. Alex imagined the anguish his father must have felt, knowing they desperately needed his help. Since the gunshot wound appeared to have entered his spine and exited through his right lung, he was evidently paralyzed from the waist down. Alex had noticed the presence of clawing marks on the ground where his father had tried to pull himself toward the ranch house, to no avail.

It was getting dark when he walked back out the front door. He struck a match and tossed it inside the house. Flames began to spread quickly. Alex also poured kerosene on his father's bloodstain and set it on fire as well. He stepped back to about halfway between the barn and the house and watched as the flames began to devour the dwelling he had known since childhood. The only home he had ever known.

He knew that if he did return to the property, he wouldn't be able to bear living in the house with memories to be brought back to mind, of the carnage he had seen there.

He decided to leave the barn intact because of all the horses stabled there. He didn't even know if he would ever return to his family homestead, or whether he'd even live through the dangers that lay ahead of him. Alex knew Buck would agree to come to the Barrington ranch to herd all the livestock back to his spread.

As Alex watched the house, which was now fully engulfed in flames, sadnesss and loneliness tore away at his insides. He'd never felt so low in all his life. He'd known other families who had suffered tragedies, but he'd never been able to fully understand their grief until now.

As he looked with a vacant stare at the burning house, he envisioned himself and Rebecca as kids, playing her favorite game of hide and seek. Though Alex was several years older than Rebecca, he'd always loved his little sister very much and watched over her like a hen brooding over her chicks.

He had never minded her tagging along when he would go to town for supplies, or even going with him to the occasional dances held at the community building. He thought of the muggy summer days, when they would swim in the creek that meandered its way through the countryside, not far from the ranch. Scene after scene of the happy years past kept replaying through his mind. He would never be able to share all those memories with his family again. He just couldn't imagine life without them. He wondered what life had in store for him now. He could see no future.

It was now an hour after dark. Suddenly Alex heard a noise, as something was approaching in his direction.

7
No Looking Back

As the sound came nearer, Alex could hear panting and recognized the sound of an animal running. Then Lobo, Alex's dog, came within view of the firelight.

Lobo frequently disappeared for two or three days at a time, out hunting jackrabbit and whatever else he could find to chase and eat. Lobo was a mix between an Airedale Terrier and Irish Wolfhound. When he stood beside Alex, his head was higher than Alex's waistline and Alex was six feet tall. He'd been a close companion of Alex for about five years now. Although he was devoted to his master, he'd get a wild hair from time to time and strike out on a hunt or the call of the wild, or whatever it was that drew him away from the ranch during those escapades.

Lobo slowed down as he drew closer to Alex and was sniffing first the ground and then the air. He knew something was wrong. Finally he eased up to Alex with a "hangdog" look, gently nuzzling Alex's hand. Alex reached out and stroked Lobo's head. Right now it was a small consolation but he said softly to Lobo, "Wul at least Ah still have you an' Storm."

Alex then rounded up the things he had packed for the trail, walked to the barn where Storm was saddled, and rode off at a trot toward Buck's ranch. Lobo loped alongside them.

Alex could hear the lonesome sound of a whippoorwill echoing through the night. There was a half moon out and Alex stared at the misty outline of Mesquite and other trees and shrubs which lined the trail. The sound of a whippoorwill had always been melancholic to Alex, but never so much as tonight. It was like a huge, invisible fist gripped his insides and a feeling of total emptiness and extreme sorrow tugged at his soul.

It seemed like an eternity had passed when he finally saw the light emanating from Buck's ranch house. It was only a five mile ride to Buck and Anna's, but it had seemed like twenty miles. Alex stepped out of the saddle, as Buck opened the front door and walked over to him, placing a comforting hand on his shoulder.

Buck said, "Alex, go on in tha house an' Ah'll take Storm ta tha barn, unsaddle 'em an' give 'em some feed."

Ordinarily, Alex would not have allowed Buck to do this for him, but under the circumstances he thanked Buck and took his bedroll, saddlebags, rifle and other gear off Storm's saddle. He set everything on the front porch except a burlap sack containing the family Bible and photos. Those he'd leave with Buck and Anna. He also carried his saddlebags inside the house. They contained all the Barrington family savings. Alex had taken the money from the closet beside his parents' bed before he had set fire to the house. Evidently, Sanchez and his men had been too obsessed with extracting their vengeance to look for valuables.

As Buck led Storm away, Alex entered the house and hung his hat on a peg by the door. He unbuckled his gun belt and hung it on another peg and walked toward the kitchen.

Anna heard Alex approaching and scurried through the kitchen door to meet him. She threw her arms around him with tears in her eyes. Alex clung to her for a few moments then Anna backed up a step, her hands still gripping Alex's arms.

She looked him in the eyes and said, "Alex, I don't have the proper words to say right now, but you remember when we lost our William, when he was only twelve. I do understand your grief some, though I've never lost my whole family at one time. I just want you to know how much we care for you and that you're welcome to stay with me and Buck for as long as you like."

Alex and William had been like brothers when they were young. Until Will, along with several others in the surrounding area, had come down with influenza and died, Buck and Anna had always been like an uncle and aunt to Alex. Anna's compassion now was the closest thing to comfort that Alex had felt since the tragedy.

Anna wiped her eyes on her dress sleeve and said, "Come on into the kitchen, Alex. I've got some food ready for you."

Alex followed her and sat down at the table. He didn't really feel hungry, but knew he needed to eat to keep his strength up. Anna's father was a Spaniard of Castilian descent and she still spoke with a slight Spanish accent. Alex had learned to speak and understand Spanish fairly well from her and had always called her tía Anna.

She was pretty much as good of a cook as his mom, although her preference leaned toward black beans, tortillas, carne asada con cebollas and the like. Tonight she had also prepared his favorite dessert, churros con chocolate. These were long strips of a special batter, deep-fried and covered with granules of sugar. They were served with a special Mexican blend of hot chocolate. Alex had enjoyed this dessert many times over the years.

It was so good that Alex had always found it difficult to stop eating this dessert and tía Anna would say, "*Vas a conseguir grasa así*," which translated means, "You're going to get fat like that." Then she would laugh in her good-hearted manner.

When Alex finished eating, he thanked tía Anna and offered to help her with the dishes. He received a good-natured rebuke from her.

She said, "Nonsense. I know you're very tired. You must go to bed now and get some rest. I've put clean sheets on Will's bed. Go on now and get to sleep. Don' worry about me and the dishes."

Alex went out to the front porch and shared a few silent moments with Buck.

Alex mostly looked at the stars, the moon and the clouds which drifted past it. Again he wondered if his family could see him. He didn't think so. He believed they were now in the very presence of God. He recalled the Bible says "In His presence is fullness of joy." Seeing Alex now would certainly not bring them joy.

He soon retired to Will's old room. He pulled off his boots and undressed down to his long johns. He cleaned up at the wash basin and got between the clean sheets.

At first, so many thoughts were racing through his head he thought he wouldn't be able to sleep, but he was so physically and mentally tired that he quickly drifted off into a restless and troublesome sleep.

When the first rooster crowed in the morning, Alex awoke, remembering some of the horrible dreams he had experienced during the night. In his last dreams, he had been at the Barrington ranch. He was in the middle of the ranch yard, watching with horror as Sanchez and his men, who in his dream had grown to about fifty in number, attacked his family.

Alex had been bound with many layers of rope and couldn't move. In the dream, there had been the thunder of the many horse's hooves and the constant explosion of gunfire, mixed with the screams of his mother and sister. Alex had been trying desperately to free himself from the ropes, but he couldn't move a muscle. He had tried to scream at the marauders to stop, but he couldn't speak. Sanchez was galloping toward Alex, brandishing a large machete, when the rooster crowed and Alex awoke.

He was awash with sweat. He sat up on the edge of the bed and looked out the bedroom window, where there was evidence of the first light of dawn. He sat there for several minutes as if in a trance. Finally he shook his head trying to clear his thoughts and walked to the wash stand and splashed the cool water on his face.

Alex pulled on his trousers and then his boots. As he pulled on the boots, he was again reminded of the past. The boots had been given to him last Christmas by his parents. They were finely crafted from soft calf's skin and fit his feet like a glove.

It seemed like everything he thought, saw or touched reminded him of his family, whom he had loved so much.

After the "good mornings" were said, Alex sat down to breakfast with Buck and Anna. There wasn't much conversation during the meal. When they had finished eating, Anna began to clear the table. Buck pushed his chair back from the table. He stood up and motioned for Alex to follow him onto the back porch.

Once outside, Buck paused for few moments with his gaze fixed on the barn. While still looking toward the barn, he began to speak rather awkwardly.

"Alex, ya know Ah never was good with words, like yur pa was . . . an' this is a more than usual hard time ta know tha right words to say. Ah jus' want ya ta know that yu'll be in me an' Anna's prayers. Ya got a long stretch o' road ahead o' ya, what can be all tangled up with danger. Jus' promise me that yu'll keep yor wits about ya an' that ya won't jus' go chargin' after these here hombres like a mad bull. Ya got ta think ahead an' plan ever' move. We los' Will an' we share tha loss o' yor folks with ya. We couldn't stan' losin' you too. Ya gonna have ta outsmart these here rascals, order ta stay alive. Promise me too, that yu'll look up marshal Tihlman in Las Cruces. Okay, son?"

Alex nodded his agreement, and said, "Buck, Ah want ta thank ya an' tía Anna for being loyal friends ta me an' my family all these years. Far as Ah'm concerned, yu're my family too, jus' like Ma an' Pa an' Rebecca were. Ah promise ya that Ah'll do everythin' ah can ta stay alive. Ah'll try ta sen' ya a wire or a letter when Ah can ta let ya know what's goin' on."

Alex and Buck shook hands and Buck grabbed Alex in a bear hug, slapping him on the back. Tía Anna joined them on the porch with a small bundle of food tied up in a gunnysack. She put it in Alex's hand as tears welled up in her eyes. She hugged Alex and said, *"Viaje por mi hijo con Dios,"* which interpreted means "Travel with God, son!"

Buck accompanied Alex to the barn carrying some of Alex's gear, including his rifle, gun belt and Colt .45s. Alex saddled Storm, slung his saddlebags behind the saddle and lashed all his gear in place. Then Lobo, who had been lying near the back porch, trotted to the barn.

Alex mounted Storm and reached down and firmly shook Buck's hand one last time before heading off at a canter. When he was about a mile down the road, he slowed Storm down to a walk. He had left at a quick pace without looking back because part of him wanted to stay with Buck and Anna. That desire, however, was far outweighed by his passion to track down Sanchez and his gang.

El Paso to Las Cruces was a good day or day and a half ride, depending a lot on the horse's stamina and ability to cover ground. Alex knew he could make it in a full day's ride with Storm. He would alternately walk and canter Storm to pace him. Storm's smooth canter was a real ground-eating pace and yet so smooth that it was easy on Alex's backside. Storm could keep this pace all day and hardly break a sweat. Lobo could keep this pace as well. He was tough as nails.

The countryside Alex was riding through was familiar to him. He never ceased to be amazed at how hills, mountains and desert all converged in this upper border of Texas, seemingly competing with one another for dominance. It was only a short distance to the border of New Mexico territory.

Alex knew that when he neared Las Cruces, the landscape would become less barren and more densely forested. Alex looked forward to the change of scenery. He just wasn't in the mood for barren surroundings right now. Perhaps because his whole life had changed so radically in *one* day and now his very *soul* seemed barren and devoid of life.

The miles, however, seemed to go by more quickly in full daylight, than they had last night. It seemed he was a bit less plagued with vivid recollections of the debauchery at the Barrington ranch. The thought also crossed his mind that Buck and Anna's prayers were helping him. Even though it had only been two days ago, it seemed to Alex that much more time had passed since that awful day.

Alex's thoughts turned again to Sanchez and his band of cold-blooded killers. Again, he thought of the different scenarios when he found and confronted the outlaws. Again, the words of his father returned to his mind. Those words were about forgiveness.

Alex just could not envision or comprehend the possibility of ever forgiving these men.

8
Badge of Honor

It was near dusk when Alex rode into Las Cruces.

He stopped at a livery stable where he would leave Storm for the night. Alex led Storm to the stall indicated by the livery owner and proceeded to remove the saddle, blanket and other tack, which he placed on the available pegs.

He took his currycomb and brushed Storm's coat in the direction of the hair growth. Then he took his hoof pick and carefully removed the dirt and small stones that almost always collected on the underside of the hooves between the hoof and the frog. When he had finished this, he took a special soft cloth and rubbed Storm's coat well. Alex then made sure that Storm had fresh hay and oats.

He could have paid a bit extra for one of the stable hands to do this, but Alex preferred to do these things himself to make sure they were done properly. Also, when the grooming is done by the horse's master, it provides an opportunity to form an even closer bond between the two.

When Alex had taken care of these details, he grabbed his rifle and saddlebags and headed toward a hotel. As he was checking in, he related to the clerk in a casual manner. He described Sanchez and his men and asked the clerk if he had seen anyone in town recently matching the descriptions.

The clerk looked a bit nervous as perspiration beaded on his forehead. He looked around the lobby tentatively, and then looked back at Alex. He spoke in a voice so low it was difficult for Alex to hear. Alex had to lean a bit closer to the clerk in order to understand.

The clerk said, "Yea, I've seen some men in town matching that description." From his accent, Alex figured the clerk was from back East somewhere. "They stayed here and checked out today about noon. I don't know if they're still in town or not."

Alex, sorry for the obvious dilemma he had placed the clerk in, put a hand on the clerk's shoulder and said, "Listen, Ah know yu're wonderin' if Ah'm not one of 'em. Ah'd hoped ya could'a told that by jus' lookin' at me. Ah' m not tha type ta hang 'round with that sort. Can ya tell me where Ah might be able ta fin' U.S. marshal Tihlman this time o' tha evenin'?"

The clerk's demeanor relaxed some, but he still spoke barely above a whisper. He said, "He usually has supper over at Maria's Cantina and grill about now. You're in luck too, because the marshal just got back an hour or two ago from some trip he was on. Went to Fort Worth I think it was."

Alex said, "Much obliged, friend."

After taking his things to his room, Alex headed toward Maria's Cantina and restaurant, where he hoped to find marshal Tihlman. As he walked along the street, he saw movement out of the corner of his eye. He turned to face that direction, instinctively grasping the butt of one of his guns as he did. There was nothing but darkness in the alley where the movement had been.

After a few moments, Alex began walking again toward the cantina. The hairs were up on the back of his neck as he had the distinct feeling he was being watched.

As Alex approached Maria's, he could hear the raucous chatter and laughter drifting from the open windows of the restaurant. The murky light of oil lanterns in front of the building vaguely illuminated the sidewalk.

Even before entering the front door, Alex was greeted by the mingled odors of beer, tequila, pulque, tobacco smoke, tortillas, beans and jalapeños. The smell of alcohol didn't agree with Alex since he didn't drink, but the familiar smell of the Mexican cuisine got his digestive juices flowing and he suddenly realized how hungry he was. He hadn't expected his appetite to return this quickly, but evidently the combination of the long ride and comforting fellowship he'd had at Buck and Anna's had brought back his love of food. Especially food that smelled like his mom's cooking or the Mexican dishes tía Anna served up.

Before entering the door completely, Alex first scanned the crowd inside to make sure that neither Sanchez nor any of his men were inside. Most of his men had only seen Alex at a distance the day they had watched the ranch house from the chaparral as Alex rode off toward town.

On the other hand, Sanchez himself and the redhead that was with him that regrettable day in El Paso would definitely be able to recognize him. As Alex checked the crowd inside, he noticed a man sitting at a corner table, in the back of the room seated with his back to the wall. There was no mistaking who this man was.

Even though seated, Alex could tell the man was tall, probably six feet two or so. He had a no-nonsense look about him. He wore a wide-brimmed black hat, black coat and gray trousers. He had a handlebar mustache that made Alex think of a longhorn steer. It was neatly waxed and meticulously curved up at the ends. Even without the U.S. marshal's badge on his lapel, Alex would have known this was a man of integrity and a ranking law-enforcement officer.

Alex's stare certainly had not gone unnoticed by marshal Tihlman. His gaze evidenced that he had been checking Alex out and sizing him up as well.

There's something about the kindred spirit of honest and honorable men. Something that made it a matter of quick observation to determine the other's character and trustworthiness.

The marshal's eyes denoted a twinkle of that recognition.

Alex had a small yet significant smile at the corners of his mouth as he approached the table where marshal Tihlman sat. When Alex reached the table he stuck out his hand and said, "Marshal? Ah'm Alex Barrington. Hope Ah'm not interruptin' yor meal, but Ah've got some important business ta discuss with ya. If ya'd rather, it can wait 'til tomorrow, or at least 'til ya've finished yor supper."

Marshal Tihlman shook Alex's hand firmly and said, "Not at all, Mr. Barrington. Please. Have a seat. Look like ya can use a good meal. Maria," the marshal spoke in an affectionate way to a Mexican lady, who had just sat food on a table a short distance away. "Ah have a friend here joinin' me for supper, if ya could come over an' find out what direction his taste buds are leanin' to'ards tonight."

Maria responded with warmth in her voice, *"Si mi amigo querido,"* as she jovially approached the table. She continued to say, "Any friend of the marshal's, must be a good man. *¿Qué quieres comer?"*, meaning, "What would you like to eat?"

Alex guessed this lovely woman must also be intuitive and somehow figured he spoke Spanish. Alex liked her right away. He responded, *"Quiero tortitas y carne asada con cebollas y papas frita, si usted los tiene, por favor, Señorita."* meaning, "I want tortillas and roasted meat with onions and fried potatoes, if you have them, please Ma'am."

Maria responded with a big smile saying, *"Si Señor. Como usted disea."*

Alex said, *"Muchisimas gracias."*

As she scurried away to the kitchen, marshal Tihlman queried, "So yor las' name is Barrington?"

He paused a moment and added, "From yor looks, Ah'd be willin' ta bet yu're related ta Dan Barrington. Got a wire from marshal Martin in El Paso, sayin' ya were headin' this way."

Alex grinned and said, "Yeah, marshal, Ah'm his son." Then reality caught up with Alex and his countenance took a nosedive.

The marshal saw the change in expression and a concerned look came over his face. He asked, "What's happened, son? Justin didn't give me much detail. Ah'd like ta hear it all from tha horse's mouth."

Alex stared at the table for a few moments, hating to have to recount the tragedy again and bring the pain back to the forefront of his mind.

Alex looked up at the marshal again and the corner of his mouth twitched a bit as he began to describe the events from the ranch to marshal Tihlman. He prefaced that account with an explanation of the events which took place in El Paso two days prior to the massacre.

The marshal's countenance also underwent a radical change. His ears and cheeks turned red and the righteous indignation was quite apparent by the look in his eyes. "Mighty sad ta hear all o' this, son," remarked Tihlman, with both a look of genuine regret and evident anger.

Once Alex had forced the last horrifying syllables from his lips, he sat there with his fists unconsciously clenched, staring at the table with the muscles of his jaws flexing.

Marshal Tihlman sat there a few moments as well. His angered expression now softened into a look of compassion.

Maria returned with Alex's meal and placed it gently on the table, evidently perceiving that a serious conversation had been shared between the two men. She looked at Alex and saw the grief etched upon his face. You could see in her eyes that she wanted to comfort Alex. She realized that this was not the time to say anything other than, "*Buen provecho*," meaning, "Enjoy your food." She then turned and walked away with a look of empathy.

Alex came to his senses enough to say, "*Gracias Señorita.*"

By this point, Alex had again lost his appetite, but he ate knowing that he needed to.

Marshal Tihlman said, "Alex, your father was a great man. Ah'm terribly sorry ta hear this. Ah met your mother too. A wonderful woman. Sanchez's trail led in this direction Ah 'spose?"

Alex shared with the marshal the signs he'd read at the ranch and included the rest of the information he had learned about Sanchez and his bunch. He also told him that the hotel clerk had recognized, from Alex's description that the outlaws had stayed at the hotel and checked out earlier today.

Marshal Tihlman said, "Alex, Sanchez an' his gang are not only evil, but they're also very cunnin' an' every man jack one of 'em are 'sposed ta be highly feared gunmen, even one-on-one. Ah'm advising ya ta let the law handle this. Not only ta keep ya from gettin' killed, but also 'cause they've never stood trial anywhere an' if ya happen ta be successful at killin' any of 'em, ya could wind up in some trouble with the law yorself."

"Marshal," Alex inserted, "maybe from Justin's wire, ya already know that's tha main reason Ah looked ya up. Marshal Martin told me ya might swear me in as a deputy U.S. marshal, ta keep me legal. Ah've been hopin' he was right."

Marshal Tihlman responded, "Yes, Alex, Ah can do that, but ya first have ta swear that yu'll try ta take as many of 'em alive as ya can. My conscience wouldn't allow me ta do it any other way an' Ah can tell enough 'bout ya, to know that you're a man o' yor word like yor Pa."

Alex responded, "Ah'll do what Ah can ta do jus' that, marshal."

The marshal said, "Okay then. Come by my office in tha morning' an' we'll take care o' that part. Ah'll try ta have tha town marshal an' tha county sheriff be there as witnesses. An' one more thing, Alex. Ah never was as religious as your Pa turned out ta be, but Ah'll be sayin' some prayers for ya jus' tha same. Yu're goin' ta need it."

"Thank ya marshal," Alex responded. "Ah *know* Ah'm gonna ta need all o' *that* Ah can get."

Marshal Tihlman then said, "Ah'll see ya in tha mornin' then an' Ah'd like ta say again that Ah'm terribly sorry 'bout tha loss o' yor family, 'specially tha way it happened. This country shor los' some prime citizens in that senseless and diabolical assault. Ah want ta go with ya, son, ta track down these vermin."

Alex said, with a sound of finality in his voice, "Ah 'preciate it, marshal, but ya've been aroun' long enough ta gain a lot o' wisdom in fightin' crime. It wouldn't do for ya ta get killed an' tha people o' this territory ta lose all tha wisdom that's taken years for ya ta 'cumulate. No, marshal. Ah've got ta do this alone. Besides, ya know it's easier for one man ta trail a group o' men without bein' detected."

Marshal Tihlman realized that this was a personal vendetta and Alex wanted to do it alone. Tihlman could identify with Alex's emotional state. He replied to Alex, "Wul, once yu're sworn in tamorrow, Ah'll become yor boss an' Ah *could* insist, but Ah'll respect yor wishes, Alex. Guess Ah'll need ta get tha whole church here prayin' for ya."

"Thanks. See ya in tha morning' then, marshal," Alex said, and with this they shook hands, Alex paid for his meal and stepped back out into the night.

As Alex walked along the street, he again had the eerie feeling he was being watched. Again, the hair on his neck and arms stood on end. He saw a man standing across the street near a saloon. The man saw that Alex had noticed him. He turned and walked quickly to the alley next to the saloon. As he passed the light coming from the windows of the saloon, Alex got a better look at him.

Unless Alex's imagination was playing tricks on him, the man appeared to have red hair and bore a striking resemblance to the man who had been with Sanchez that day in El Paso. The eerie feeling left Alex as suddenly as it had come when he began aggressively walking toward the man, anger mounting in him. Before Alec could get halfway to him, the man disappeared into the darkness of the alley.

As badly as Alex wanted to follow him, he knew it would be foolhardy to follow the man into a dark alley. Instead, Alex went on back to the hotel and when he got inside his room, he shoved the deadbolt in place.

He found an out-of-date newspaper on the washstand and crumpled pieces of it placing it on the floor in front of the door and the window. With this preparation, plus the fact that Lobo was in the room with him, Alex was assured that no one could enter his room without him knowing about it. He would have time to draw a pistol from its holster, which hung on the bed post at the head of his bed.

There was one last thing Alex remembered thinking before he became drowsy. *If* indeed, one or more of Sanchez's men *had* lingered in town *and* if the man he had seen in front of the saloon *was* the red-headed man that he'd seen in El Paso with Sanchez, then the outlaws would know that he was on their trail. They would also know he had visited with marshal Tihlman. This would greatly complicate matters for Alex and he'd lose the element of surprise that *had* been to his advantage.

This brought a sense of frustration to Alex, if only he'd somehow anticipated the possibility one or more of the Sanchez gang had lingered behind in Las Cruces, Alex would have gone out of his way to use side alleyways to get to and from the cantina. This would have perhaps lessened his chances of being spotted by the red-headed man.

Alex drifted off to sleep. He didn't know how much time had passed when he was awakened by a muffled growl from Lobo.

9
Pit of Darkness

Alex snatched a Colt .45 from its holster and slowly got out of bed, trying not to make any noise. Usually, Lobo didn't growl when he heard an unknown noise unless Alex was asleep. He normally raised his hackles and bared his teeth, knowing instinctively that his master would see his alarm posture while not giving away Alex's position.

Alex crept in sock feet as close to the door as possible without stepping on the newspaper. Lobo was looking in the direction of the door, but had stopped his muffled growl. Alex waited a few moments in suspense when he heard a soft taping at the door. Alex asked, "Who's there?" He immediately sidestepped quietly two steps to his right, so that if anyone shot through the door, in the direction his voice had come from, they would be shooting empty air.

But Alex was beginning to relax because he figured anyone intent on shooting him wouldn't knock at the door first. Unless, of course, they were trying to get a fix on his position.

Then he heard the voice of marshal Tihlman. "Alex, it's Tihlman. Ah need ta speak with ya. It's urgent."

Alex answered, "Okay marshal." He pushed the newspaper out of the doorway, pulled back the deadbolt and opened the door. Marshal Tihlman stepped inside the room as Alex struck a match and lit the lantern.

As the soft glow of the lantern illuminated the marshal's face, Alex could see concern creasing his forehead and tugging at the corners of his mouth. "Alex," the marshal continued, "wanted ta let ya know that tha hotel clerk came ta me a short while ago. Said ya'd spoken ta 'em 'bout men fittin' tha description o' Sanchez an' his men. Ah told him that ya'd talked ta me 'bout 'em too. Ah guess he wanted confirmation from me that ya really were on tha up-and-up an' had actually talked ta me."

Tihlman paused for a moment, then continued, "Anyway, he says he saw one o' tha men shortly after ya spoke with 'em. Said it was tha red-headed one ya described. He jus' figured he needed ta let me know. Also said that shortly after ya went back up ta your room here tonight, he saw tha red-headed hombre ridin' out o' town. Said he seemed kind o' in a hurry. He rode out headin' toward tha northwest edge o' town."

Alex responded, "Yeah, Ah saw who Ah thought was tha same man myself after Ah left tha cantina. Couldn't be sure though, 'cause tha light wasn't too good where Ah saw 'em. Guess this confirms my suspicion though, an' soun's like they're still headin' up tha Outlaw Trail. Probably will stop in Silver City. Well, marshal, o' course this means they know Ah'm followin' 'em. Goin' ta make things a lot harder."

Marshal Tihlman frowned in deep thought and then queried, "Alex. Ya shor ya don' want me ta go with ya? The odds are stackin' up against ya more all tha time."

Alex answered, "No marshal. Ya know how Pa believed? Well, Ah don't know for sure what Ah'm supposed ta do with these rascals when Ah catch 'em, but Ah *can* say Ah have this feelin' that tha good Lord has His hand involved in my affairs right now. It's just a feelin' Ah have on tha inside o' me. If that feelin' is right, then Ah can't help but think o' tha Scripture that says He'll close tha wrong doors an' open tha right ones."

Alex paused briefly and added, "Ah don' believe Ah'm exactly thinkin' maybe tha way Jesus would right now, but Ah figure He'll work on tha inside o' me while Ah'm on tha trail. Ah can't 'splain how Ah feel so sure 'bout these things, but somehow Ah jus' do. If Ah'm wrong an' tha good Lord doesn't lead or protect me . . . Well . . . that's okay too, 'cause Ah really won't have much of a life anyway, 'til Ah get this stuff resolved one way or another. That's tha best Ah I know how ta 'splain it ta ya right now, marshal."

"Wul son," said the marshal, "somehow ya kind o' encourage my own faith jus' hearin' ya put it that way. By tha way, tha newspaper here is pretty good thinkin', an' Ah did notice ya spoke firs' from tha left side o' that door an' tha next time ya answered from tha right side. Yu've got a lot o' savvy, son. Put all that together with that sprinklin' o' faith yu've got, an' ya jus' might get through this here mess alive."

After a moment more of reflection, Tihlman added, "Well, Ah'll see ya in tha mornin' then, ta swear ya in."

"Okay," Alex replied, "Thank ya for bringin' tha warnin'."

"Goodnight then, Alex."

"Goodnight marshal."

With that, the marshal left. Alex pulled out his father's pocket watch, now one of his most cherished possessions, and saw that it was nearly midnight. He blew out the lantern and laid back on the bed, with his hands clasped behind his head and just stared at the ceiling for a while, thinking. He thought of the possible reactions of the outlaws, now knowing he was on their trail.

At this point in his life, he didn't really understand yet how criminals, given over to such ungoldly acts as these men were, would likely react to varying situations. He figured they would assume that he would now, perhaps, continue hot on their trail.

It seemed to Alex this would be a reasonable assumption, but again, these were not exactly reasonable men. Alex thought to himself, a man must be at least bordering on insanity just to be able to commit the unthinkable deeds these devils were capable of.

If ever a gang of men were influenced by the powers of darkness, which his father had so often alluded to, then *these* men were surefire candidates. They appeared to have rings in their noses, put there by the evil spirits Alex's father called demons.

Another passage came to Alex's mind now. His father had often spoken of the verses which said that the weapons of our warfare as Christian, God-fearing men and women, are not fleshly weapons. They aren't like guns, fists and the like, but are *spiritual* weapons.

Alex now wished he had gotten into more deep discussions with his father, about things like this. At this point, all he really understood how to use were the fleshly weapons and a bit of prayer. Well, the way he figured it, he'd just have to use what he had and what he understood for now.

Alex determined, however, that he would pull out his father's well-worn Bible while on the trail of these men and see what else he could learn about those other weapons. The spiritual ones Dan had so often alluded to.

Alex felt a need to pray, but right now he just didn't have it in him. He felt that God wouldn't hear him right now anyway, because of all the hatred, bitterness and the significant lack of forgiveness he felt inside of him.

Alex had prayed at the church altar as a young boy, giving his heart to God, but unfortunately he hadn't pursued the things of God much after that except for memorizing Scripture passages. He hadn't gotten deeply involved in the kind of prayer that his father practiced. He guessed that he'd kind of thought that deep religious practice was more for older folk. One thing that came to his mind now, was something his father had said many times, "God has no grandchildren."

In other words, you can't depend on the closeness of your parents' relationship with the Almighty to provide you, as an individual, with a free ticket into His kingdom. You had to receive that on your own knees and by your own commitment to God and His Word. Alex had memorized a lot of Scripture, but it was mostly head knowledge and hadn't really penetrated down into his spirit yet.

He wondered if the vile feelings he had inside him now could be the trap and tool the powers of darkness might use to dislodge what little faith and knowledge he *did* have.

He remembered well the sermons Dan Barrington had so eloquently delivered, stating that the lack of forgiveness was a major tool used to snatch souls out of God's hands and bring them to isolation from their loving, forgiving Father, thus making them vulnerable to the fiery darts of wicked spirits. We must forgive others before God can forgive us. Dan had said that a soul, once efficiently isolated from communion with the loving Heavenly Father, was treading on perilous ground indeed.

With these thoughts running through his mind, once again Alex finally drifted off to sleep.

He awoke as sunlight peeked through the window. He splashed water on his face and got dressed. As he opened the door of his hotel room, he called Lobo to come with him. He went over to Maria's for breakfast and saved some for Lobo, who was patiently waiting outside. He knew Lobo hadn't had a chance to catch his own meals for a day or two now. The dog met his master with wagging tail, whining in anticipation of the food in Alex's hand.

When Lobo had finished gobbling the food and had drank his fill at a horse trough near the sidewalk, the two started off toward marshal Tihlman's office.

As Alex stepped through the door, he saw that the town marshal and local county sheriff were seated in the office, as planned. Introductions were made and U.S. marshal Tihlman told Alex he had informed the two men of the situation.

The sheriff said that if he had known sooner he could have rounded up a posse to pursue Sanchez's gang. He was sure, however, that by now the outlaws would be out of his jurisdiction before a posse could be organized. He said he'd send a wire ahead to the sheriff of the next county.

Alex doubted the sheriff's sincerity, because of the lack of enthusiasm in the man's voice. He figured him to be one of those lawmen who held the position strictly as a means of earning a living, and that he had no real desire to chase after a group of desperados as dangerous as Sanchez and his gang. Alex, however, didn't display these feelings in his demeanor, but spoke respectfully to the sheriff and thanked him for his promise.

Marshal Tihlman then swore Alex in as a U.S. Deputy marshal. As Alex took the oath and repeated the mandatory words, he was surprisingly moved by the promise he made to uphold the law and conduct himself in a manner befitting a law officer representing the United States government. Until this point, he had thought of the badge he would receive only as a mere formality. As he took the oath, however, and the badge was pinned on his shirt, he felt a sense of responsibility and honor, which he realized he'd have to live up to.

Little did he know at that moment, the impact that this would have on him in the near future. Neither did he realize that the Lord would use this as one of the *many* tools in His omnipotent hands to fulfill a promise in His word that *all* things work together for the good, to those who love Him and are *called* according to His purpose.

When you got right down to it, Alex hadn't the vaguest idea that it was even possible there *was* a *call* of God *in* his life. If he had known this, his question to himself certainly would have been, "Could Ah ever attain unto ta such a callin', from tha Creator of all Heaven an' Earth?"

Indeed, this very issue would manifest itself and greatly challenge him in the weeks and months to follow. What exactly would Alex's reactions to these spiritual promptings be?

These thoughts and questions had not yet materialized in Alex's conscious thinking, but were a mere shadow lurking in his subconscious mind. He sensed something occurring on the inside of him, but was clueless as to what these stirrings in his heart were.

If these questions and challenges had somehow made their way into his conscious thoughts at this time, Alex would most likely have dismissed them as tricks that his highly charged emotional state had evoked upon him.

Nevertheless, wheels were indeed in motion in Alex's heart, which would ultimately lead him to the brink of the most important decisions he had ever faced, in his entire life. His eternal destiny would hinge upon these decisions. Would the Words of the Master Alex had so often heard his father allude to in his sermons be sufficient and significant enough to ensure that Alex would make the right choices when the time came?

With the small weight of the new badge on Alex's shirt and the far greater weight of the new responsibility on his shoulders, Alex left marshal Tihlman's office and went back to his hotel room to get his things.

He then went to the livery stable, saddled Storm and situated the rest of his gear in its proper place. As he led Storm from the stable with Lobo at his heels, marshal Tihlman approached meeting Alex just outside the stable entrance.

He shook Alex's hand firmly and said, "Godspeed, son, an' may that big dog o' yor's an' any angels tha Lord might be able ta spare, help ya watch yor back."

"Thanks again for everything, marshal," Alex replied. "Ah won't forget all ya've done ta help me an' Ah'd be honored ta be considered a friend by a man such as yorself."

"Ah'm honored ta be yor friend, son," responded the marshal. "Hope ta see ya back here, alive an' kickin'."

"Thanks, marshal," Alex concluded, as he mounted Storm. He then put Storm into a canter, again not wanting to look back.

Alex thought of the badge on his shirt. He'd never thought he'd follow in his father's footsteps, other than to be a rancher. He'd never had aspirations in any other direction. So many things had happened and Alex's life had changed so drastically over the past few days, that Alex had difficulty adjusting to the reality of it all. He still felt as if the past few days had been a dream.

The further away he got from Las Cruces and the closer to Silver City, the more trees and wildlife he saw. Juniper woodlands, spruce, pinion, douglas fir and ponderosa pine appeared at the higher elevations. The douglas fir was especially fragrant. The ponderosa pine had a smell which reminded him of vanilla beans. This aroma, he knew, emanated from the tree's bark.

The lazy drone of bees and other insects could be heard all around. The sound of a Gila woodpecker hammering on a nearby tree echoed through the forest. If it hadn't been for the recent tragedy Alex had experienced, he would have enjoyed all of this immensely, but his mind didn't focus directly on these sights and sounds. Instead, he was aware of them subconsciously.

His thoughts were alternately focused. First on the past happy years he'd spent with his family. Then, on the cruel, gruesome acts of the treacherous men he was trailing.

Thus was his state of mind when Lobo suddenly stopped. Alex noticed that the breeze had just shifted and was now coming from the Northwest, instead of the South. Lobo's hackles went up on his back and he bared his teeth. Storm had also begun to act very nervously. Alex reached for his rifle.

Storm suddenly reared up on his hindquarters. Alex felt an impact on his chest, followed by the cracking sound of a rifle. That was the last sensation he remembered, before all went dark and he lost all awareness.

10
Angel of Light

At first, there were only brief recollections of vague sounds and blurred images. They would come and go sporadically, interlaced with sensations of horrible pain and mental anguish. A haunting pattern of thoughts and questions without an awareness of whose they were.

It was as though Alex was at times partially in touch with an agonizing reality, then a black void of time would follow. He struggled with great effort of inner will to bring himself *out* of the darkness he kept slipping into, and *toward* a light that seemed to be at the end of a long tunnel.

It seemed he had fallen into a deep, cavernous well, like a bottomless labyrinth, and was trying desperately to climb out.

At times, he was indistinctly aware of the soft touch of velvety smooth hands. His ears were caressed by a gentle, soothing voice that seemed like the whisper of the wind in the trees. That voice had the effect of a beckoning call toward the light. It was as if someone was there, like an angel of light, assisting his own will to *live* and return from the darkness, back to the world of light and warmth.

Little by little, awareness increased. Then the fuzzy thoughts began to take focus.

When Alex finally came to, he opened his eyes and found himself in a room which he didn't recognize, yet which seemed familiar in a sense. He was in a soft bed. The mattress and pillows were evidently filled with goose down.

Alex looked around the room. He saw a vase of fresh flowers on the washstand. A bright shaft of sunlight entered the room through a window to the left of the bed. It appeared to be early morning.

This was evidently a woman's bedroom because Alex noticed several dresses hanging from a rod in the right corner of the room. He could also detect the faint presence of perfume, mingled with the odor of the hand hewn pine logs the room was constructed of. Woven Indian tapestries hung from the walls.

Alex tried to raise himself to a sitting position and winced with pain. He discovered that his chest and right shoulder were wrapped in clean bandages.

He also discovered a bandage wrapped around his head.

How had he gotten here? What had happened to him and how long had he been unconscious?

These questions now baffled him.

Slowly, Alex began to remember being on the trail. He remembered the scenery he had ridden through. Then he remembered Storm rearing up and the impact to his chest. He remembered hearing the crack of a rifle.

Evidently he had been ambushed, but how had he wound up in this room? Whose room was it and how was he still alive? Alex sensed a motion beside the bed and he looked down to see Lobo lying there, looking up at him with devotion in his eyes. Lobo whined excitedly.

As Alex pondered these things, he heard soft footsteps approaching outside the room. The door opened and a young woman entered carrying a pan, which evidently contained water. The young woman was walking carefully, looking down at the pan, making sure not to allow any of the liquid to spill onto the floor.

She placed the pan onto the washstand and turned toward the bed. When she saw that Alex was awake and watching her, she gasped and clasped a hand over her mouth. Then, as she regained her composure, she lowered her hand and a brilliant smile lit her countenance. Alex couldn't help but return the smile.

At that moment, she looked like an angel to Alex. She was the most beautiful creature he had ever seen in his entire life!

At once an awareness came to Alex, that this was the source of the velvety touch, of the soothing, gentle voice. She was the angelic-like presence he had been aware of during his times of semi-consciousness.

During that moment, when their eyes met for the first time, Alex was overwhelmed with an emotion that was unfamiliar to him. Goosebumps ran onto his arms and down his spine. His heart began to beat faster and he felt the warm tingle as his face began to blush. The young woman also blushed and she opened her mouth slightly, as if to speak, but it seemed that the words lodged in her throat.

The young woman sat down in a chair beside the bed, seemingly a bit overwhelmed with emotion. It then occurred to Alex that she must have already spent a lot of time in that chair during his unconsciousness.

After a few more seconds, she was able to vocalize her thoughts. In a soft voice as smooth as silk, she said, "Thank God you're awake . . . I" . . . She paused for a second, stood up and looked out the window which was near the foot of the bed. "We have been so concerned for you! We have been praying you would pull through! It looks as though our prayers have been answered!"

"Ah'm very grateful ta ya," Alex said. He paused a moment in reflection, then said, "Ah guess we're both wonderin' 'bout some things. Ah'm wonderin' how Ah wound up here, and Ah know you're probably wonderin' who Ah am an' how Ah wound up in tha condition Ah was in. First off, my name is Alexander Barrington." Then he paused and looked at the young woman.

She replied, "I am Rachel McPherson and I'm very pleased you're alive and also very pleased to meet you . . . awake that is."

She blushed again and once more revealed her dazzling smile.

Alex had taken a more thorough look at Rachel moments earlier as she was staring out the window regaining her composure. It had only taken him a brief moment to assess her appearance, and Alex was definitely pleased with what he saw.

She had long, light brown hair with golden highlights. Since she'd been standing in the shaft of light, while she gazed out the window, he'd noticed she had beautiful bright green eyes. The beam of sunlight caused them to sparkle like diamonds. Her complexion was creamy olive and slightly tanned. Her dress was very modest, yet he could tell she was firm and shapely and appeared to be about five feet six inches tall.

Rachel said, "As for how you wound up here, my father and I were sitting on the front porch a few days ago—"

"A few days ago ya say!?" Alex interrupted, with the sound of amazement in his voice. "Ah'm sorry, ma'am, Ah didn't mean ta interrupt."

"That's quite all right," she said with an understanding glance at Alex. "Please call me Rachel. You make me seem so old, calling me ma'am."

Alex, in an apologetic tone, said, "Alright. Please tell me tha rest of it."

"Well," continued Rachel, "we were sitting there, having a cup of coffee when this magnificent gray stallion, which is evidently your horse, came galloping toward the house. We watched with amazement because we could tell that he had a saddle, but no rider. He ran right up to the front porch and stopped. He stood there, pawing the ground with one hoof and then began to trot back toward the direction from which he had come. Then he trotted back to the porch, snorting and shaking his head. It didn't take us long to figure out he wanted

70

us to follow him. My father went to get a couple of our horses saddled, while I tried to calm the stallion down some."

Rachel paused a moment, gazing out the window again with a distant look in her eyes as if she was seeing the whole situation again, for the first time. Then she continued, "I've never seen such an intelligent horse, or one who evidently had such devotion and concern for his master. I knew his owner must be someone special . . ."

She paused and looked back at Alex, blushing again. "I was finally able to calm him down a little and by that time Father led two of our saddle horses around to the front of the house. Just before he returned, I had noticed blood on the gray's saddle. I told Father about this as we mounted our horses. We knew we needed to hurry . . . That someone was badly injured."

Rachel paused and gazed out the window again, taking a deep breath, as though recounting the story pained her. She took another deep breath and continued, "Your stallion began galloping back, in the direction from which he had come. We could barely keep up with him, though I could tell he occasionally slowed his pace, in order not to leave us behind. Finally, about three miles down the road, he stopped. When we rode up to the point in the road where he stood, we saw you lying on the ground. The gray was nuzzling you gently. Your big dog was by your side, guarding you. He seemed to know that we were there to help you."

Rachel again paused briefly, then continued, "Father and I lashed together a travois. Your stallion allowed us to tie it to his saddle. We brought you back here to the ranch. Mother and I have been doctoring you. The gunshot wasn't that bad. It had gone through your shoulder and evidently it didn't hit any bones, though it appeared to have come close to your left lung. It became infected. You also evidently hit your head when you fell. We had no way of knowing how bad that was. The infection brought a high fever and you were delirious for a few days. If I hadn't believed in miracles already, I surely would now, because I think that without one, you wouldn't be alive right now, marshal."

Alex had a bewildered look on his face for a moment. "Marshal?" Alex queried. Then he remembered the badge and the fact that he was, indeed, a deputy U.S. marshal now. Alex added, "Oh, yeah." He tried to prop up on an elbow and winced with pain.

Rachel said, "Oh, please be careful. You might open the wound again." She leaned over him to check the bandage on his chest. A wisp of her hair fell across his cheek as she reached over. Alex could smell the fresh fragrance of her hair. He wanted to touch that beautiful golden hair, but he managed to refrain from that impulse.

When Rachel assured herself there was no sign of blood on the bandage, she sat back down in the chair. She seemed unaware of the stir of emotions her nearness had caused. But, was she?

Rachel said, "I assume you're on the trail of some outlaw, or gang of outlaws, marshal, and that they laid an ambush for you?"

Alex responded in like manner, as Rachel had earlier. "Please. Call me Alex. Ya make *me* feel old." Then he grinned at her.

Rachel said, "Of course . . . Alex. Anyway," she continued, "Mother and I used a recipe for an old Pueblo Indian herbal poultice on your shoulder to help fight infection. But mostly, we kept the wound clean and prayed a lot."

"Ah'm sure both helped plenty," replied Alex. "Ah'm greatly in yor debt. Ya've been very kind."

"Please don't feel indebted to us," said Rachel. "I know you're the type of man that would do the same for others."

Again their eyes met and they both blushed. Alex had never given much thought about what kind of woman he would like to have in of his life, nor had he ever considered himself as having an unfulfilled heart. But now, two issues became clear to him. He realized now since the loss of his family, that there were at least two voids in his life. The first was his need of a closer walk with God.

Now, by encountering this wonderful and inspiring young woman, he felt a need for completion that only a woman like Rachel—and the God she so obviously knew on an intimate basis—could bring.

Alex's mind argued that he had only known Rachel for a few brief moments. He questioned how he could possibly have such strong emotional, spiritual and physical attraction to her this soon. Yet, a voice deep within him was whispering, "*She's the one.*"

Alex quickly rationalized these thoughts and feelings could be attributed to the fact that, though he had just awakened from a state of semi-unconsciousness, he had been aware of her presence for days now.

Thus began a raging battle between Alex's heart and mind. He was, at present, unaware of its gravity, length and significance. Neither did he have any idea how this chance encounter—or was it chance?—would impact his life in the weeks and months to follow.

Alex suddenly realized he had been staring out the window. He caught a glimpse of things which, though not yet tangible to his conscious understanding, gripped the far recesses of his soul. He glanced back at Rachel. She had been watching his gaze, longing to know his thoughts during that brief interlude.

She, however, did not reveal her curiosity but said, "Well . . . Alex, I believe it's your turn to tell me *your* story."

Alex hesitated for a moment, bringing his thoughts back into focus. "Yes . . . O' course," he responded.

Rachel asked, "Have you been on the trail of many outlaws in the past?"

"No . . ." Alex hesitated. "Actually this is tha firs' time. Ah was recently sworn in an' given the badge in Las Cruces. This is kind of a special case. Tha men Ah'm after are very vile bank robbers, murderers an' rapists. Ah've been on their trail for several days. One o' tha gang had lingered behin' tha others in Las Cruces an' recognized me. Now they know Ah was after 'em. They probably think Ah'm dead now an' will likely slow down for a while. Ah need to get back on their trail right away though."

Rachel then said, "Oh, but you mustn't go after them again! Not for a while anyway. You need to finish healing first and regain your strength. I'll go get you some breakfast and tell Mother and Father you've regained consciousness. They'll be so thrilled!"

She stood up and grabbed Alex's hands excitedly, with that velvety touch.

"You must promise me you'll at least think about recovering before you continue to pursue these men," she concluded.

She leaned over impulsively and kissed him lightly on the forehead, then blushed again when she realized what she had just done. It was just that she felt she had already known Alex a long time because of the days-on-end that she had spent nursing his wounds. But, there was a deeper reason. That reason, however, hadn't yet made it to the forefront of her conscious thoughts.

As she pulled away, Alex impulsively grabbed her arm not wanting the moment to end. Their faces were only inches apart as they looked into each other's eyes. Rachel's lips began to tremble and Alex released the gentle grip he had on her arm. She slowly stood upright as her breathing quickened. She stammered, "I'd . . . I'd better go . . . get your breakfast."

Then this lovely creature disappeared through the door, leaving Alex perplexed and bewildered. He wondered if she had already kissed his forehead while he was unconscious, since it had seemed so natural. Somehow he sensed that she had and the thought sent a warmth flowing through him.

11
New Folks

When Rachel returned with breakfast, she brought her father and mother with her. Their faces showed the excitement and happiness they felt, learning that Alex had regained consciousness.

Rachel introduced them to Alex. "Alex," she began, her face beaming, "I'd like you to meet my father, Patrick McPherson and my mother, Allison McPherson."

Alex greeted them with a smile and said, "Ah want ta thank ya for all yor kindness."

Allison McPherson replied. "You're more than welcome, marshal."

"Mother, I think he would rather we call him Alex," Rachel said.

Alex agreed, "Yes . . . Please."

Patrick McPherson joined the conversation, "Welcome to our home, Alex," and with a twinkle in his eye, he added, "and back to the land o' the living."

Both Rachel's parents spoke with a heavy Irish brogue. Alex liked the sound of their accent and the way the letter "R" seemed to roll off their tongue. Their voices lilted up and down with a captivating rhythm. Rachel had the accent as well, but not as strongly as her parents.

Patrick was medium height with a thick chest, a solid, square chin and ruddy complexion. Allison was about the same height as Rachel, but looked a bit more frail. She had auburn hair and the same green eyes as her daughter.

Patrick McPherson, understanding the awkwardness of the situation for Alex, said, "Well, lad, we know you're probably starved, since you haven't eaten for days. The women folk here were only able to get a little water and some occasional broth into you, since we got you back here to the ranch. I know I wouldn't want three people just standing around, watching me eat, so the wife and I will go on about our business. I would suggest, though, that you let Rachel at least sit here and hold the plate for you. It'll be a wee bit before you'll have much pain free use of that right shoulder again. By the way, are you right-handed?"

Alex responded, "Yes, unfortunately. Thanks for your consideration. Ah've never been in a situation quite like this before an' it does make a fellow feel a bit foolish."

With that, Alex smiled. He too, like Rachel, was gifted with a smile that could light up a room.

The McPhersons took great pleasure in his smile and Alex could see that they were genuinely happy to have him in their home and to witness this breakthrough in his recovery. Alex liked them right away.

Then they left the room. Patrick had brought another small table into the room, when they had come to greet Alex. Rachel now pulled it up close to the bed and set the plate of food and coffee on it. She sat in the chair and began to cut the steak into small pieces. She said, "I also understand that this is awkward for you, Alex, but please allow me to hand feed you for a couple of days or so. I don't want you to risk aggravating that wound. You have to let the nerves and muscles mend properly or you just might not get full use of your shoulder back."

Alex gave an understanding nod and said, "Ah know yo're right about that an' Ah guess Ah'll jus' have ta swallow a little pride, along with tha food. Thank ya, Rachel."

There was steak and potatoes, fresh vegetables, evidently from the McPherson garden, and biscuits, which looked good and smelled very mouthwatering to Alex.

As Rachel continued to cut the steak up, she noticed Lobo looking up from where he was lying on the floor. He cocked his head from side to side and licked his chops. Rachel laughed and tossed him a sizable chunk of meat, which he caught in midair and downed with two quick jerks of his jaw and neck.

Rachel commented, lightheartedly, "I want to tell you that your dog has not left you more than a few times, since you've been here and then only to go outside to take care of his necessaries. This is the first time he has even accepted food. What's his name?"

"Lobo," said Alex with a sparkle of pride in his voice. "My stallion's name is Storm. This may soun' silly, but from tha beginnin', when Ah first lassoed that mustang, fresh off tha plains, Ah knew inside that tha good Lord had sent 'em my way for a special reason. He saved my life out there on tha trail when he reared up, jus' before tha rifle was fired. If he hadn't done that, the bullet would surely have gone right through my brisket." Then Alex added, "Plus, he came an' found you kind folk ta come ta my aid."

"He was a Mustang?" Rachel asked with amazement.

"Yup," Alex countered. "That he was."

Rachel looked a bit perplexed. "But how did a horse with his breeding ever wind up feral, I wonder?"

"Ah asked myself tha same question, time an' again. Tha only thing Ah can figure is that he ran off from a remuda somewhere, or tha like."

"Will you please tell me about how you caught him sometime?" Rachel asked.

"Sure," responded Alex. "That's a story Ah enjoy tellin'. Actually, Ah had some Divine help with that one."

"You mention God a lot, Alex. I really like that. He has been my best friend and source of strength for most of my life. It makes my heart glad that you know Him also. That's something else I would like to hear about, sometime."

"Wul," said Alex, "Ah'll give ya a real short version, right now. Ya see, my father was a preacher. Actually, it would be more accurate ta describe 'em as a diplomat, an' a emissary for God. A very eloquent speaker, in a Texan sort o' way."

"You speak of him in the past tense. I assume he has passed away?" Rachel asked.

Alex looked down at the floor, for a moment, sadness dominating the expression on his face. "Yea," was all he could muster, at the moment.

With remorse showing on her face, Rachel said, "I'm sorry. It must have happened recently. I . . . shouldn't have asked."

"That's all right," responded Alex. "But it's still kind o' hard for me ta talk about."

"I understand," said Rachel.

She had finished cutting the steak and forked a piece, guiding it to Alex's mouth. He accepted it and began to chew slowly, savoring the taste. He felt like gulping it down as Lobo had done, but realized he needed to get his stomach used to eating solid food slowly.

After finishing the first few bites of the meal, Alex remarked, "Yor mom is a good cook, or did *you* fix this food?"

Rachel responded, "Thanks. Actually, we both pitched in on this one. In fact, we usually work together at preparing the meals. During roundup, we have to cook for quite a crew of men. It takes both of us and we enjoy working together in the ktichen."

Alex then commented, "It's not hard ta figure yor folks are from Ireland. Do ya mind tellin' me some o' their story?"

"Not at all," replied Rachel. Her face expressed her pleasure that Alex was interested in hearing about her family.

"My father grew up on a farm in the Irish countryside, near Dublin. My grandfather leased the land. Even as a boy, my father had heard many stories of the free land available to settlers, in the American frontier. He is from a rather large family and with Ireland being a small country, most of the land is already in the possession of wealthy families who have owned it for generations. My father wanted land of his own and dreamed of coming to America, to stake his claim."

Rachel paused, to give Alex another bite.

There was a warmth and glow about her that drew Alex like a magnet. He realized that it was something more than her physical beauty and personality.

There was, it seemed to Alex, an almost unfathomable depth of purity and innocence, which he thought had to come from her heart. It was an inner beauty and strength that Alex intuitively knew came from her closeness to the Creator.

Rachel continued with the story of her parents, "Mother's family owned a small boardinghouse, nearby. That's where she first learned to cook. Mother and Father both attended the same school. Father says that since he was about twelve years old, he knew he wanted to marry Mother, someday. During their teen-age years, they began to dream together about coming to America."

Alex could see in the expression on Rachel's face and could tell by the tone of her voice that she was enjoying sharing this story with him.

She continued, "Father began, at an early age, to do extra work for neighboring farmers, saving up for their dream. He also learned to make furniture to sell. He's a very disciplined man with foresight for the future. He and Mother were married when he was twenty and she was nineteen. Mother had also made extra money taking in laundry and the like. Together they had saved up enough to be able to buy passage to this country and when they had only been married for a year, they sailed across the Atlantic to begin a new life here."

Rachel held the coffee mug for Alex so he could wash down the food he had eaten so far. Then she gave him some steak and potatoes.

While doing this, she continued with the story. "They lived in New York for the first two years, continuing to work and save. That's when I was born. Times were difficult for them then. They were so anxious to move on out west, that they lived as meagerly as possible in order to build a nest egg sufficient to buy livestock, simple farming equipment, supplies for the journey and a wagon to make the trip in. They decided it would be best to move to Independence, Missouri for a brief time and keep their eyes and ears open for news of a satisfactory wagon train, going further west."

Alex found himself intrigued with the story and he was mesmerized by Rachel's smooth, silken voice as she recounted the adventure to him.

"They finally made it out here," she said, "only to find out that the land which speculators had painted such a fine picture of in their hearts and minds wasn't suited for farming. They staked their claim anyway, after finding out that livestock could do okay, on this land. They also thought the countryside here was beautiful. So they turned their dream around, from one of farming to one of ranching."

Rachel noticed Lobo had come and laid down near her and was still staring at the plate of food so she smiled and tossed him some more.

Alex grinned and said, "Looks like you two have hit it off pretty well. Ah think ya have a frien' for life."

Rachel looked at Alex and blushed as she said, "Well . . . I hope I have *two*."

12

A Beautiful Dream

When Alex slept that night, he had several dreams. He figured the pain had him in a half wakeful state during some of the night because when he awoke he could remember most of what he had dreamed.

Of course he had at least one nightmare about the massacre of his family, but the good thing was that he could only remember one. He did, however, remember some very pleasant dreams about the McPhersons.

The last dream he remembered just before fully awakening, involved him and Rachel. They were walking through a field of beautiful green, waist high prairie grass, which a gentle breeze caused to sway in roles like the waves of the sea. They were walking along in silence, but each very keenly aware of the other's presence. Soon, they came to a meadow fringed with bluebonnets.

The sky was clear and a brilliant blue except for a few white billowy clouds. The landscape was open, gently rolling hills as far as the eye could see. There were some perfectly shaped trees scattered here and there, but they did not block the view of the undulating hills. They entered a circular meadow of shorter, softer and more emerald green ground cover. It was surrounded by the hills of undulating grass they had just walked through. The gentle breeze made a soft whispering sound as it caressed that grass.

In the middle of the meadow were Greek style columns which were the purest white Alex had ever seen. In fact, everything seemed to have a luminous quality which was rather unearthly. Alex could see other such columns scattered over the distant landscape. Rachel was wearing a long white dress with the same luminous brightness.

As they approached the columns in the middle of the meadow, Alex could tell these were set in a circle. In the center was a beautiful ornate fountain with the tranquil sound of water running down from statues of cherubs, blowing long trumpets, which turned gracefully upward at the end. The water ran down into a pool made of white marble. Around the fountain, and scattered throughout the meadow were resplendent flowers in clusters of astounding color, whose beauty was spectacular as well as peaceful. It seemed that God encompassed them with a tangible, tender loving affection. The tenderness of this love far surpassed anything Alex had ever experienced.

There were three crescent-shaped marble benches around the pool and he and Rachel sat down on one of them. There was a serenity about this place that he dreamed of, which held such calm and comfort that it seemed beyond comprehension of human understanding.

There was no visible sun in the sky, yet, everything was brightly lighted. The temperature was like that of the most beautiful and perfect spring day. He and Rachel had turned toward each other and had clasped each other's hands when Alex awoke.

He closed his eyes, fervently wishing to fall right back to sleep and continue the dream. It was the best dream Alex had ever experienced and he didn't want it to end.

The dream was so real that Alex couldn't help wondering if it possibly could have come entirely from his mind. Alex had only seen columns and statues like that once, in a book at school. They had been mere drawings. How could everything he saw in that dream seem so vividly real and have such crystal clear detail? Just thinking about it caused chills to run down Alex's spine.

Alex had been lying there thinking about the dream for a few minutes, when Rachel entered the room carrying breakfast on a tray. Alex had a strong sense of déjà vu when he saw her, for she was wearing a white dress much like the one in the dream.

The smile, which Alex now looked forward to with anticipation, flashed across her face. There was nothing pretentious about that smile. It was completely natural and Alex thought to himself that she probably didn't realize how often she smiled, or how beautiful it was.

Alex wished he had the joy in life which Rachel possessed. He had a desire to be with her, feeling it possible for some of her joy to rub off on him.

Rachel sat the tray of food on the small table. The tray held a plate of eggs, salt pork, biscuits and fresh milk, along with a cup of Arbuckle's.

Tentatively, Alex tried to raise himself up on one elbow again. To his surprise, the pain was only about half what it had been the previous day. He commented, "That poultice sure mus' work well. There's much less pain this mornin'."

"Yes," Rachel responded, "but you still shouldn't rush things. Please, let me continue to feed you, at least for today . . . Okay?"

"If ya insist," replied Alex, good-naturedly. "Ah don' see Lobo. He mus' be takin' care o' business."

Rachel said, "Yes. I quietly opened the door a while ago and let him out. He seems a lot spunkier since you're awake and getting better."

Alex, grinning, said, "Hope he gets on back ta catchin' rabbits again. By tha way, how's Storm doin'?"

Rachel responded, "Oh, he's doing pretty well." There seemed to be a touch of mischief in her voice. "He spends part of the day loooking toward the house, wondering how you are,

I'm sure. The rest of the time he's showing interest in a mare of ours in an adjoining pasture. It's her time and Storm has taken an interest. She's our finest mare. Storm evidently has good taste." She chuckled and then turned a bit red.

When growing up on a ranch, talk of breeding livestock was common of course, but nonetheless, Rachel became suddenly bashful about it.

Alex acted as if he hadn't noticed and said, "Maybe yor father would like Storm ta breed with 'er."

Rachel's embarrassment quickly vanished and was forgotten. The thought of the magnificent foal, which Storm could sire with their top mare, brought an excited expression to her face. She said, "Alex! That would be wonderful! I've noticed father watching them and knew he was thinking of the same thing . . . and so was I, of course. He would never ask of you what he would consider to be a trivial question while you're laying in bed, recovering from such a serious injury. I know him. He would think it rude to do so."

Alex said emphatically, "Rachel! You an' yor family have saved my life! There's no way Ah could ever repay ya! Tha very least Ah could do, would be ta allow Storm ta breed with yor mare, an' Ah know Storm would consider it an honor as well," he concluded with a rather impish grin.

Alex had also become enthused about the prospect and asked Rachel to describe the mare to him.

Rachel said, "Okay, but first I need to give you some of this food, before it gets cold." Her face lit up with that brilliant smile.

The thought of the dream Alex had experienced last night returned to him again as Rachel hand fed him a few bites of the breakfast. She had a gentleness about her, which was quite overwhelming to Alex. Her presence was intoxicating to his senses. He wanted to tell her about the dream he had been blessed with last night, but felt he should keep it to himself. He wondered how long he could keep such strong emotions bottled up inside?

As Rachel gave Alex more food, she looked tenderly into his eyes for a moment and it seemed that she sensed his discomfort. She leaned back and gazed out the window with a wistful look. She then remembered her promise to describe the mare to Alex. Unknown to Alex, her thoughts had made her temporarily forget where their conversation had left off.

She began, "Father had heard of a fine stable of horses in Virginia. He had corresponded with the owner through telegraphs. This breeder's stock are all direct descendants of Justin Morgan."

That statement got Alex's attention in a hurry. Every horse breeder worth his salt knew of the famous horse, Justin Morgan. He was a stallion named after his owner, a school teacher in Vermont. So strong had been the blood of this horse, his owner had begun a whole new breed of horses with that one stallion. Although barely over fourteen hands tall, the stallion had been able to outpull most draft horses and outrun most racehorses.

Alex said, with a definite show of interest, "So tha mare's a Morgan?"

"Yes," responded Rachel. "Father really wanted a Morgan stallion, but was only able to purchase the mare. Aye, but she's a beauty, though! She's rather large for a Morgan. She's fifteen and a half hands, but still has the straight, clean legs, the muscled quarters and the deep body. Until I saw Storm, I had never seen a better horse."

Alex said, "Yea. Ah'm convinced Storm has some strong Morgan blood too, mixed with some Quarter Horse an' Thoroughbred, which gives 'em his height. Ah'm more eager than ever now, ta get back on my feet, so Ah can see yor mare. Can ya tell me more 'bout 'er?"

"Well," responded Rachel, "she's a chestnut with a fine, intelligent head, which of course she carries high, and she has a clean-cut throatlatch. She's all grace n' glory, that one!"

85

Alex could certainly tell that Rachel shared the same love of horses he possessed. He now had several reasons to hope he could get up and about soon. First, for sure, was his desire to get back on Sanchez's trail. This, however, was now magnified by his desire to see the McPherson's mare. But an even stronger and more immediate reason was his need to get out of this bedroom.

Alex was now torn with conflicting emotions. On one hand, he had a desire to be with Rachel every moment. On the other hand, he felt a need to become mobile enough that he could escape such close and frequent contact with her. He just wasn't used to the kind of feelings he had for her, nor did he want those feelings to hinder his getting back on the trail of Sanchez and his gang.

Their conversation dwindled at this point and was replaced by a comfortable silence. Words were not a constant necessity for them in order to enjoy each other's company, just as in his dream.

Alex was able to finish all the food on the plate, which he washed down with the milk. Then he began to enjoy the coffee. It had been kept hot because Rachel had wrapped a thick cloth around it. Despite some objections from Rachel, he insisted on using his left hand to hold the coffee mug himself.

Rachel excused herself, saying that she would bring the pot of coffee and join him for a cup. While she was gone, Alex's mind raced. Conflicting emotions and thoughts raced through his gray matter, until he felt as though mentally he was riding the wildest of bangtails and about to blow a stirrup. He felt he must get a grip on his feelings and head them off at the pass.

To Alex, the timing for all of this was not in his scheduled plans and there simply was no time for it. He realized it would take him longer to recuperate than suited his wishes right now. He had the feeling, once again, that the good Lord may be trying to speak something to his heart.

Rachel returned with the Arbuckles. They alternately talked more about the horses and then enjoyed moments of silence.

Finally, Rachel said, "Well, I've got chores to do. I'll ask Yang Ling, the Chinese man who has been helping us here at the ranch since I was a child, to come help you bathe. He and father are the ones who removed your outer garments and got you ready for Mother and I to dress your wounds when we first got you back to the ranch."

Alex had been wondering who had accomplished this, hoping that it hadn't been Rachel or her Mother who had to take care of such a matter. Alex was painfully modest and had worried about that. He felt relieved hearing that it had been men who had taken care of this detail. It was bad enough that he didn't yet have a shirt on. He had always felt embarrassed for any woman, except his mom or sister to see him shirtless even. He felt the same way about being seen in his long handles. For Rachel or her mom to have had to completely undress him would have troubled him immensely. Alex was thankful that Yang or Rachel's father had at leaset put a pair of trousers back on him. He understood that he'd been left without a shirt on because a wound needs as much air as possible in order to heal more quickly. Even bandaging needs to be as porous as possible.

Alex said, "Thanks. Ah believe Ah'll be needin' my clothes in a day or two. Ah have a couple o' clean outfits in my bedroll."

Rachel replied, "Yes, I know. That's where we found the pants you're wearing now." She blushed slightly and added, "Of course Yang and my father were the ones that put them on you." She said this with a rather impish grin and then added, "I washed the ones you had on and darned the two bullet holes on the front and back of your shirt, as well."

Alex paused for a moment and said, "Thanks." He felt nonplused and frustrated not being able to express his gratitude more effectively. The simple word "thanks," seemed so terribly weak, but his mind drew a blank when he tried to think of more appropriate words to show his gratitude for all the McPhersons had done for him. He didn't yet have his father's way with words. He remembered his father telling him once though, that he had also been shy and awkward with words when he was younger. Alex thought to himself that perhaps one day he too would be able to express himself more eloquently.

For now, the only way he knew to expand the significance of the single word was to say it with his most sincere smile and by an open, honest and direct look into Rachel's eyes. The smile and look, which she returned, spoke volumes to Alex. He kneew she understood what he really wanted to say from his heart.

As she left the room his pulse was racing yet again. He silently petitioned God from the bottom of his heart. "Lord, please don't let me hurt Rachel's tender soul. Don't allow tha anger an' rage Ah carry inside, ta bring any pain or sorrow inta her life."

Alex hoped and prayed that the anger and rage inside him would abate over time and that he'd be able to approach his continued pursuit of the outlaws with level-headed control. He knew that only God could accomplish this. Even the strongest of those who follow in Jesus' footsteps to the best of their ability, would need a real miracle in order to abandon the temptation of rage and vengeance he was faced with. But, Alex knew deep within his heart that *all* things are possible with God.

He now made a silent vow to do his best at allowing the Lord sufficient opportunity to produce this miracle he so desperately needed. He had no idea of how strongly this vow would be put to the test in the near future.

13
Mixed Emotions

By the next day Alex was feeling much better, although his right shoulder still pained him when he tried to use it. Today, however, with assistance from Yang Ling, he was able to put on the clean outfit Rachel had brought in. He was also able to sit on the edge of the bed and feed himself with his left hand. The ability to do such a simple thing would never before have been a big thing. Now, however, this accomplishment brought a feeling of encouragement. Alex would never again take the simple things in life for granted.

After breakfast Rachel brought a sling she had made of cloth to give support to Alex's right arm. With help from Rachel, and enduring some tooth-grinding pain, Alex was able to get his arm into the sling. Rachel made adjustments to the length of the sling. Finally, it was a perfect fit and helped considerably at reducing the discomfort and pain.

Of course, all of this required close contact between Alex and Rachel. When all was said and done, Alex couldn't decide which had been the toughest for him to endure. The pain in his body, or the sweet ecstasy of physical contact with Rachel. Both were certainly a test of his strength and endurance. He had to exercise strong self-control in both circumstances. The latter was both a source of consternation *and* bliss for Alex.

When Rachel left the room, Alex decided to make his first attempt since regaining consciousness to stand up and perhaps even walk around a bit. He was anxious to regain mobility as soon as possible. He turned around the chair by the bed so he could use it for support. He slowly pulled himself upright.

Though the pain in his shoulder had subsided again, once Alex stood up, he realized how weak the wounds, fever and lack of eating had made him. He wasn't quite in a full standing position when the room began to spin. Alex first saw spots before his eyes and everything grew dark. He felt that he would surely faint. However, as suddenly as it had begun, the dizziness, and the faint feeling left him.

Alex noticed he was still clinging to the chair hard enough to make his knuckles turn white. Now, in place of the faint feeling, severe nausea swept over him. He felt he was going to lose his breakfast. All the hard work he had invested in getting it into his craw would be wasted. He headed for the window and opened it, just in case. He sure didn't want to return Rachel's benevolence by skunkin' up her room.

After opening up the window and sticking his head out, the fresh air seemed to help. In a few minutes, the cold sweat and clamminess had left him. Apart from the minimal discomfort of his shoulder, the only remaining symptoms were a feeling of weakness and the accompanying shaky feeling. He felt like a newborn pup facing a sandstorm.

Alex stayed at the window for some time, soaking up the sun and the beauty of outdoors. He had never been cooped up inside this long. He felt a tremendous sense of gratitude to be alive and to be near the time when he could walk outside and see Storm and McPherson's mare. He looked forward to this with great anticipation.

Suddenly, Alex became aware that though he had thanked Rachel and her family, he hadn't thanked God for the obvious miracles he had been given. The miracle that Storm had reared up at just the right moment. The miracle of Storm going for help. The miracle that there had been a compassionate and Godly family nearby who knew how to pray in faith. There was also the miracle of his recovery from such a close brush with death. He realized that he certainly had a lot to be thankful for and that without the Lord's grace and mercy, he'd probably be pushing up daisies right now.

He felt compelled to offer some words of thanks to his Creator. Alex never dreamed that he would encounter a situation so quickly after the demise of his family that would make him glad to be alive and feel thankful in his heart. He slowly and carefully got on his knees in front of the window. He spoke words of great sincerity and thankfulness. He spoke in a soft voice because he realized the Lord isn't hard of hearing.

He said, "God . . . Father . . . Ya know Ah'm not much with words. But Ah believe Ya can fill in tha gaps an' hear the right words from my soul. Thank Ya for sendin' Storm my way an' for using 'em ta be a part o' savin' my life. Thank Ya for tha McPhersons an' their willingness ta take a wounded stranger in an' help Ya ta nurse 'em back ta health. Ah ask Ya ta bless 'em abundantly in return. Help 'em ta reallize how grateful Ah am, 'spite o' tha fact Ah'm not good at 'spressin' what's on my mind. Ah give Ya thanks from tha bottom o' my heart. In tha name o' Yor Son, Jesus', Amen."

As Alex concluded his prayer, he heard a slight rustle of cloth behind him. He turned and looked behind him to see Rachel standing inside the doorway with two mugs of coffee in her hands. He wondered if she had heard his prayer. One thing was for sure. She had definitely seen him in his kneeled position and with his head bowed. The way she reacted next made him almost certain she had heard the words he had prayed.

She stammered, "I . . . I'm sorry . . . I . . . I didn't mean to interrupt."

Alex said, "It's okay. Ah was done anyway." Alex, using his left hand on the window sill, pulled himself to his feet. He turned to face Rachel. He already thought she glowed all the time. Though her smile was somewhat demure in that moment, the resplendent spark of life now revealed in her eyes made even her normally brilliant smile pale slightly in comparison. Alex's first reaction to being caught in the process of offering a prayer was to be slightly embarrassed. Not that he would ever be ashamed of prayer, but in his opinion, prayer, except for around the dinner table and the like, was a private matter. The wondrous look, however, that he now received from Rachel, eradicated any discomfort and assured him that there was absolutely *nothing* to be embarrassed about and *everything* to be proud of. This realization served to heighten his already deep respect for her.

Neither of them had spoken since Rachel's awkward comment after entering the room. But, Alex intuitively knew that her respect for him had just climbed to a new level as well.

Alex was simultaneously pleased *and* disconcerted. In his heart he was glad for her approval, but in his mind he was also bothered because he knew that soon he must return to tracking Sanchez and his men.

He was also confounded by the thought that Rachel may somehow soon be able to read his innermost secret thoughts. That she might be hurt or deeply troubled by the darkness of hatred and revenge that lurked there, hidden in the secret recesses of his soul. If indeed she were able to perceive this, Alex would feel a deep humiliation. He was also haunted by the thought that this might have some effect on her view of his character.

This, however, wasn't likely since Rachel was intuitive enough to understand the difference between his *current* emotions and his *normal* nature. He would soon likely be faced with the necessity of sharing with her the events which transpired at the ranch. Rachel would then *certainly* understand the darkness which now plagued his soul.

His deep preoccupation with these thoughts was interrupted when Rachel said, "Well, I'm glad to see you are up 'n about, but I hope you don't overdo it."

Alex responded, "Actually, Ah've been thinkin' it's 'bout time Ah got outside a little. Maybe see tha mare an' all."

Rachel asked, "Why don't we talk about it over a cup of coffee, on the front porch?"

Alex answered, "That soun's great."

Soon, they were seated in two of the six rocking chairs, on the veranda. They sipped their coffee in silence for a few moments, before either of them spoke. Then, each of them spoke at the same time and each asked the other's pardon.

So Alex said, "Please, you first."

Rachel responded, "I was just going to say that I'm sure you're glad to get outside again."

Alex answered, "Yo're shorely right about that. Ah haven't spent so much time indoors, since Ah was a kid an' had tha measles."

"And what were *you* about to say?" Rachel inquired.

"Well," began Alex, "it was actually somethin' along the same lines. Ah was goin' ta say that Ah really 'preciate ya giving up yor room for me, but Ah think it's 'bout time for me ta move out ta tha bunkhouse. Where have ya been bunkin' anyway, since Ah kind o' took over yor bedroom?"

Rachel replied, "Oh, it's been no hardship for me. I've been using my brother's old bedroom."

After that statement, she had a far-off, melancholy look in her eyes and was staring into the distance. This was the first time Alex had seen any sign that Rachel had anything but joy and happiness in her life. He could tell both by her countenance and by her tone of voice that something had happened to her brother. He didn't comment or question her about it, concerned he would, "meter la pata," the Spanish equivalent to, "put your foot in your mouth." So often had Alex conversed in Spanish with Tía Anna that he sometimes *thought* in Spanish.

After a few moments, Rachel voluntarily explained to Alex, "We lost Sean, my younger brother, to influenza a good number of years ago."

Alex said in a warm and understanding manner, "Sorry to hear 'bout that. Ah los' my bes' frien', who was as close as a brother ta me, ta influenza also. We were both twelve when he died. That was 'bout nine years ago."

Rachel said, "That's about how long ago we lost Sean. It was evidently during the same epidemic. I'm sorry about your friend as well."

"Thanks," said Alex, gently. "Anyway, he continued, "Ah would feel less in tha way an' less burdensome, if Ah move ta tha bunkhouse. Ah really want ta get in shape as quickly as possible too, so Ah can help out 'round tha ranch for a while. It'll be good medicine for me ta do so. O' course Ah won't be able ta be much help at firs', but once Ah've recuperated some Ah can carry my share. Ah know Ah can never repay you an' your family, but if it's all right with yor folks, Ah'd like ta do my best, at leas' ta show some of tha 'preciation, that's in my heart. Then . . . Alex paused and stumbled around a bit, trying to get the last sentence out . . . "Then, Ah've got ta get back on Sanchez's trail. Ah figure Ah'll be ready ta do that in a couple or three weeks, maybe."

Rachel's countenance saddened again for a moment and Alex could see the slight struggle she had returning to her normal joyous self. She smiled that heartwarming smile of hers, only this time it was just a trifle less brilliant than normal. Alex could sense she was trying to hide some kind of disappointment. He assumed it was more about his mention of leaving instead of his moving out to the bunkhouse.

Rachel then said, "Oh, I'm sure Mother and Father would love to have you stay around for awhile. For as long as you like actually, but just for the record, I want you to know that none of us expect you to feel obligated. As I said before, we know you're the type that would do the same, given a similar situation."

"Rachel," Alex began, "there's . . . something Ah need ta . . . tell ya . . ."

Rachel put her index finger across her lips and then placed it across Alex's mouth in the same manner. It was a gesture saying he didn't have to talk right now about the sort of thing she had already guessed was bothering him. With her eyes fixed on Alex's, she responded, "Shhhh . . . Alex," she continued, "I can tell that you've recently been through some kind of horrible experience other than being shot from ambush. Of course I don't know exactly what it was, but I want you to know that there's plenty of time for you to share that with me later, if you'd like. I see the struggle and the pain you're going through right now trying to explain it. Maybe you should just let your mind and feelings settle down for a while and tell me about it when you're more comfortable doing so."

Alex had actually wanted to tell her about all that had happened in order to overcome the suspense and dread he faced. He dreaded her reaction, if and when the dark battle raging inside of him was revealed.

Rachel would then be able to see the rage and anger now temporarily constrained within his soul. Held at bay by the tender innocence and peaceful presence of an extraordinary woman.

For now, though, he felt a sense of relief that Rachel had persuaded him to wait. Thinking about it, he realized he would have less difficulty telling the story after he'd had more time to contemplate how he would explain the events which had precipitated his pursuit of the outlaws. Alex marveled at the wisdom Rachel was gifted with.

Then his mind drifted into a cavernous web of thought. While he felt his hatred and rage would be totally justifiable for a man who didn't know the Savior, he loathed and even felt a sense of shame that those feelings had managed to gain a rather recondite root in his heart.

He couldn't yet fully understand the reason for the conflicting emotions battling within him. He was presently unable to grasp the wondrous *gift* of forgiveness made available to those willing to allow the inner working of the Spirit of God. The gruesome events which had occurred at the ranch had even somewhat suppressed his memory of that powerful message on forgiveness his father had preached that Sunday prior to the horrific debacle.

He and Rachel finished the rest of their coffee in silence. Then Alex remarked, "Ya know, Rachel, Ah really feel like Ah'm ready ta try out my legs, with a bit of a walk. Ah'd like ta see Storm again an' Ah'd also, like ta see that mare o' yor's. Do ya have time ta accompany me?"

Rachel replied, "Yes. With the condition that you promise to hold onto me if you should get dizzy."

"Ah promise," Alex replied in a rather teasing way.

"All right then," concluded Rachel. "Just let me take the coffee mugs inside and I'll be with you in a minute."

She then took the empty mugs and disappeared inside the house for a few moments. When she returned, she brought a walking stick which she handed to Alex. She explained her father had used it once after injuring his leg in a riding accident. She wanted to take no chances of Alex losing his balance due to his weakened condition. He thanked her and accepted it. He carefully rose from the rocking chair and started toward the porch steps.

They slowly made their way toward the barn. There was a large enclosed area just behind the structure and extending a good distance to the right and left of it. It was divided into three pastures. Alex spotted Storm about fifty yards out in the left pasture.

He whistled in the special tone he used to call Storm. The stallion, whose head had been down grazing, immediately looked in Alex's direction and sprang into a gallop toward the fence, tail high and flying like a flag behind him.

So eager was he to get to his master that it appeared he would surely either burst through the fence or jump over it.

Instead, when he was a few feet from the fence, he braced himself with stiffened front legs and lowered quarters, sliding to a standstill right in front of it.

Alex, grinning ear-to-ear, began to stroke Storm's muzzle and scratch between his ears while talking to him in his soothing manner. He glanced over at Rachel who was standing in awe at such a display of affection between man and horse. She was smiling her brilliant smile. She reached out and joined Alex in caressing the horse. Rachel knew that if horses were able to smile, Storm's would match that of his master. In amazement, she watched the two harmoniously rekindle their bond.

After a few minutes of this joyful reunion, Alex said, "Ah would like ta stay here with Storm a lot longer, but before my energy runs out, Ah'd like ta see yor mare."

Rachel responded with a question, "Alex, are you sure you're up to it? It's a good walk to the third enclosed pasture where the mare is."

Alex assured her that he could make it, so they walked to the opposite side of the barn, following the fence line until they came to the third, fenced pasture area. There were at least two dozen mares out grazing there, but even at a distance Alex had no trouble spotting the chestnut.

He glanced at Rachel, with an excited expression on his face, and said, "She's everything ya said an' more!"

Rachel smiled and then whistled. It was a softer and more feminine whistle than Alex's, yet it got the attention of most of the mares in the pasture and several of them, including the chestnut, began trotting toward the fence. Head and tail high, the chestnut was easily the first one to reach the fence. Alex had the same opinion of her that Rachel had. Except for Storm, she was the finest horse Alex had ever seen. Rachel informed him the mare's name was Ginger.

Alex inquired of Rachel, "Have ya talked ta yor father yet, 'bout breedin' Ginger an' Storm?"

Rachel replied, just a bit sheepishly, "Yes, I hope you don't mind. I thought, afterward, that you might have wanted to tell him yourself."

Alex responded, "*What?* An' take that pleasure from ya? No, Ah'm pleased ya went ahead an' told 'em. What was his reaction?"

"Oh, he was thrilled, of course," responded Rachel. "If you're feeling up to it tomorrow, maybe you and I can watch Father open the gate and lead Ginger into Storm's pasture."

Alex could feel the same excitement Rachel had in her voice. "Oh, Ah think Ah'll find a way ta make it out here again," he replied with a grin.

With that, they returned to the ranch house. By the time they got there, Alex was pretty much beat. As much as it hurt his pride, he had to allow Rachel to support him a bit as they climbed the front porch steps. He didn't even feel up to going inside yet, so he sat back down in one of the rockers.

Rachel looked at him with compassion and understanding. Her heart ached to see him in such pain, yet she understood a man's indomitable nature to disguise any appearance of weakness. She also recognized that the male ego was placed in man by God as a natural mechanism to insure his motivation to provide for his family. It could easily be perverted, as can all good things, turning into an ungodly desire to dominate with cruel and insensitive demands. But Rachel knew this definitely was not the case with Alex. She merely said, "I'll go get us some more coffee."

She turned and went inside the house. As soon as she was inside, Alex allowed a sigh to escape, brought on by his fatigue and pain. He was amazed at how weak he was. He certainly didn't want Rachel to know the extent of his physical distress. He would have suffered a blow to his manly pride.

He was also concerned that perhaps Rachel would want to postpone their plans to put Storm and Ginger together in "*horsely*" matrimony, to have and to "*foal*" 'till the next mare did them part. He certainly didn't want to put *that* off. He felt like a little kid at Christmas in anticipation of the event.

Rachel returned shortly with the coffee. Alex was too preoccupied with his thoughts and pain, to notice her quiet return in time. When she looked at Alex, his face still reflected the pain he had been struggling to hide. He quickly plastered a smile on his face in an attempt to conceal it.

Rachel acted as if she hadn't noticed. She handed him his coffee and sat down next to him trying to conceal a concerned look on her face. She said nothing about her apprehensions, understanding a man's stoic desire to hide pain and suffering. Alex knew she must have seen the pained look on his face. He marveled at her ability to constrain herself. It had been his experience that *most* women would have *voiced* their concern and attempted to persuade a change of plan concerning Storm and Ginger. He was quite aware, however, that Rachel was *not* a typical woman by *any* means.

Although she had previously expressed general concern, she was evidently satisfied to trust his judgment. Alex understood that unless he himself said he wasn't up to it, they would still unite Storm and Ginger tomorrow. Alex had yet another reason to appreciate the consistent quality of Rachel's character. Her inner lack of desire to control others pleased him very much.

After finishing her coffee, Rachel went back inside, to help her mother prepare dinner. This would be the first time Alex would sit at the dinner table with the McPhersons.

14
The Horror Revealed

After Rachel went to assist her mom with preparing dinner, Alex returned to Rachel's bedroom to take a short nap. He needed to recover some strength. He intended to move his things to the bunkhouse, after dinner.

When Alex awoke, he felt refreshed. He could smell the appetizing aroma of the food Rachel and Allison were preparing. Alex's stomach began to rumble and he could hardly wait to satisfy his suddenly strong craving to eat. He knew that fried chicken was on the menu, for its tantalizing smell wafted into the bedroom, beckoning him to the dinner table. Alex couldn't remember the last time he had been so hungry. He felt like going ahead to the table to sit there and wait with fork and knife in hand.

When Rachel finally came to tell him dinner was ready, he tried hard to hide his eagerness, hoping that his attempt to do so would be successful. He had washed his face, shaved and combed his hair to be as presentable as he could.

As Alex entered the dining room for the first time, he took note of the sturdy, yet beautiful, table and chairs. He asked Rachel about their origin. She informed him that her father had built the dining set from cherry wood, he had ordered from back East. He greatly admired Patrick's craftsmanship. When Rachel had told him her father learned to make furniture back in Ireland, he'd had no idea how very gifted he was.

There was also a matching china hutch and a beautiful grandfather clock. When he asked, Rachel informed Alex that her father had ordered the face, pendulum and other inner workings for the clock and had handcrafted the case to match the other dining room furniture. Alex was amazed.

How had Patrick found time to make all of this furniture while simultaneously maintaining what appeared to be a quite sizable and industrious ranch?

There were also intricately embroidered doilies upon which the china was set on the table. Alex learned that Rachel's mother had made them. She had taught Rachel her skills with a needle as well.

Judging by Rachel's slight hesitance and her mild embarrassment as he asked her about these things, Alex knew that there was no arrogance in this family concerning their talents. Conversely, he sensed an attitude of modesty and humility.

Once everyone, including Yang, was seated at the table, Patrick McPherson bowed his head and took his wife's hand in his own. Alex also bowed his head. He was seated next to Rachel. As Patrick began to say grace, Alex felt Rachel's soft, warm hand grasp his own.

Alex's intense hunger for food was momentarily forgotten as the blood rushed to his head and his heart raced. He felt very much alive and glad to be so in that moment.

As Patrick McPherson ended the prayer, Rachel gave Alex's hand a quick squeeze before letting go. Alex opened his eyes but just sat there dumbfounded for a few moments staring down at the table. He didn't even remember his intense hunger until Rachel passed him the platter of friend chicken. The sight and smell of the chicken finally brought him back to his senses. He felt concerned that everyone else at the table must surely have read him like an open book and that they had seen the tide of emotions which had washed over him.

He had glanced quickly at Rachel as he forked a drumstick from the platter. She was staring at the wall on the opposite side of the table and he could see a slight smile playing at the corner of her mouth. He noticed that her plate still had no food on it. He glanced quickly at Patrick, Allison and Yang's plates and noticed that they too were empty. Then, as he passed the chicken across the table to Yang and was passed the mashed potatoes by Rachel, it dawned on him that he was being served first. His ears grew hot as he began to blush when he hadn't realized that he was being given this honor.

Maybe Rachel's father noticed Alex's predicament because he began the conversation then by asking Alex what he thought of Ginger. He was so self-conscious and flustered that he had to think for moment, asking himself, "Who's Ginger?"

Finally, after a second which seemed to last an eternity, he got his wits back and managed to stammer, "Ah . . . uh . . . oh . . . why she's tha . . . fines' horse Ah've ever seen . . . next ta Storm."

Alex glanced at Patrick and noticed that he was now apparently focused on selecting a piece of chicken from the platter. He was looking at the platter with a smile on his face a yard wide, which he was attempting to make less obvious. Alison appeared to be in the same situation. As for Rachel, when her father passed her the platter of chicken, he had to clear his throat in order to get her attention. This effectively drew her eyes from the wall. Then Alex had the pleasure to see her blush as well. At least he wasn't in this boat by himself. He began to grin to himself now.

In the meantime, Yang dropped the spoon from the bowl of mashed potatoes onto his plate with a loud clang. Alex noticed that Yang, too, looked like he was about to pop a gut. Alex had to look back down at his plate and think of what to say about Ginger and Storm in order to keep from bursting out in laughter. The thought of the Scripture, "A merry heart, doeth good like a medicine," came to Alex's mind. He felt better inside than he had felt for a long time. He found it quite pleasing to share the company of folk he not only held in high regard, but who also had a refreshing sense of humor. His heart was warmed by sharing their company. He felt as though he'd known them for years.

Once everyone had their plates full and the intense humor of the moment was pretty much under control, the conversation began in earnest. The main topic, of course, was the potential breeding of Storm and Ginger. About bringing together two of the finest horses that had ever been seen in that region of the country.

Both horses had an extremely strong and rock solid ancestry. Patrick couldn't imagine the two horses conceiving anything but the best. Alex and Rachel both had to agree with her father's deduction.

Alex discovered during the conversation that Yang Ling had come to live with the McPhersons as a young boy. His mother had died giving birth to him. His father had been a laborer for the railroad and had died in an accident. Yang had run away from the railroad construction outfit after his father's death. The McPhersons had encountered Yang in Silver City. They had noticed his half-starved condition and had brought him back to the ranch. He had only been ten years old at the time, and Rachel had been four. He was like a big brother to her. He had learned about horses over the years and was now the wrangler at the McPherson ranch.

Yang joined the conversation about Storm and Ginger with much enthusiasm. Even Allison McPherson displayed a love of horses and gave her own input about mating the two equine anomalies.

During that first meal with the McPhersons, Alex was reminded of his own family. The warmth and camaraderie deeply touched Alex. For the first time since the nightmare of what had happened to his family, Alex realized that for every Sanchez, there were many good people like the McPhersons, attempting to live out their hopes and dreams.

His personal hope of a happy life began to resurface.

After dinner, the men retired to the front porch and continued the conversation with more coffee.

The women joined them after a while. The conversation explored many different avenues. Among the new topics, Alex wanted to know more about how Patrick had learned to make such fine furniture. Alex expressed that one day he would like Rachel's father to teach him how to make such furniture. Patrick's face lit up with a broad grin when Alex mentioned this, and Alex could tell that his genuine interest in the furniture pleased Patrick very much.

Alex was surprised, yet relieved, that no one questioned him about his background during the conversation. Alex knew that sooner or later he would have to share his story with them. Although he was proud of his family and under different circumstances would have enjoyed sharing insight about his life, he dreaded telling of the horror which he had recently experienced. This, of course, would have to be included once he began to tell of his past. He just didn't want to end such a beautiful evening on such a gloomy note.

Alex knew that the McPhersons sensed some catastrophe had put him on the trail of Sanchez and his men. He also knew that they were too polite to pry into his business. They would allow Alex, in his own time, to tell them of his past.

As daylight began to fade and the night insects began to sing their rhythmic songs, Yang and Rachel's parents went inside.

One of the most beautiful sunsets Alex had ever seen formed on the horizon. It was a brilliant mix of orange, crimson and lilac. Rachel was seated in a rocking chair next to Alex.

Lobo was sprawled on the porch nearby. He would occasionally bite or scratch, at an annoying flea.

Alex was enjoying this peaceful moment with Rachel. He thanked God in his heart for allowing him the privilege of getting to know this wonderful family. In the short time he had known them they had already become very special to him. He was amazed that it seemed like he had known them for many years.

While pondering these things, the thought suddenly crossed Alex's mind that he was perhaps being selfish, not opening up to Rachel and her family about his past. He felt a sudden urgency to bare his soul to her. It baffled Alex that not even an hour ago, he had thought it would be quite some time before he told all. Now, however, he felt strongly that it would be impolite and unfair of him to wait any longer in getting it all out in the open. The thought even passed through his mind that maybe the Lord was behind this prompting. Suddenly, he felt like there was a damn inside him that would soon burst if he didn't get it all off his chest.

Alex reached over and took Rachel's right hand in his left, solidly committed to take the verbal and emotional plunge into the past. Rachel looked over at him with an expression that was a mixture of intrigue and expectancy. She squeezed his hand, as though she understood. She read in his eyes that he was about to say something of great significance.

Alex began, "Rachel, Ah feel Ah need ta ask yor forgiveness."

After a moment, Rachel, responded with a question, "What on earth for?"

Alex paused for just a moment, gathering up more courage for the task he had now undertaken. Then he continued, "You an' your family have been so wonderfully honest an' open with me an' have asked for no explanation from me. Ah know ya mus' be curious an' would probably also find some relief from concern, if ya just knew *somethin'* 'bout my circumstance. That's 'cause Ah know ya can all tell somethin' bad happened in my life recently. It jus' hit me, how thoughtless Ah've been, not havin' already opened up ta ya."

As Alex hesitated for a moment, struggling somewhat for the right words, Rachel said, "Alex. Of course we're all curious. That's just the nature of mankind. Please don't think, though, that any of us would dare to be upset with you for keeping things inside for a while. We know . . . I . . . especially, speaking for myself . . . understand, that you've evidently been through some sort of horrible tragedy recently. If you feel, however, that this is the right time and that you're ready for this, then rest assured that I will listen, not only with my mind, but also with my heart."

Alex, upon hearing these words from Rachel, took a deep breath and as he released it, he felt more relaxed and confident about continuing. Rachel sure did know just how to say the right things at the right time. He squeezed her hand as a gesture of appreciation.

Alex continued, "Ah thank ya for tha words o' encouragement. A more kind an' givin' spirit Ah've never seen. It's in yor parents as well . . . but 'specially in you."

Alex noticed that Rachel appeared to blush. He couldn't be sure because it was now dusk dark. The lanterns glowing from within the house were insufficient to see any color change in Rachel's face. Alex detected her embarrassment by the way she looked down momentarily and because her grip tightened slightly in his hand as he paid tribute to her character.

Alex moved on, not wanting to make her uncomfortable. "Rachel," he said, "tha only four things ya know 'bout me so far is that my father was a preacher, my best frien' died o' influenza, Ah was recently deputized, an' Ah'm on tha trail o' some bad hombres."

Alex paused again for a moment, then added, "Ah want ya ta know that Ah had a normal an' happy childhood. Ah had lovin' an' God fearin' parents. Sure, we had our hard times, like every other farmer or rancher. Tha hard winters an' tha drought. Tha rustlin' of our livestock sometimes. Yor normal, every day difficulties. All in all though, we did pretty well. The Lord blessed us. My mother, father, younger sister an me, all went every Sunday ta tha church my father pastored in El Paso."

Alex was temporarily out of words struggling to find ones to describe the scene of carnage he had come home to on that day he'd never forget. It pained him greatly to pull those horrible events back to the forefront of his mind.

He then explained about his father's past which he had only learned about a little over a year ago himself. He told Rachel of the men he'd overheard outside Al's barbershop. He related the heart to heart talk with his father that night around the campfire, on their way home with the prize bull. He described his parents and Rebecca to Rachel. He told her of the plans they had, to build up their herd of cattle to match the quality of their horses.

In fact, Alex told Rachel pretty much all he could in an attempt to postpone for as long as possible, the story of how things went terribly wrong. When he was unable to delay the gruesome facts any longer, Alex leaned forward, cradling his face in his hands in an attempt to camouflage any tears that might come.

He had thought he would never be able to shed another tear, but being here with Rachel now and with such compassion oozing from her every pore, he felt a tight lump in his throat that literally ached.

Rachel had placed her soft hand on his back as he leaned forward. A tear or two did indeed begin to roll down his face. It took him a minute to regain some of his composure.

Rachel said nothing, but continued to gently rub his back. Just her touch brought comfort to his soul. Alex's right shoulder began to ache. In his state of mind, he had forgotten and had used his right hand to help support his head as he was bent over. He had no choice but to sit back up in order to lessen the pain in his shoulder. He hid the pain from Rachel, not wanting to cause her to worry about that right now.

Finally, Alex was able to continue. He told her of the incident in town with Sanchez and one of his cronies. He once more felt a numbness in his heart and mind, like he had felt when he had discovered his family, slaughtered by the Sanchez gang. The feeling that he may never be able to shed tears again returned. Alex was astonished at how this feeling of not being able to ever cry again could come and go so quickly.

Alex then told Rachel of his errand in El Paso. Of the warning passed on to him by marshal Martin. He told her of his wild ride back to the ranch and the sheer horror he experienced upon his arrival in the ranch yard. He told her of his father's last words. Of the numbness of mind he'd experienced as he entered the house and found his mother and sister.

Rachel now had her arm around Alex. He continued relating the main details of burying his family and burning the ranch house, the only home he had ever known.

He told her of the advice by marshal Martin to look up U.S. Marshall Tihlman and of his doing so. He told of the marshal swearing him in as a Deputy U.S. Marshal and of the red-headed outlaw spotting him in Las Cruces.

When he had finished getting it all out, Rachel said with great emotion and compassion in her voice, "Oh . . . A-lex . . . I'm so . . . *sorry!*" Tears were now coursing down her face.

Alex could tell by the sound of her voice and the hesitancy that she had been crying silently as she had heard his story. She leaned over and kissed Alex tenderly on the cheek. Alex held her close to him as they sat there for several minutes in silence.

Finally, Alex asked a favor of Rachel.

He said, "Rachel! Could ya please relate all o' this ta yor family? Ah don't want ta have ta go through tha telling of it again."

Rachel responded emphatically, "Of course, Alex! I understand!"

Alex then looked at Rachel's face and this time, by the lantern light, he was able to see tears glistening on her cheeks. Their faces drew nearer and Alex could resist no longer. He gently kissed her trembling lips. Immediately, Alex's emotions arose from the depths of despair and soared toward the starry sky. How was it possible to feel such horrible pain in one moment and then to feel such joy in the next? Alex had no answer to this question, but there was one thing he did know for sure!

He wanted *this* moment with Rachel to last forever!

15
The Wrong Words

After about half an hour of sitting in silence just enjoying each other's company, Alex remarked that he should go ahead and get his things and move out to the bunkhouse that evening. Rachel insisted that he stay at the house one more night, using the argument that he would be able to get situated better in the daylight. So Alex gave in.

It had been a long day for Alex physically and emotionally and he was exhausted. He hadn't offered much resistance when Rachel insisted he stay in the house one last night. He felt bad about putting Rachel out of her bedroom so long, but he was too exhausted to think much about it.

Rachel had told him, they had put him in her bedroom instead of her brother's because it gets more sunlight which would help in his recovery. He was barely able to get his boots off and wrestle through the pain of getting his arm out of the sling to remove his shirt. As soon as he had accomplished this and put his arm back in the sling, he just collapsed on the bed and was asleep in a matter of minutes.

When he awoke in the wee hours of the morning, he felt rested and refreshed. It was still dark out and the first rooster hadn't even crowed yet, so Alex lit a lantern. He took the sling off his arm and was surprised to find that his shoulder was much less sore. After washing up at the basin and using both arms to do this, Alex was pleased to discover that even after using his right arm, there still was only minimal pain in the shoulder.

Shortly after pulling on his boots and a clean shirt there was a soft knock at the door. Alex said, "Come in," and Rachel opened the door. This caused the thought to return to Alex that he needed to give Rachel's room back to her today. It was still quite dark out, but Rachel said she had heard him stirring around and just wanted to check and see how he was.

When Alex moved his right arm around some for her and told her how much better it was this morning, Rachel's face lit up with a smile.

She told Alex that breakfast would be ready in about half an hour. Alex thanked her and told her that, since it would be daylight enough to see pretty well in a few minutes, he would go ahead and start moving his things to the bunkhouse.

Rachel went back to helping her mother prepare breakfast as Alex took his things out to the bunkhouse. He saw that a lantern was lit inside, so he knocked on the door and heard Yang Ling's voice telling him to come in. Alex opened the door, picked up his bed roll and saddlebags and stepped through the doorway. He was surprised to find out that Yang stayed in the bunkhouse. He seemed such a natural part of the McPherson family that Alex had assumed he stayed at the main house.

Upon asking him about it, Yang explained to Alex that he had always stayed in the bunkhouse and preferred it that way. He said that when a roundup was underway, he was able to work more closely with the temporary help, if he lived among them. Plus, he added, he liked the solitude when there were no extra hired hands around.

Alex made apology for interrupting Yang's privacy, but Yang immediately responded, "No, no. On the contrary. I've been looking forward to your moving out here, so we can get to know each other better."

Alex expressed his pleasure, but then added, " 'Fraid Ah won't be a lot o' help for a few days yet."

Yang then said, "Don't worry about that. We all know you've had a very serious injury and don't expect you to be busting Broncos in the next couple of days."

They both had a laugh at that and Yang had effectively made Alex feel welcomed.

It seemed a bit strange coming from a Chinese man, but Yang actually spoke with a bit of an Irish accent himself. Alex figured Yang had been around the McPhersons so long that some of the Irish brogue had worn off on him. In fact, Alex figured Rachel to be about twenty years old and that would mean that Yang would have been at the McPherson Ranch about sixteen years now.

Alex asked Yang about Rachel's age and found out that he was exactly right. She was indeed twenty. Yang got a rather mischievous look in his eye when quizzed about Rachel, but he didn't say anything to kid Alex about it. Alex really appreciated that.

Once Alex had put his things on one of the bunks, he and Yang walked to the ranch house for breakfast. They arrived just in time for Allison and Rachel were putting the food on the table as he and Yang entered the dining room.

Alex sat by Rachel again, as it just felt natural and right to do so. This time, as everyone bowed their heads for the blessing, Alex took Rachel's hand, instead of waiting for her to take his. He felt a bit more in control of his feelings this way, because he wouldn't be caught off guard. Rachel held his hand just a bit firmer than the day before. Alex figured that to be for two reasons. First, because the bond between them had grown closer after he had opened his heart to her last night. Secondly, he had initiated the holding of hands this morning.

After the blessing was finished, Alex could tell there was a more serious attitude at the table this morning. While everyone helped their plates, Patrick broke the silence by saying, "Alex. Rachel shared your story with us like you asked her to, and I

112

just want to offer you my condolences. I knew you had gone through a tough ordeal, but I didn't realize just how bad of a situation it had been. I certainly understand the cause for you to be anxious about getting on the trail of those outlaws. I only hope and pray that you'll wait until you're healed sufficiently and ready, once more, to take on such an arduous task."

Patrick then ended his short speech by clearing his throat and looking down at his plate and fiddling with his food a bit nervously, as if he were hoping he had expressed his sympathy and understanding adequately.

Allison then took up where her husband had left off, saying, "Yes, Alex. We will all have you in our prayers." She paused for a moment, tears welling up in her motherly eyes. She then continued, "Often, we don't understand why certain things are allowed to happen, but just remember the Lord's Word says that all things work for good, to those who love Him."

Alex responded by saying, "Ah thank y'all for yor kindness an' yor prayers. It comforts me ta know folks, like yourselves, will be rememberin' me ta tha Lord."

After a few moments of silence, Yang piped in, saying, "Well, I'll be praying too. As soon as *somebody* lets me know what I've missed out on here." He said this with a mock attitude of insult followed by a big grin.

Everyone laughed a bit then and Rachel reached across the table, patting Yang's hand and sayin, "*pobre sito,*" which is Spanish for, "poor little one," at which everyone had to chuckle.

Yang, in his good-natured way, had managed to break the slight awkwardness of the moment. After that, all began to eat and regular conversation ensued.

Of course, enthusiastic mention was made of putting Storm and Ginger together this morning. Then Patrick said, "Aye! But we've been doin' a wee bit o' forgetting around here lately, with all that's been going on and all. Remember. There's the big race in Silver City coming up before long!"

Rachel gasped and said, "Aye! Yes! Alex, if you're well enough by then, I know you will want to enter Storm in the race. They've got a four mile course laid out. I've been planning to enter with Ginger. I did have high hopes of winning. That is, until you and Storm entered into the picture," she added teasingly.

Alex joined in the fun and scratched his chin for moment, uttering a contemplative "Hmmmm . . . How 'bout it Mrs. McPherson? Do ya think Ah might encounter a woman's wrath, if Ah were ta win?"

Again everyone laughed as Rachel elbowed Alex gently in the ribs. Then, Allison injected, "Well lad. If you *should* happen to stir up the wrath of an *Irish* woman . . . Lord have mercy on you!"

Again, more laughter made its rounds. Alex liked the lighthearted bantering and enjoyed himself, as this type of conversation continued throughout the remainder of breakfast.

Alex had learned during the talk that the first prize for winning the race was a full rigged saddle and bridle decorated with silver conchos plus a Henry repeating rifle. There was a $5 entry fee. Riders from all over the territory were coming to show off their mounts and riding skills and also to take a shot at first prize. A picnic was planned as well.

There was to be a pie baking contest, for the ladies. Allison and Rachel kidded each other about which one of them would win the contest. Patrick with a huge grin on his face, said, "Aye. But I think you both should bake a pie this week. Alex, Yang and I can do some early judging and tell you where you need improvement."

Allison said, "Patrick McPherson. Don't you go putting Alex on the spot now. You know he'd have to fib and say both were equally good."

Rachel inserted with a grin and wink at Alex, "Mother, you know Alex wouldn't fib just to make you feel good."

After some more laughter, Alex joined in, "If it has anything ta do with apple, peach, or cherry pie, Ah'll be willing ta take a chance on tha fibbing part."

Patrick responded, "Aye. It's a diplomat we have here and a man after my own heart in the choice of pies."

When everyone had finished breakfast, Rachel and her mother began to clear the table. Alex pitched in as Patrick and Yang left to start the chores. Allison said, "Now, Alex. You need to rest your shoulder."

Rachel evidently understood Alex's need to feel useful. She said, "Mother. Why don't you go ahead? Alex and I can do the dishes."

Alex insisted that though he couldn't swing an ax yet, he needed to start helping in the ways he could. He said light use of his arm would be good. Allison McPherson looked at Alex, with a twinkle in her eye. It was evident that she was pleased a man would not think of himself as above doing what was considered to be woman's work.

She then beamed and said, "Aye. Well, if you insist, I could sweep the porches. When you and Rachel are done though, remember, we have an appointment to help Storm and Ginger to decide if they're meant for each other." She then grabbed a broom and left the kitchen.

Alex and Rachel started the task of washing the dishes after they had scraped all the scraps together and took them out to Lobo. Alex insisted that he'd do the washing and Rachel the drying.

He told Rachel, "Hands as beautiful as yor's shouldn't be in dishwater with lye soap, any more than necessary, so they'll continue ta match your face."

He turned to grin at Rachel and found that she was blushing. This time, instead of her normal dazzling smile, she was looking at him with a warm tender smile of appreciation. This was the first time he had seen that particular smile. It affected him even more deeply than the beautiful brilliant one. Then it occurred to him that this was the first time he had made any reference concerning her appearance. From the look of this smile, you would have thought that no one had ever mentioned anything about her beauty. Alex couldn't believe that was possible.

In a way, he wished he hadn't said it to her. He had decided not to let things get too serious between them because he didn't want anything to distract him from his immediate goal of catching up with Sanchez. He felt it would also be better for Rachel if they didn't become more involved because it was entirely possible that he may not return from the manhunt. The odds were stacked against him and he'd already been ambushed and shot once. The complimentary words he had just spoken to Rachel were from his heart and they had just popped out before he knew it. In the future, he would have to think before speaking.

When they finished the dishes, they went outside to find Rachel's mother. Allison had finished sweeping the back porch and was halfway done with the front porch. Rachel took over for her mother and finished the sweeping. Alex felt bad that he'd only been able to help with the dishes. Even wielding a broom was more than his shoulder could withstand at this point. He marveled to himself how easy it was to take one's health and mobility for granted. This being his first serious injury, he had never thought about or fully appreciated the health and vitality he had enjoyed all his life.

With the sweeping done, the three of them walked back toward the barn. As they approached, they could see that Patrick and Yang already had Ginger tied to the fence, near the gate of the pasture she had been in. She now had to be led to the gate of the pasture Storm was in.

Storm was evidently already aware of Ginger being nearby. He was waiting at the gate, snorting and shaking his head. Ginger was behaving in like manner. Once Ginger had been released in Storm's pasture, they both frolicked off like a couple of yearlings. Alex was grinning and when he glanced around, he saw that the others were equally enjoying the moment.

After a few more minutes, Rachel's parents and Yang began to head off in their separate directions, leaving Alex and Rachel still standing there. They continued to admire the two horses for a while longer. They both were savoring this moment and Alex, without thinking about it, grabbed Rachel's hand in his own.

Then he remembered his inner commitment to limit his time and romantic involvement with Rachel and said spontaneously, "Well. Now that we've had the pleasure o' seein' Storm an' Ginger gettin' together, guess Ah'll mosey over ta tha bunkhouse an' get myself settled in. Thanks again for lettin' me have tha use o' yor room, Rachel. Ah know yu'll be glad ta have it back now, though."

Alex, to his dismay, suddenly felt his words had been too abrupt and informal. That he'd perhaps gone too far in his attempt to temporarily distance himself a bit from Rachel. He hadn't *at all*, however, wanted to give her the impression that he was losing interest in her. Not in *any* way had he intended his words to come out the way they had! Sure, his motive was to make an attempt at protecting her from the likelihood he might not return from his mission alive. As intuitive as Rachel was, however, she might fail to realize the true intent of his words. After all, she *was* mostly intuitive, *not* a mind reader!

The smile on her face dimmed a bit as Alex spoke. He really hoped he hadn't overdone his attempt to politely establish a bit more formality in their relationship. The *last* thing Alex wanted to do was to hurt Rachel's feelings or to cause her to feel they had no hope of a deepening relationship in the future.

As he watched her smile lose some of its brilliance, Alex had a sickening feeling in the pit of his stomach.

After a moment, her smile regained much of its normal brightness and she responded, "Actually, I'll miss you being in the house. I'll also be concerned that you'll try to use your shoulder too much." Rachel paused and then added, "Well, I'll see you at supper."

She turned and walked slowly away. Her step didn't seem quite as lively as normal and her posture not as erect.

She seemed to be making an attempt to hide deeper feelings obviously left unspoken. Just before she turned to walk away, Alex thought he saw the beginning of a tear in the corner of one of her eyes. Alex really hoped it was his imagination.

He began to walk toward the bunkhouse, wishing all the while that he was limber enough to kick himself in the rear good and hard. The sickening feeling in his stomach grew worse. How he wished that he had said something else. He remembered one of his father's favorite adages: "Words spoken are like water spilled on tha ground . . . Once spilled, ya can't put it back inta tha bucket." Right now, he could hear those words echoing in his mind. It was as if Dan Barrington was standing beside him, talking to him in a voice which was almost audible. Alex now felt like the slime covering a stagnant pond. Like a carbuncle on a skunk's rear.

His mind raced as he thought back over the words he had said. What *could* and what *should* he have said, instead of what he *had* said? As he pondered the words he had used, he now thought they sounded too careless and had *minimized* much of the warmth he had in his heart for Rachel. Once again, he realized he needed to think before opening his big mouth.

16
The Lazarus Effect

Alex slept fitfully that night. He tossed and turned and couldn't shake the worrisome thoughts he had concerning what he had said to Rachel that morning. These thoughts even invaded his dreams.

At dinner, Rachel had seemed a bit reserved. Not pouting or anything of that nature. That would be so unlike her naturally warm, exuberant personality. Alex interpreted it more as the cautious reaction of a person who had trusted their emotions into the hands of another, and now felt the risk of being hurt.

Alex had done a lot of soul-searching since that morning and had come to some unsettling conclusions. After a lot of introspective thought and some silent but earnest prayer, he began to see his recent thoughts and actions in a different light. He had the distinct feeling that this "different light" was the result of God's Spirit dealing with him.

He saw himself as a man who was currently being pulled in at least two, very different and conflicting directions. On one hand, he was being driven by bitterness, rage and a desire for justice and revenge. On the other hand, he sensed the gentle yet potent call to be true to his heart where Rachel and her family were concerned.

He was feeling the need for a heightened sensitivity, *especially* concerning Rachel's feelings. He sensed a need to be *very* aware and cautious of *what* he said to her and *how* he said it.

He remembered his father had often said that the forces of darkness speak to a person's inner thoughts in a *harsh, demanding* and *forceful* manner. He had also said that *God's Spirit* communicates in a small, still, and *gentle* voice which speaks to the person's spirit with a beckoning call. The Lord will *not* try to *force* you. If He *did* you would no longer have a *free will* and could never *love* Him from your *heart*. The *ability* to *love requires* a *choice*. One *must* chose obedience to *one* of *two* diametrically opposed entities. Either to <u>God</u> (the source of *all* things good), or to <u>Satan</u> and his henchmen, (the source of *all* things bad). Man's <u>own will</u> is positioned *between* these two. Alex remembered yet another thing his father had often said: "Ya can't ride tha fence forever . . . Ya've gotta 'ventually choose whose army yur gonna join forces with."

In a way, he thought he knew how Lazarus may have felt when Jesus had raised him from the dead. Lazarus, though brought back from the dead, was still bound by the grave cloth wrapped tightly around him. Rachel and her family had been the main instruments in the hands of the Almighty in bringing him back from death's door. Surely he would be dead now, if they had not found him and prayerfully nurtured him back to life. Yet Alex was still all bound up with hatred and the desire for vengeance.

Lazarus *must* have felt confused. Alex's emotions, *likewise*, were confused by the conflicting passions coursing through his soul. Lazarus wouldn't have been able to see until the grave cloths were removed and would have stumbled around blindly.

Alex had allowed his judgment to be clouded by his obsession to seek justice and revenge. Yielding so completely to that driving force had caused him to hurt the one person in his life he now cared the most about. It wasn't just the actual *words* he had spoken but the seemingly callused and indifferent *tone* in his voice. He hadn't *at all* meant for it to sound that way.

Rachel seemed to have a distinct talent for reading *people*, similar to the way Alex could read *horses*. She had evidently read between the lines, and clearly distinguished his attempt to distance himself from her. As intuitive as she was, however, Alex realized she had no way of knowing the true depth and strength of his feelings for her. One kiss and a few kind words were simply insufficient to convince her heart of his true feelings and intentions. Alex was in a quandary because he realized Rachel needed encouragement right now, yet he wasn't sure how to provide that for her without compromising his desire to not increase their romantic involvement.

Alex was truly between a rock and a hard place. He had fumbled in his attempt to protect her from the greater pain she may experience should the outlaws be successful in their next attempt at taking his life. He simply lacked the verbal skills to adequately convey his true feelings for her, while at the same time help her to understand the driving force he had to contend with. Try as he might, he couldn't yet think of the right words to help her understand his dilemma. He desperately hoped he would be able to do so before the day when he would leave to continue his quest of apprehending Sanchez and his gang.

For now though, the task at hand was to treat Rachel as kindly and gently as possible, while trying not to allow their relationship to escalate. This was a task that, at the moment, seemed as insurmountable and formidable as taking down Sanchez and his men.

After wrestling with all these thoughts at great length, Alex surmised his best hope was to commit it all into God's extremely capable hands. This dilemma was simply beyond his own puny ability to resolve. Recognizing his inability to handle this situation adroitly, Alex uttered a simple prayer from the depths of his heart. "Lord," he said, "Ya know all o' this is gonna take more wisdom than Ah possss on my own. Ah ask Ya ta guide me along an' give me tha 'bility ta straighten out tha mess Ah've made here. In Yor Son's powerful name Ah pray. Amen!"

Alex finally drifted off again about an hour before dawn. When he heard a rooster crow, he awoke feeling rather dismal about his situation. He understood, however, that the Scriptures say in 2nd Corinthians 5:7, "For we walk by faith, not by sight." He knew this also meant we can't go by how we "feel" but by the truth and promises in God's Holy Word.

His shoulder was improving remarkably well. He felt confident that he could not only help with the dishes today, but he could also handle the sweeping. He knew continued careful use of his arm and shoulder would greatly speed up his recovery. He badly wanted to be of more use and found it difficult to feel he wasn't pulling his own weight with the chores on the ranch. At this juncture in his life, *patience* was not his greatest virtue. That was yet another area he really needed to patiently work on. As he realized the irony that it *took* patience to *gain* patience, he chuckled to himself.

At breakfast he made a special effort to pay particular attention to Rachel. The thoughts of the previous night still lingered with him. He made a point of making eye contact with Rachel as often as he could. The times he achieved looking into her eyes, he smiled a very sincere and warm smile. Unknown to Alex, Rachel's soul was greatly encouraged within her due to these heartwarming smiles.

She responded in like manner with a slightly baffled look, as if the purposeful attention directed toward her was unexpected, yet very welcome. She looked rather like a calf at a new gate, not sure exactly what to expect after their last conversation on the previous day. She appeared to be proceeding with caution toward the unknown. Even toward the possible depths of love and passion. She definitely appeared somewhat apprehensive though her face betrayed a newfound hope, encouraged by Alex's gentle attention directed toward her.

Evidently she *had* significantly misinterpreted his little speech of the day before, much the way he'd figured she had. Seeing the change in Rachel's demeanor now, made Alex feel *much* better and tended to eradicate the worries he'd struggled with for so many agonizing hours last night. He was genuinely amazed that the Lord had begun to answer last night's prayers so quickly and profoundly!

When it was time to say grace, Patrick asked Alex if he would do the honors.

Alex was caught totally off guard. However, as he bowed his head and grabbed Rachel's hand, his mind began to rapidly fill with things he wanted to say in addition to the normal giving of thanks for the food and asking the Lord's blessing over it.

He took a deep breath and then began the prayer gripping Rachel's hand with a little extra firmness. He said, "Heavenly Father, Ah want ta take this opportunity ta thank Ya for a number of things. Ah want ta thank Ya for sendin' tha McPhersons ta save my life. Lord, Ya weren't a minute late in providin' tha help Ah needed. Ah want ta thank Ya for bringin' me inta tha lives o' this wonderful family. May Ya help me ta someday be a blessin' ta them in return. Like Mrs. Mac said, "Ya work all things for good ta those who love Ya." Ah don' know jus' how Yo're goin' ta turn tha death o' my family aroun' for good, but Ya sure made a great start of it by allowin' my path o' life ta cross tha path o' this family . . ."

Alex paused for moment, then continued, "Oh yea, Lord, Thank Ya for tha food an' please bless it . . . In tha name o' Yor Son Jesus, Amen."

Everyone else said amen and the meal began. After a few moments, Allison said in a heartfelt manner, "Alex, that was a beautiful prayer and I can tell it was from your heart. We also count it a privilege that He brought *you* into *our* lives. You've already been more of a blessing to us than you realize, and I'm sure you will be even more so in the future."

Alex responded seriously, "Thank ya, Ma'am." This was followed by a couple minutes of silence, which Alex broke by saying, "My shoulder's feelin' much better this mornin'. Expect Ah'll be able ta start helpin' out more real soon. Ah'd like ta start by helpin' both with tha dishes *an'* tha sweeping today."

Patrick rejoined with a grin, "That'll be fine. Just don't let your pride keep you from giving that shoulder a break when you need to. Do you promise me, lad?"

Alex said, "Ah promise, but if Ah'm goin' ta be in tha race, Ah've got ta start limberin' up for it. Ah don't want ta be like an old rusty hinge, a creakin' an' a groanin'."

This rather humorous analogy elicited a chuckle from Patrick and grins from all the others at the table. Though Alex wasn't very eloquent with words, he *did* have a way of getting his point across in an ardent and colorful way.

Most of the rest of breakfast was spent talking about the coming race. As he had promised, Alex helped Rachel with the dishes and then swept both the front and back porches. He experienced some discomfort in his shoulder and chest muscles, but overall, he was pleased with his rate of recovery.

Shortly after he finished sweeping the back porch, Rachel came out the back door carrying a bucket to fill with water from the well. Alex convinced her he was able to draw the water for her. He used his right arm until it began to ache, then switched to his left arm. It took three times to fill the larger bucket from the house, using the smaller pail which was attached to the rope and lowered into the water by means of the crank handle attached to the well shaft.

When Alex finished cranking the final pail full and had poured it into Rachel's bucket, he felt relieved. He found it hard to believe how much stamina he still lacked. After carrying the now full bucket inside, Alex took a breather in one of the rockers on the front porch. He felt drowsy, not having had much sleep last night, and he soon dozed off.

The next thing he knew, something was nudging his foot. As he awoke, he saw Rachel standing in front of him, holding two cups of coffee. She had gently nudged him with one of her feet to awaken him. He noticed that a quilt had been draped over him. Evidently this was Rachel's doing. It was early fall and the air was beginning to chill.

Alex noticed by the position of the sun that it was now late afternoon. Rachel must have been concerned that he would catch a cold, thus the quilt and coffee. Alex accepted the coffee with a "thank ya." She sat down next to him. Alex *was* actually a bit chilled and the coffee felt good going down. He felt a deep-seated gratitude for Rachel's nurturing disposition.

Rachel explained, "I figured you must have overdone it this morning." She had a bit of concern apparent in her voice and reflected on her face. She obviously didn't want Alex to catch pneumonia, thus causing a big setback in his recovery. In his weakened condition he would be more susceptible to such infections.

Alex replied, "Na. It wasn't really that. Ah jus' didn't sleep well las' night."

Rachel asked, "Aye, so you had a lot of pain last night?"

Alex paused for a few moments, thinking how to answer the question without letting her know the anguish he had suffered about what he'd said to her on the previous day and the manner in which he'd said it. He finally managed to give her a laconic explanation, "Ah jus' had a lot o' thoughts runnin' 'round in my head."

Rachel looked at him with uncertainty for moment. Then, a look came across her face betraying the fact that she perhaps knew what may have been bothering him. She said nothing, but shifted her gaze out upon the rocky outcropping of a distant mountain.

Alex thought to himself that Rachel would never be able to conceal a lie. Not only because of her character, but also because her thoughts were discernibly reflected in her face. She was honest as the day was long and more beautiful than any glowing sunset or vibrant delicate flower.

In that moment, beholding the dazzling exquisiteness of her countenance, he strongly hoped and prayed with all his heart that he would make the right choices in the near future. A woman like Rachel was *extremely* rare and Alex hoped he wouldn't push her out of his life forever. He realized, however, that the personal demons he was now struggling with made this a possibility. He would have to tread as carefully as he could upon the grounds of their relationship. He certainly didn't want to *lose* her.

17
Danger on the Trail

During the following days, Alex continued, day by day, to do more work using his right arm. It continued to get better, only not as quickly as at first. He saddled Storm numerous times and went for a ride in the countryside. Naturally, Storm was eager and raring to go.

Alex rode by himself the first time and then, at his request, Rachel would sometimes join him with Ginger. Usually, however, Alex rode alone. Rachel seemed to sense and understand his need for occasional solitude. Alex was grateful for her understanding and patience. He was now well enough to ride in the Silver City race and looked forward to the challenge.

Whenever he rode alone, he strapped his pair of Colts on and rode out far enough to be out of hearing distance from the ranch. He would set some pinecones or rocks, on a bolder and practiced drawing and firing at the targets.

Alex had always had a natural talent for speed and accuracy with a pistol. He now, however, was impeded by his right shoulder. Though he could use it adequately for lifting and pulling, the attempt to accomplish a fast draw with it produced more pain than the steady controlled lifting he did around the ranch.

He simply was unable to come close to his old speed of the draw with his right arm. He decided, therefore, to practice with his left. He had never spent much time attempting to improve his speed and accuracy with his left hand. Now, however, he felt it was a good time to do so. It didn't make much sense anyway to carry the extra weight of two guns if he was incapable of using both effectively. Day-by-day, he began to gain more proficiency with his left hand.

Eventually he could hit the rocks or pinecones he set up at about twenty paces, rarely missing. This was an extraordinary accomplishment. Most men would need to take careful aim with a pistol and some would even have to use a rifle to accomplish this. Alex was now able to do it firing rapidly from the hip. After much practice, he could accurately shoot with either hand, and incredibly enough, with both simultaneously!

Alex was also now able to help out with more difficult tasks at the ranch. Even though his shoulder wasn't completely healed, his stamina and strength had returned to normal.

The morning arrived when it was only three days before the big race in Silver City. Being a good day's ride from the ranch, Alex, the McPhersons and Yang set out three days prior to the race. They wanted to get there in time to find sleeping accommodations and to give Storm, Ginger and Yang's horse a couple days to rest up and be ready for the race.

Rachel and her mother also wanted to see if their hotel would allow them use of the kitchen to bake their pies. To bake them three days early at the ranch meant that they would not have the freshness needed for the pie contest.

On his forays into the countryside when he had taken his guns, he had stowed them in his saddlebags and hadn't strapped them on until he got out of sight of the ranch. The day they left for Silver City, however, Alex had his Colts buckled around his waist. Though it was common for men to wear six shooters on their hips, including Rachel's father who also wore one, Rachel had never seen Alex wearing his guns.

He also had his deputy's badge tucked away in one of his shirt pockets in case he needed it. The time had come when Alex couldn't afford the luxury of *not* wearing his Colts. When

Rachel had first noticed the presence of the Alex's guns, a look of concern was vaguely visible in her expression.

Alex felt he should offer an explanation to Rachel, although he knew she probably already understood. However, he wanted her to hear it from him candidly. Her expression was not at all one of disapproval, or reproach, only that of half-masked anxiety.

Alex attempted to put her at ease, the best he could. He told her that he didn't really expect Sanchez and his men to be in Silver City, but that he wore his weapons as a precaution. He explained to her that though the race may be a temptation to Sanchez's gang, he didn't think they would be foolhardy enough to linger that long in Silver City.

Rachel accepted this logic as he spoke in a calm manner and smiled reassuringly at her. She seemed to place a lot of faith in his judgment. This was very gratifying to Alex. He couldn't think of a single thing he'd want to change about Rachel. She evidently felt the same toward him.

Though he realized Rachel was anything but gullible, he greatly appreciated her trust and confidence in his judgment. He firmly believed the old adage that a man was only as great as the woman who stood beside him allowed and encouraged him to be. Alex's thoughts were that Rachel would definitely make a wonderful wife and lifetime partner, to *some* man one day.

It was a long trek, through some pretty rugged terrain. They made brief pauses now and then to stretch their legs and give the horses a break. About halfway to Silver City, they stopped and had lunch from the basket of food Allison and Rachel had prepared for the trip.

The brief rest stops were not only for the purpose of stretching their legs, but also to allow a breather for the horses Rachel's parents and Yang were riding. Although they were all fine mounts, none could keep the same rigorous pace set by Storm and Ginger.

It was during the last of those rest stops that a near disaster was encountered. As they dismounted, the horses seemed very nervous. Alex knew something wasn't right and kept a vigilant eye on their surroundings. He was about to suggest remounting the horses and finding another rest area further down the road. Rachel had also noticed the nervousness of the horses and Alex's look of concern. She was watching him.

Allison had already found a small boulder and had just sat down when the unmistakable sound of rattles noised their fearful warning. Alex saw the snake less than two feet from Allison's right leg, fully coiled and ready to strike. Before Alex had time to think about it, his left hand moved with lightning speed as he drew and fired from the hip.

It was so fast Rachel's eyes couldn't even follow the blurring speed of motion. One moment she was watching Alex's face and the next moment she was hearing the roar of the Colt. Her eyes looked at the smoking revolver for a moment and then followed the direction of the pointed gun. She then saw the snake, its head blown off and body now writhing a bit as its nerves continued to twitch.

Alex holstered the Colt and walked over to Allison to make sure that fragments of rock or lead hadn't harmed her. Allison was just sitting there in shock. Her face was pale but she appeared to be unharmed. Alex glanced around at the others and found that they were all still standing where they had been the moment the rattles were heard. Rachel, Patrick and Yang, were staring at Alex and Allison with their mouths open and their faces as pale as Allison's. After a few moments, Patrick and Rachel regained their composure enough to hurry toward Allison. Yang was still glued to the spot where he'd been, with a look of disbelief on his face. Finally, he turned his attention to the horses to calm them down. They were still nervous because they could smell the snake and didn't realize it was now harmless.

When she had finished checking on her mother, Rachel looked up at Alex with a tear rolling shamelessly down one cheek. She grabbed Alex in a grateful hug. She was trembling as the emotions of the moment caught up with her. Alex tenderly patted her on the back as he looked over her shoulder at Patrick.

Rachel's father still had a look of awe on his face. He said, "I thought you were *right*-handed."

"Ah am," replied Alex, with a slight look of embarrassment on his face.

Patrick added, "Then if you can do *that* with your *left* hand, I'd pity the man or varmint, that had to face up to you *right*-handed, Lad." He paused for a moment and then added, "Even if I could have gotten my gun out in time, I could never have hit the snake. Most likely, I'd have hit Allison instead." Patrick had still been squatting beside his wife as he spoke. He then stood up and continued, "Well, you *surely* don't have any need to feel indebted to us *now*, Lad. You've earned your keep and *then* some!"

That "mile-wide" grin of his split his face as he stepped over and stuck his hand out. Rachel released her hold on Alex and he grabbed Patrick's hand. Patrick shook Alex's hand vigorously. He said, "God bless you, son!" He then turned and headed toward the horses with Allison walking beside him, each having an arm around the other's waist.

Allison glanced back at Alex with a look of gratitude which spoke volumes. Patrick was shaking his head and muttering in disbelief, "I didn't know a man could *move* that fast!"

Alex hooked his right arm in Rachel's left and escorted her back to Ginger. He held the reins of the nervous mare while Rachel climbed into the saddle. Once everyone was mounted and ready to ride, Patrick led them down the road once more.

As they rode along, Alex thought about the incident. He knew he had *never* drawn a gun that fast or shot that accurately, even with his *right* hand. Of course, he had never *had* to draw and fire under such desperate circumstances either. He gave a silent word of thanks to the Lord, for helping him with the situation.

Alex sensed an ever-increasing awareness of destiny at work in, not only in his own life, but also in the lives of those around him. He pondered with his heart where it would all lead. What he once would have considered as coincidence, Alex was now beginning to see, as a seamlessly executed plan. A plan obviously being woven together by a Supreme mastermind. This was beyond Alex's scope of comprehension, and he felt strongly in his heart that this plan had been set into motion even before he was born into this world.

He began to realize that such a plan was written in the heart of the Almighty for *everyone* who had ever *been*, or ever *would* be, born. He also began to understand, that we all have a choice to make. A choice to either *seek after* and *accept* this plan, or to *reject* the *perfect* will of God and go our *own* way. Many of the scripture verses his father had quoted in sermons over the years passed through Alex's mind. They confirmed his present thoughts and made much more sense than they ever had before.

Alex thought about Sanchez's gang. He believed they'd be tempted to stay in Silver City for the festivities but knew they probably wouldn't. They wouldn't want to take the chance of being seen by so many people. They would have to know that folk from miles around would be flocking to town. If anyone recognized them, there would certainly be enough men of fighting caliber to make up a formidable posse. Surely the outlaws wouldn't want to take that big of a risk.

Alex was still deep in thought about these and other things, when they topped a hill and saw Silver City, nestled in the valley before them.

18
The Nature of Man

As they rode down the hill toward Silver City, the sun was just beginning to dip behind the distant mountains beyond the town. The sun had an ethereal quality about it. The lower it sank behind the mountains, the more beautiful the scene became. The clouds took on a predominantly golden glow, streaked here and there with areas of crimson and violet gray. In the twilight, the night insects began their peaceful serenade. In the distance, an owl added its nocturnal call.

When they were close to the town, the barking of dogs could be heard, along with the muffled crying of a baby.

Soon, they rode down the main street and located a livery stable. They reached an agreement with a livery hand and all began to unsaddle their horses and groom them. Once they had made sure that the horses had adequate food and water, they inquired where they might be able to find lodging. They took their saddlebags and other personal gear and headed toward the hotel the worker had recommended.

Yang and Alex had decided to share a room, and Patrick and Allison secured one for themselves. Rachel's room was next to Alex and Yang's.

Alex had made a point of describing Sanchez and his men to the livery stable worker. He recalled them all exactly. He informed Alex that men matching their descriptions had indeed been in town until about two weeks ago. They had left early one morning, refusing to pay their livery bill. The worker said he had told the town marshal about the incident, but realized there was little the marshal could do about it. Alex decided he would seek out the marshal in the morning. If there was a county sheriff in town, Alex intended to have a talk with him as well to get as much information as he could.

After Alex and Yang got settled in their room, Alex pulled a small tin of boot black and a soft cloth from his saddlebags. He sat on the edge of his bed and began to shine his boots. Yang lay on the other bed with his hands clasped behind his head. He looked over at Alex and remarked, "I've never seen anyone pamper a pair of boots the way you do." He paused a moment and then asked, "Is there a particular reason for that?"

Alex continued to buff the boots and without looking up, he replied, "Yup. My parents gave me these boots las' Christmas. Besides my Colts, my father's watch, his Bible an' ole Storm, Ah guess they're tha most important possesions that Ah own. 'Course, Ah can't leave Lobo off tha list an' tha *family* Bible an' photos Ah saved."

Yang said, "Sorry, I didn't mean to pry."

Alex countered, "No need ta 'pologize. Everyone's got a right ta be curious."

Yang, then asked, "Speaking of curiosity, where in the world did you learn to shoot like that? I still don't believe it, and I saw it with my own eyes."

Alex, now finished with his boots, set them down near the foot of his bed. He then leaned back on one elbow and stared at a lantern glowing on the washstand. Yang could tell he was thinking on how to answer that one.

Finally, Alex replied, "Wul, Ah learned ta shoot from my Pa. When tha McPhersons told ya 'bout my past, did they tell ya he used ta be a lawman?"

Yang responded, "No. They only mentioned him being a rancher and a preacher. Seems like he had a real duke's mixture of professions."

Alex chuckled at that and shared with Yang about overhearing the two strangers, in front of Al's barbershop. He also told Yang about his father opening up about his past on that trip back from San Antonio.

Alex and Yang exchanged bits and pieces of their past with each other. After that conversation, they both knew and understood one another even better. A closer bond was forged between them.

While Alex lay upon his bed after the last lantern was blown out, he tried to envision what the coming days and weeks may hold for him and his newfound friends. Friends who already seemed like family. He also churned thoughts around in his head about the decisions he would be forced to make. All decisions so important, that each had the potential of altering the entire course of his future, possibly even the futures of his newfound friends. Especially Rachel's.

Now *there* was a tough subject to figure out. Maybe *that* was his biggest problem. Trying to figure things out in his head, too far in advance. Alex was certainly finding himself drawn frequently back to thoughts of the many Scriptures and words of wisdom he had heard so often from his father over the years.

He realized now, more than ever, the great wealth of wisdom, God had entrusted to Dan Barrington. The light of understanding was also growing in Alex that he needed to follow his father's example of trusting more in God's Holy Spirit, inspired Word and less in his own mental faculties.

One scripture especially voiced its truth in his heart. That verse says, that man's carnal mind is enmity against God's Spirit. He remembered hearing his father explain that this verse, understood more in modern vernacular, meant that our natural minds are an enemy of God's Spirit and would lead us astray if we listen to our finite way of thinking. Our thinking is contrary to God's way of thinking.

Another passage which supported this truth says that God's thoughts and ways are *much* higher than man's. It states that, "As high as the heavens are above the earth, so are God's thoughts and ways, above the thoughts and ways of man." Our earthly minds are brimming over with latent disaster and hostility toward the Lord.

Yet another favorite verse his father often quoted was that Jesus is the Good Shepherd and once we get to know Him on a personal basis, we become His sheep and the Bible says that the sheep hear the voice of the Shepherd and recognize it. They would not follow the voice of a stranger. That stranger could be our own thoughts or the voice of the forces of darkness, speaking either *directly* to our thoughts or speaking to us *through* another person. The other person may be well-intentioned but unfamiliar with the voice of the Shepherd themselves.

Soon, Alex drifted off to sleep.

When he awoke in the morning, he washed up and got dressed. He walked out onto the small balcony of the hotel room. He found that more people, either in groups, or alone, were drifting into Silver City. Alex could sense an atmosphere of excitement and anticipation building in the town.

Yang soon joined him and they watched the activity together. The people arriving represented a cross section of the folk that lived probably within a 100 to 200 mile radius from Silver City. For the most part, they appeared to be honest, hardworking families and nonchalant drifters of a fairly high caliber.

Alex and Yang, however, noticed a number of men who had the appearance of being unsavory and shady characters. Among this sort, there were bound to be some of ill repute. The kind that seemed to have trouble and mischief in their eyes and written on their faces.

Alex and Yang were in agreement that some of these men could spell trouble. Although Alex saw no one that fit the description of any of the Sanchez gang, he was nonetheless reminded of that fateful day in El Paso. The day which had led to the demise of his family. This made Alex uncomfortable and he vowed to himself to keep his eyes open and not allow *any* harm to come to Rachel or her family.

The contempt he felt for such men resurfaced inside of him. There was a growing *difference*, however, in the *level* of disdain and hatred he *now* felt. He was subliminally aware of a *slight* degree of softening on the raw edges of his hatred.

Because the Holy Spirit had been actively injecting *innumerable* Scriptures into his thinking lately concerning Sanchez and his men, Alex was discovering that *some* of the hatred and repulsion he felt for the men was being spontaneously *redirected* toward the forces of *darkness* at work *in* those men. His *anger* was not abated, yet the *blame* was more focused on the *spiritual* influences these men were *controlled* by.

Now as he stood on the small balcony, Alex reflected on the days of his childhood. He had always been aware of the *positive* influence God *could* have on individuals. He remembered the first time, however, he had given much thought to the negative evil influence the powers of darkness have upon people. He thought of God's adversary, Lucifer, a high-ranking archangel, who had allowed the sin of pride to enter his heart which ultimately led to his expulsion from the Holy presence of God.

According to the scriptures, he had been isolated on earth and within earth's immediate atmosphere. In the 28th chapter of Ezekiel, a prophecy was spoken to the Prince of Tyrus which also alluded to the fall of Lucifer, the Prince of Darkness. It described Satan's fall from Heaven.

He was cast down to Earth because he had said in his heart that he wanted to be <u>equal</u> to and <u>even greater</u> than God. He wanted, and <u>still</u> wants to be worshipped as God. Absolutely NO being <u>created</u> by God can be <u>equal</u> to Him! Simply put, <u>only</u> God can <u>be</u> God. It is utterly <u>impossible</u> for <u>any</u> being to become <u>equal</u> <u>to</u>, let alone, <u>exceed</u> God in <u>ANY</u> way!

The same chapter says in verse 13, that Satan had been in the Garden of Eden during the creation. Having been cast down from Heaven, he is extremely jealous of God and ALL His creation. *Especially* man. From the very moment God created man and gave *him* dominion over the Earth and *all* living creatures on Earth (which *included* the Devil), Satan was biding his time and looking for a *weakness* in man which he could *exploit.* If he could find such a weakness, then he would have a possible way of deceiving mankind into unknowingly *relinquishing* their God-given *dominion* over the Earth. Not only that, but having been the highest created archangel in Heaven before his fall, he has great wisdom and knew that *if* Adam and Eve *fell prey* to his *deception, he* would then have *dominion* over Earth.

That *included* control over all Adam and Eve's offspring, if they would just *believe* his *lies* instead of *trusting* in God's Word, they, like him, would fall from God's grace. Like him, they would become enslaved by a sinful nature. *He* would be their *new Master.* The extremely important thing Satan overlooked and had no revelation of, was the fact that God *already* had a *plan* of *redemption* in place, *knowing* that man *would* indeed fall prey to the subtle temptation which would be set as a snare by Satan.

God *created* time, yet lives *outside* its boundaries and can see *everything* that *has* ever or *will* ever occur. Unlike mankind, *He* is not *limited* by time. We see time as one long, unending line. God sees it from His Heavenly vantage point. *Natural* man views time as their *only* means of *identifying* an Earthly *reality,* at the end of which, *physical* <u>death</u> awaits. The Lord sees time as an *object* He *created* and as an *arena* in which man acts out his *fleshly* life. According to Scripture there are *two* separate and distinct *forms* of <u>death.</u>

As Alex meditated on these things, Scripture verses began to flood back into his memory. He remembered that in Revelation 2:11, the Bible says, "He that hath an ear, let him *hear what the Spirit saith* unto the churches; *he that overcometh* shall *not* be hurt of the second death." He also remembered Rev. 20:6, "*Blessed* and holy *is he* that hath part in the *first* resurrection; *on such* the second death hath no power, but *they* shall be priests of God and of Christ, and *shall reign with Him.*"

Also, Rev. 21:8 says, "But *the fearful and unbelieving*, and the abominable, and murderers, and whoremongers, and sorcerers, and idolaters, and all liars, shall have their part in the lake which burneth with fire and brimstone: *which* is the second death." In other words, from these and numerous other verses, one can see that the *second* death (which of course comes *after* the 1st *physical* death) is eternal separation from the presence of God. Those who place their *faith in* and are true *followers* of Christ will escape the *second* death because they will live for all eternity in the very presence of God!

Then Alex recalled the verses *written to Christians*, in 1st Corinthians 15:51–55, "Behold, I tell you a mystery: We all shall not sleep, but we shall all be changed, in a moment, in the twinkling of an eye, at the last trump: for the trumpet shall sound, and the *dead* shall be raised incorruptible, and we shall be *changed*. For this *corruptible must put on incorruptin*, and this *mortal must put on immortality*. But when this corruptible shall have put on incorruption, and this mortal shall have put on immortality, then shall come to pass the saying that is written, Death is swallowed up in victory. O death, where is thy *victory?* O death, where is thy *sting?*" Alex realized that these verses would *terrify* unbelievers, but would bring *peace* and *great joy* to those who have *placed* their *faith in Christ!*

Since the beginning of man's history on earth, there has always been an ongoing struggle between satanic powers and mankind. The one-third of heaven's angelic host who had rebelled against God along with Lucifer, and were cast down to earth, *with* Lucifer, are known collectively as fallen angels or demons.

Together, they form an evil unseen army invading the thoughts of mankind, enticing them to doubt God's Word. Tempting them like Eve to believe that God's Word is not true and that *man*, by pursuing his own desires, can obtain wealth, power and recognition among men and a fulfillment of all his lustful desires which he believes will bring him happiness.

Many aspire to being like God, some even believing that they can become greater than God. Lucifer's current <u>main</u> victory over mankind, however, is in *deceiving* man to believe that God *doesn't* even *exist* and that, he, Satan, himself, *doesn't* exist. The main purpose of Jesus' ministry on earth was to destroy the authority of these hate driven evil forces. Adam and Eve had relinquished the authority over the earth that God gave them to Satan when they gave heed to his *lies*, instead of God's *promises* and *commands*.

Jesus' purpose was also to open not only *physically* blind eyes, but *most* importantly the *spiritual* eyes of all mankind. This applies to those who desire to *know* and *understand* the *truth*.

So basically mankind is now divided into *three* major groups.

The *first* group consists of those who *give* themselves to the lies of the forces of darkness to follow a selfish path of life oblivious to or uncaring of whoever they hurt along the way.

Alex recalled that the *second* group is composed of those who, although not perfect, have a hunger and thirst for righteousness and truth. These are those of whom Jesus had spoken, saying they would experience a new birth, their spirits snatched from darkness and transformed into new creatures of light with spiritual understanding. *These* have an arduous task of learning to engage the enemy in spiritual warfare. They are spiritual babes after the rebirth of their spirit, and through learning God's ways begin to mature to spiritual adulthood.

He also remembered the *third* group consists of those who haven't yet committed themselves to *either* the forces of darkness or to God's Spirit of light and understanding. These persons can be good in a basic sense and according to *man's* standards. They can be honest, hardworking people and even go to church. But, until they *fully* give themselves to God, accepting the cleansing of sin, made available through the sacrificial blood of Jesus, they are, as Alex's father put it, "walking on perilous ground indeed."

As a young boy, Alex had often wondered why a God of Love would place mankind in such a hostile environment. Once, he had asked his father about this. Dan Barrington had told him that the only two creatures God ever created with a spirit and a *free will* were *angels* and *mankind*.

The angelic host has always had a free will, which is what made it possible for Lucifer and other angels to sin. He had explained to Alex, that *all* other animals on earth react either out of an instinctual or environmental stimulus. And that man is the *only* being, created *on* earth who has a distinct knowledge of good and evil and who is therefore capable of committing sin, and thus, will be held *accountable* for sin. The only way to be forgiven of sin is to believe that Jesus was God's Son, that He shed His own blood to provide forgiveness for our sins and that we ask for and accept this forgiveness by *faith*.

After Alex had pondered these things, which his father had told him, he had several other questions which came to mind. Alex remembered clearly the day he had asked his father two of the main questions which still bothered him. They had been out mending a fence when Alex had presented these questions to his father. The first question, was, "What *is* faith an' why do some people *have* it, an' others *don't?*"

Dan Barrington had rested an elbow on a nearby fence post and looked off into the distance as he answered Alex. He had said, "Son, tha Bible says, in tha eleventh chapter o' tha book o' Hebrews, that, 'Faith, is tha *substance* o' things *hoped* for an' tha *evidence*, o' things not *seen*.' Jus' think of it this way. Ya can't *see* the wind, yet ya know it's real, 'cause ya can feel it an' see tha mighty things it does. Tha book o' Romans, says, in tha first chapter, that, since tha beginnin' o' time, creation *itself* has proven that there *is* a Creator. Some folk believe that all life happened by chance, but God, knowin' that this kind o' doubt would tempt us, put other verses in His Word ta help us out with that kind o' foolish thinkin'. Tha Bible says, for example, that we can't make our own selves grow, even an inch. We can't even make one gray hair turn back ta its original color jus' by thinkin' 'bout it, yet *God* knows *exactly* how many hairs are on each person's head. When ya get right down to it, it takes a lot more faith, son, ta believe that there *isn't* a God, than to believe that there *is*."

Dan had paused a moment in reflection and then continued, "If ya choose ta believe Satan's *lies* more than ya believe God's *Word*, you're puttin' more faith in tha *Devil's* word than in *God's* Word. Ah sure don't want ta be guilty o' that! Tha Good Book, also says that we're *all* given the *same* measure o' faith. A piece o' that same faith that God Himself, used ta speak this ole world into existence, outta nothin'. Yup . . . We *all* have faith son. We jus' gotta decide *whose* story we're goin' ta *believe*."

Alex's second question had been, "Did all tha people that lived on earth before Jesus died on tha cross, go ta hell? That wouldn't be fair."

Alex remembered that his father had looked at him with a twinkle in his eye, which Alex intuitively knew reflected pleasure that Alex had been seriously thinking of such deep, spiritual matters and was seeking the truth about them.

His father had then responded, "Son, Ah'm glad you're askin' these questions. Ah've talked about 'em before in church. Guess Ah need ta talk about 'em again. There's probably other children, like yorself, who weren't old enough ta remember or understan' these things."

He remembered his father's next words had been quite enlightening. "There have been three separate dispensations which means, periods o' time in history. The *first*, was tha Dispensation of Conscience. That time lasted from Adam an' Eve, 'til tha time o' Moses. Then, God took Moses up ta a mountaintop an' gave 'em the Laws o' God. That began tha *second* dispensation. This second one was tha Dispensation o' Law. That lasted from Moses 'til Jesus came ta earth. That started tha *third* dispensation. This *third* one was tha Dispensation o' Grace. That's tha period o' time that we're livin' in now."

Again Dan had paused and Alex could tell he was thinking of the right words to help his son's young mind understand these things. Then he had continued, "During the time o' *Conscience*, God judged man accordin' ta whether or not he did tha things that he knew in his heart were right or wrong. We've all got that built right into us. After God gave us His *written* Laws, man was responsible for a new level o' understandin' 'bout what God required of 'em. Tha Good Book says in tha third chapter o' Galatians that tha Law was our schoolmaster an' that it was sent ta show us that we couldn't be saved by good works. That we needed a special gift o' Grace in order ta be cleansed from our sins. That Jesus would <u>be</u> that gift o' Grace."

Dan had continued to expound upon these truths, "Tha first prophecy that God gave us, tellin' us that Jesus would come ta earth an' die for our sins was written in tha book o' Genesis. Faith is tha same Alex, whether ya were lookin' *forward* in history for tha <u>first</u> *comin'* o' Christ, or if you're looking *backward* in history believin' that He has *already* come. There are still folk alive today who have never heard about Jesus. They will still be judged under tha Dispensation o' *Conscience*. God is always fair, son. Ya can count on that. There's another very important thing that ya need ta remember. The Bible says that 'Ta whom much is given, much is required.' One thing that means is that if a person has ever heard about Jesus, an' has rejected tha truth about 'em, they'll be held accountable. That's a very soberin' thought, son. Jus' make sure that ya remember that one, 'cause ya've heard a lot."

When Alex stopped to think about it, he was *amazed* at the *vast* amount of scripture he could recall. He'd never before realized that hearing his father quote the Bible *so many* times over the years, had caused such a *great* volume of verses to actually be *implanted* within his heart and soul! He was deeply thankful for this. He realized that *without* the exposure he'd had to Bible truths during his youth, he'd now have *very little* to drawn upon. How would he *possibly* be able to have *any* understanding or insight into things which can only be discerned by God's Word and His Spirit?

Two additional verses now came to Alex's mind: One was Proverbs 22:6: "Train up a child in the way he should go, and when he is old he will not depart from it." Also, Hebrews 4:12, "For the Word of God is quick and powerful, and sharper than any two-edged sword, piercing even to the dividing asunder of soul and spirit, and of the joints and marrow, and is a discerner of the thoughts and intents of the heart." In other words, *God's Word* has the inherent ability to show us the difference between what is revealed to us by His Spirit, and what is merely our *own* thoughts, *or* reasoning placed in our minds by the powers of darkness.

Alex was suddenly jolted from his thoughts by the distressed voice of a woman. With a sense of horror, he recognized that the voice belonged to Rachel.

19
Intervention

Alex and Yang's eyes met for a brief moment of surprise and anguish. Then Alex peered anxiously over the banister. He spotted Rachel almost directly beneath him on the board sidewalk. She was facing away from Alex. One of the men of questionable character, whom Alex had watched ride into town just a short while before, was standing facing in Alex's direction. He had a firm grasp of Rachel's right arm with his left hand. Rachel was struggling to break free of his grip.

Alex heard this slovenly-looking man saying, "Come on Honey, jus' one dance at tha Cantina." He had a devious grin on his face, showing brown-stained teeth and a big lump inside his left cheek. He then spat some tobacco juice out onto the street, a streak of it remaining on his chin.

At that moment Alex experienced the strongest sense of déjà vu he had ever felt. It seemed like he was in a dream. He thought to himself, "This jus' can't be happenin' *again.*"

Suddenly Alex snapped out of the momentary disbelief of what he was witnessing below him. He suddenly sprang into action. He had no conscious plan, other than to end this situation immediately. It was as if his body began to act on its own, grasping the banister with his left hand, he swung his legs over it, plunging downward upon Rachel's antagonist. It was about a 12-foot jump. The man who was gripping Rachel's arm looked up about a second before Alex's knees impacted his chest. Alex landed on his feet like a cat. Rachel's assailant, however, went sprawling backward, landing on his back in the street, almost directly underfoot of a couple of horses tied to the hitching post.

The startled horses pranced about nervously, pulling against their reins and almost trampling the man as he rolled out of harm's way. A cloud of dust arose around the man and the horses.

Then, to his left, Alex noticed another man lunging toward him with fists clinched. This second man was huge and almost a head taller than Alex. The training which Alex had received from Julius paid off now, and Alex automatically knew from the man's body movement that he was going to throw a haymaker at Alex with his right arm. Easily anticipating this, Alex dropped to a squatting position while simultaneously sweeping his right leg out. The man had already thrown the punch which contacted nothing but air. Alex's right leg found its mark, knocking the huge man's legs out from under him. He hit the boardwalk on his left shoulder, letting out a wail of pain. He rolled onto his back and grabbed the top of his left shoulder. The awkward fall, coupled with his great weight, had evidently broken the man's collarbone.

Alex recognized this probability because he had seen a couple of men over the years being thrown from a Bronco and afterwards, grabbing their shoulder near the area of the collarbone.

Alex hadn't yet buckled on his Colts this morning, so he was unarmed. Although it didn't appear the injured man had plans of drawing his gun, Alex retrieved it from him anyway in case the man in the street, who was just now getting on his feet, might intend to escalate the fight.

Alex just held the gun down by his side as he faced the man in the street. The man, however, seemed to have no intention of going for his gun. Instead, he held both hands out to his side to prove he had no such intention. He had a look of fear on his face. Alex said to him, "Take yor gun out o' yor holster real careful like an' empty tha bullets on tha groun'." The man did so, very slowly and deliberately, so Alex wouldn't get the wrong idea.

When the man had accomplished this, he said stammering, "We didn't mean no . . . harm . . . We . . . was jus' foolin' 'round."

Alex replied in a firm tone of voice, "That kind o' foolin' 'round can get a man hurt. Ya' owe the lady an apology."

Alex had already noticed that there were several witnesses gathered around who had evidently seen all that had happened. They continued to watch in silent amazement.

The man in the street looked around rather sheepishly at the witnesses and then at Rachel. He began to speak with what sounded like genuine sincerity, saying, "Ma'am, Ah'm real sorry 'bout all this. My partner an' me has jus' come from a pretty wild an' open town. They got a couple o' dance halls there an' lot of women workin' in those places will dance with ya if ya buy em' a drink. Guess we was there too long an' forgot that mos' towns ain't like that an' mos' women are ladies, like yurself. Please forgive me fur forgettin' that."

Alex had been listening intently as the man was making his apology. He had now come to the conclusion that though these two men were very uncouth and ignorant, they didn't seem to have the same type of underlying propensity of extreme violence and savagery which characterized Sanchez and his men.

Alex glanced at Rachel and saw that she was watching his reaction to the man's apology. Alex nodded slightly at her, indicating that it was his opinion that the apology seemed sincere enough. She was inclined to agree with Alex, therefore, she looked at the man in the street and said, "Your apology is accepted."

The man visibly breathed a sigh of relief. Alex then said, "Ah believe ya meant what ya said, but jus' in case yor partner might have had other ideas . . ." Alex then emptied the gun of the other man and held it out toward the man in the street saying, "Ya might want ta get yor partner to a doctor. Ah think he may have a broken collarbone."

The man in the street then walked up to Alex and accepted the six-shooter. He stuffed it in his belt with a nervous grin and then went to his partner to help him to his feet. The two of them walked off, the big man still holding his shoulder and grimacing.

Rachel then walked over to Alex and expressed her gratitude for his intervention on her behalf. She also said, "You seem to have an uncanny way of being there right when you're needed."

Alex responded, "Ah'm sure tha Lord had a hand in that."

They turned, arm-in-arm, to enter the hotel, but before they made it inside a man wearing a marshal's badge walked up to them.

As Alex and Rachel paused in anticipation of a conversation with the marshal, Yang exited the front door of the hotel, evidently out of breath from hurrying down the stairs.

He said, "I couldn't see the second fellow, from where I was on the balcony or I would have jumped down to help you out."

Alex replied, "Ah know ya would've, Yang."

The marshal then spoke up, "Ah've already talked with some o' tha' witnesses an' got tha lowdown on what happened here. Ah heard tha 'pology an' feel ya did tha right thing." He paused a moment and then added, "Ah'm sorry, Ah forgot ta introduce myself. Ah'm Bob Clancy, town marshal." He stuck out his hand and Alex accepted this polite gesture. He said, "Thanks, marshal. Ah'm Alex Barrington an' this is Rachel McPherson an' Yang Ling. Rachel's family owns a ranch 'bout a day's ride east o' here."

The marshal rejoined, "An' ya must be their foreman."

Alex explained, "No marshal. Yang here is tha wrangler an' foreman for tha McPhersons. Ah was actually going ta look ya up today 'bout another matter. Will ya have time for us ta talk more, sometime today?"

Marshal Clancy replied, "Sure thing. Ah'll be in ma office after Ah finish makin' my roun's. Ah should get back there in 'bout a hour or before. Ah'll have some coffee ready."

Alex said, "Soun's good marshal. Ah'll see ya there then."

"Okay," replied the marshal. He tipped his hat to Rachel and said, "It's been a pleasure meetin' ya an' Mr. Ling." Rachel and Yang returned the compliment and marshal Clancy walked on down the boardwalk.

Alex, Rachel and Yang went inside the hotel and made their way to the dining room. Once they were seated at a table, the thought came to Alex that it might be a good idea to go up to his room and get his guns and holster. He was beginning to feel rather naked without them. He excused himself, saying he would be back in a minute. He added, "Ya can go ahead an' order breakfast for me if tha waitress comes while Ah'm gone."

While Alex went to get his guns, he thought to himself that he now understood better than ever how his father must have felt that day in El Paso. It must have been virtually impossible for Dan Barrington not to be furious with Sanchez.

Following on the heels of this thought, Alex wondered how the outcome could have been changed if his father had indeed controlled his rage that day. Would Sanchez have walked off? Alex seriously doubted that. Men like Sanchez usually wouldn't back down from anyone. If Dan had asked Sanchez either in a polite way *or* in a firm manner to walk away, the odds were extremely high that Sanchez would've continued to goad Alex's mother. In actuality, only God knew the answer to these kinds of questions. Alex intuitively understood that many things that happen in life are a mystery to mankind.

How could Alex's father have ever guessed that Sanchez and his men would do the unthinkable acts of depravity which they committed that day at the ranch. Alex finally shook these thoughts out of his head. He realized that this type of speculation was futile. There are some things in life that we just have to accept for what they are. Alex figured we would all wind up with "bats in the belfry" if we tried to understand *everything*. He headed back downstairs.

When he returned, Rachel's parents had joined them at the table. Alex greeted them and asked if they had slept well.

After Alex sat down, Patrick said, "Rachel and Yang just told us what happened outside a bit ago, Lad." Patrick grinned as he continued, "We're now officially and deeply in your debt. It seems the Lord has sent us a guardian angel."

Alex was a bit embarrassed and countered, "Now jus' what kin' o' a man would Ah be, if Ah didn't watch out for tha family that saved my life? Why, tha Lord would revoke my guardian angelship."

Everyone at the table chuckled and Allison said, "Aye, Lad, you're far too modest."

A waitress then brought two plates of their breakfast and said she would be right back with more of their order. She returned with the rest of the food and then brought a coffee pot to refill their cups. She had served Yang's food and coffee first and had a special smile for him each time. When she left after refilling their coffee mugs, Patrick said, "Yang, I hear they're having a dance after the race to celebrate the pie contest and the race. It seems to me like you've found a good candidate to ask to the dance."

Yang blushed a bit and said, "Maybe you're right. I'll give it some thought."

Allison joined in saying, "Aye, Lad, just don't think about it too long. I'm sure a number of men will have noticed that philly's smile and good looks."

After this statement the humorous atmosphere continued throughout the remainder of the meal.

While everyone was enjoying their last cup of coffee afterwards, Rachel said to Allison, "Mother, I was on my way to purchase the ingredients for our pies. I have already spoken with the lady who is in charge of the meals at the hotel and she said we are more than welcome to use the kitchen. She said she had already been asked the same question by a number of women and that plans have been made to make the kitchen available after dinner tonight. Would you like to go with me now to the store?"

Allison showed enthusiasm as she responded to Rachel's question. "Yes, of course. Let's get at it."

Patrick and Yang decided to check on the horses while Alex went to find marshal Clancy's office. When Alex entered the office, he could smell coffee. The marshal had evidently kept his promise. Marshal Clancy got up from behind his desk, saying, "Come in. Come in," and motioned to a chair in front of his desk saying, "have a seat." Clancy had taken off his gun belt and jacket, down to his red long john top. His trousers were supported by a pair of suspenders and his big belly was hanging over the waistline of his pants.

As Alex sat down, Clancy walked over to the coffee pot and poured two mugs of the hot liquid. He then handed one of the cups to Alex and sat down behind his desk again. Alex took a sip of the coffee, discovering that it was very strong. He thought to himself, "Ya could float a horseshoe in this java!" He had already had three cups at the hotel. He feared that if he drank *this* cup, he'd be as nervous as a cat in a roomful of rocking chairs and wouldn't be able to sleep for a week. He had noticed the marshal spoke rather fast and jerky. Alex felt he now understood why if Clancy drank much of his own brew.

"So, what's on yor mind, Mr. Barrington?" the marshal queried. Before Alex could get a word out, marshal Clancy said, "Yor name sort o' rings a bell for some reason."

Alex waited a moment to make sure the marshal didn't have *another* question or comment before he began to answer the *first* question. Clancy just sat there twiddling his thumbs, so Alex began explaining that he was on the trail of the Sanchez gang. After a brief summary of this, Clancy slapped his knee and said, "That's it! Ah knew yor name sounded familiar."

He then opened a desk drawer and pulled out some papers, tossing them onto the desktop. He fumbled through the stack until he found the particular papers he was searching for, and then said, "A U.S. Marshal Tihlman sent these ta me 'bout three o' four weeks ago. Yup," he continued, "tha first page there explains he also sent copies o' these papers ta tha marshal's an' sheriff's offices in St. Johns an' Page, Arizona. He mentioned yor name. Said yu're a deputy U.S. Marshal on tha trail o' those men ya jus' spoke of. Said these men 're evidently followin' tha Outlaw Trail an' he hoped tha messages would catch up ta ya here, or maybe in St. Johns or Page. Said he was able ta get more information 'bout those there hombres. There's descriptions o' each one of 'em an' a drawin' showin' their likeness."

Clancy offered the papers to Alex. Alex took them and mused through them for a moment. He then turned his attention back to the marshal, who was now sitting there curling the ends of his mustache between a thumb and forefinger and squirming around in his chair. It seemed that Clancy just couldn't sit still. Alex didn't know why, but this annoyed him. It wasn't that he necessarily disliked the marshal. He just definitely wouldn't want to be stuck bunking with the man all winter in a line shack somewhere. In that case, Alex would surely wind up sleeping outside.

Alex said to the marshal, "Ah 'preciate ya hangin' on ta these for me. From a talk Ah had with a livery han' here, seems like ya had a visit from these rascals couple o' weeks ago." Alex didn't understand why the marshal hadn't noticed the outlaws since he'd had the information on them for some time now.

The marshal looked out the fly specked window of his office, as if trying to recall anything he could about the Sanchez gang. He stopped twirling his mustache and began picking his nose. At that point, Alex looked down at his mug of coffee and decided to set it on the desk, having lost his desire to drink any more of it.

The flies on the window had evidently been swatted with a newspaper last summer or even before. Alex couldn't imagine just letting them stay there that long.

Finally, the marshal said, "Now ya mention it, there was a' outfit, matchin' their descriptions, came through town. Believe Ah remember they skipped town without payin' their livery bill."

Alex was dumbfounded that the marshal had even needed to think for a while before remembering the outlaws. Alex then said, "Well, marshal, thanks again. Guess Ah'll see ya at tha race." Alex shook hands with the marshal. As he walked toward the door, he heard Clancy belch loudly. Alex glanced over his shoulder in time to see the marshal walking toward the coffee pot, scratching his rear as he walked.

Alex left the marshal's office and as soon as he had gotten a couple of buildings away he stopped at a horse trough, tucked the papers under an arm and washed his hands off in the water, drying them on his trousers. He hoped he wouldn't have reason to visit the marshal again. Alex thought to himself, "The man must o' been raised by a pack o' coyotes or somethin'."

Alex, however, couldn't help but chuckle to himself as he walked back to the hotel. He was just glad he hadn't taken Rachel with him to the marshal's office. It was good she and Allison were out buying the ingredients for their pies.

20

The Purity of Compassion

When Alex got back inside his room at the hotel, he found that Yang wasn't there. He began to take a closer look at the papers marshal Tihlman had sent him. Tihlman had mentioned that he had sent duplicates of the same pages to St. Johns and Page, Arizona. He said that he hoped Alex received at least one set of them. Also, that the drawings, pictures and information enclosed were all that he was able to come up with so far.

Alex began to pour over the information. He studied the drawings of the men's faces and their descriptions.

The information about Sanchez, of course, was already familiar to him. His first name was unknown. He was a mix of Mexican and North American. His father, a gringo, had abandoned him and his mother when he was a young boy. He had beaten him and his mother during the few years he had stayed with them.

Sanchez had never been accepted by his mother's family or by gringos, which had all contributed to his hatred of Anglos and all people in general.

There was a difference, however, as Alex thought about this information for the second time. He sensed that some chord deep within him was struck, as he thought about this man, who to Alex, was the epitome of evil. He didn't permit himself to allow these feelings to mature into actual thought. Instead, he began to think of his loved ones and purposefully brought the memory of that horrible day back to the forefront of his mind to reinforce the bitterness he'd become used to.

Alex felt a confusion of emotions within. Not understanding the cause, he returned to focusing his thoughts on the pages of information about the outlaws.

The next man described was known only as Slim. He was a tall, wiry white man who was unkempt and had yellow rotting teeth of which the two front top ones were missing. He was said to have a wicked sneer and to be a very sneaky type individual. He carried a big Bowie knife on his left hip, his gun on the right, and was supposedly proficient with either.

Next, was Raul Vargas, who was rather short and muscular and said to be handsome. He was reportedly lightning fast with a gun, preferring the "border draw." This was when a man wore his gun butt facing forward, drawing it with the opposing hand. He was said to have a dark goatee, which he kept meticulously trimmed.

Then, there was Tom Coleman, who like Julius, was a former prizefighter, and supposedly had never been defeated. He was known to enjoy street fights and reportedly had killed a man with his bare hands. He was said to be short-fused, with an extremely bad temper, always itching for a fight with gun or fist. He was known to carry a sawed-off shotgun rigged with a custom-made holster, which enabled him to swing the gun up from the hip and fire quickly. Alex knew that such a gun would be very deadly at close range when loaded with buckshot, but at more of a distance, the pellets would scatter and become ineffective. Coleman was also described as having red hair. Thinking back, Alex remembered the red-headed man with Sanchez had, indeed, been wearing such a gun.

Next, was Vance Smith, suspected of being some other well-known gunslinger that used an alias to help avoid prosecution for several questionable killings. It was said he preferred to shoot a man in the back because, though good with a gun, he liked to always have an ace in the hole and had no scruples or sense of honor.

The last man described was called Ace, real name unknown. In fact, not much of anything was known of him. He was an unknown variable who was described as being the quiet, deadly type with no fear. He was thought by some who had met him to possibly have a death wish. The only physical characteristics mentioned were that he had salt-and-pepper hair and an icy stare. People who encountered him once had no desire to look into those eyes again, for to look into his eyes was to see undiluted hatred and the look of death, which sent shivers down the spine. It was like looking into the eyes of the devil himself.

Personally, as he read this last description, Alex wanted all the more to look into those eyes. The eyes of one of the men who had helped in terrorizing his family before murdering them. He desired to look into those eyes partly because of the bitterness which clutched his gut with an iron fist, but also because he too, had no fear. Ace probably had no fear because his life was empty and void due to his murderous and sinister soul, hence his possible death wish. Alex's lack of fear, on the other hand, was due to the fact that he had a personal knowledge of God. Maybe he wasn't as close to Him yet as he knew he should be and wanted to be, but Alex still remembered that day all fear had left him. That special day when as a young boy he had given his life to God.

Before that, Alex had the normal fears of a child. One of the most pronounced was a fear of lightning. He remembered the first lightning storm he had experienced after his encounter with the Lord. He had suddenly realized he was no longer afraid of lightning and had never been since. He literally had peace in the midst of a storm. He remembered, even now, his father often quoting the verse that says, "There is *no fear* in the perfect Love of God, for perfect love casts out *all fear*." Another verse he always kept in the back of his mind and in his heart says that

God has not given us a spirit of fear, but of love, power and a sound mind.

Alex set the papers down and lay back on the bed with his hands clasped behind his head. He had purposefully brought back the memory of his folks' death in an unconscious effort to subdue the unknown, unrecognized, and uninvited emotions he had sensed trying to take form inside him. He didn't know what they were, but even now he was mustering his will to keep them at bay. If he could've been honest with himself at that moment, he would have resisted the hardness of his heart and the scales of hatred blinding the eyes of his soul. He had now grown accustomed to these feelings, but if he'd had an open heart, he would have realized that the Almighty and Merciful God of all creation *Himself*, was behind those emerging thoughts and feelings.

Now that Alex *had* stirred up the memories of his family's brutal demise, they struck his heart like an enormous swarm of potent hornets, causing his soul to writhe with unimaginable grief and overwhelming sadness. He rolled onto his side as tears welled up in his eyes, which he shut tightly in a vain attempt to quell their flow. A hard lump formed in his throat and his chest felt as if it were encased in tight bands of steel.

Such was Alex's condition when he heard a soft knock at the door. He knew from the soft rhythm that it was Rachel. He cringed inside as he felt a duality of desires. He wanted to see Rachel and for her to hold him in her arms and help calm the storm within him, yet his all too normal male pride made him want to run for cover. After a moment, he answered in as calm and casual voice as he could produce under the circumstances. "Who is it?" he asked, knowing good and well who it was.

Rachel detected the gloom, dark thoughts and emotions by the sound of his voice. Most women, without even realizing it, simply have an intuition and sensitivity to such things. She knew something was deeply troubling him and her heart yearned to reach out in compassion and nurture. She softly said, "Alex . . . Can I come in? I need to talk to you."

Alex hesitated, panicked at the thought of her catching him in what he considered to be a weak moment. If only he'd had the ability to know her thoughts and feelings at that moment as she waited outside the door, he wouldn't have been the least bit reluctant to open the door. Despite his embarrassment, his desire and need to see her overruled and he finally sat up on the edge of the bed with his back facing the door as he said, "Come on in."

Alex heard the door open and was aware of the gentle rustling of Rachel's dress as she softly walked toward him. Rachel noticed the papers describing Sanchez and his men spread out on the bed. She quickly had an inkling of what had triggered Alex's obvious pain. She lightly placed her hand on his shoulder. Something in that warm, gentle touch had a deep effect on Alex. It was as though her thoughts and compassion were wonderfully transmitted to his heart. He couldn't help but to stand up and turn around facing her.

Rachel was an extremely intuitive and special woman. When she saw the tears on his face, she did not in any way perceive this as weakness in Alex. She had the innate ability to see all his strengths of character and, ironically, she even saw those tears as yet another of his strengths. It was the strength of a compassionate heart which caused those tears. Alex saw the tears as weakness because of society's general view of what constituted strength in a man, *and* because of his acceptance of this shallow, yet nearly universal view. As he looked into Rachel's eyes, however, he realized that she was not one that accepted *any* philosophical view merely because it was the status quo.

Once more, Alex's perception of Rachel and his respect and appreciation for her soared to a new level. In that moment, looking into Rachel's eyes and reading her soul, Alex knew he loved her in a way he could never love another woman. He *wanted* to tell her of this love, but due to his desire to *protect* her from possible future grief in the event of his death, he was still reticent to express his heart as yet. He felt sure, however, that Rachel could read it in his eyes.

Alex was drawn as if by a powerful, irresistible magnet into Rachel's arms. This, he seemed to have no control over. Rachel seeemed to have been mutually drawn by the same irresistible pull and they held each other in a passionate and tender embrace. Alex had never imagined such ecstasy was possible from a mere hug. They stood there in that embrace for quite a few moments, neither wanting this beautiful point in time to end. Alex lovingly stroked Rachel's hair and caressed her cheek with gentle fingers.

Alex's thoughts also focused on God during those moments. He was humbly thankful to Him for sending such a rare and wonderful woman into his life. Soon, Alex's grief and sorrow vanished, melted away by the bliss of holding and being held by such a pure and inexplicably virtuous and selfless woman.

The door then opened and Yang entered. When he saw Alex and Rachel, his face turned red with embarrassment at having intruded on such an intimate moment. He stammered, "Uh . . . I'm uh . . . sorry." He then backed out of the door, closing it quietly as he left.

Alex and Rachel released one another, both blushing a bit at having been caught in their private moment. They stood facing each other for a few seconds, holding each other's hands in a tender moment, each looking deeply into the other's eyes.

Rachel then softly said, "I'd better be going."

They exchanged a warm smile and Rachel then turned and left the room.

Alex sat down on the edge of the bed, amazed at the extreme change in his mood that only a few moments with Rachel had brought about. He was once again faced with the dilemma of his desire to protect Rachel by not allowing their relationship to gather more momentum. Although he had wanted and desperately needed her comforting presence just now, in a sense he regretted it.

This was yet another incident which had drawn them closer together. Would this perhaps bring more hurt and pain to Rachel in the future? Alex certainly hoped not. He then said a prayer, asking the Lord's help with this perplexing situation.

21
Love's Revelation

Late that night, numerous women were on hand at the hotel kitchen to bake their pies for tomorrow's contest. Alex and Yang couldn't help but visit Rachel and Allison in the kitchen and found that several other men had also been drawn in by the alluring smell of the baking pies.

The kitchen wasn't large enough for them and the women too, so after a while of stepping around the men, the women finally had to shoo them out. The men all hastily retreated through the kitchen door and Alex thought with amusement that if they had been hound dogs, they would all have had their tails tucked between their legs.

The men found their way into the hotel parlor. They joined a group of men already gathered there. They sat around talking and exchanging tales, known among cowboys as "windies," about their skills as horsemen and the valor and speed of their mounts.

Of course Alex, not being inclined to brag even if it *was* only in fun, just sat there listening and enjoying the pleasure the other men were deriving from the exchange of their tall tales. Unless a man was a drinker, there was little else to do that night. It was a mutual understanding that each man could use a bit of imagination and his most prized stretching techniques to embellish the stories.

In daylight, the men could have engaged in target shooting on the outskirts of town or thrown horseshoes in a side street.

Alex found out there was to be a prizefight in town after the race. Several men who had seen how he had handled the two men earlier that day, tried to talk Alex into participating. Alex had declined each time, even though it was told there would be a $50 purse for the winner.

He had enjoyed the challenge of learning the fighting skills from Julius and had certainly now seen the usefulness of his knowledge. Alex, however, felt that prizefighting as a sport, was often not so much about the money, as it was about the vanity of a fellow wanting to prove his manhood. He felt no need to prove anything and preferred not to take the risk of seriously injuring someone, unless it was a case of necessity. Each time an attempt to get him to enter the fight was made, he opined his lack of desire to do so.

While they were all sitting around talking in the lobby, the men finally ran out of windies and began to discuss the big race which would take place after the pie baking contest tomorrow. The men began to discuss wagers on the race. There was one gentleman dressed in a business suit who had stated earlier that he was not a contestant in the race. He now spoke up and said he thought it would be best to place the bets tomorrow, just prior to the race, after everyone had the opportunity to see all the horses and riders. He added that, being a town banker, he would be glad to hold the wagers in his bank until after the race. Alex didn't like to wage money, so he stayed out of that part of the conversation. His father had taught him that betting, while not necessarily immoral itself, could bankrupt a man. He'd also said that if a man had a *family* and wagered away his money so that he couldn't provide for them, then it *certainly* became immoral at that point.

Everyone agreed the man's idea was a good one. The topic of conversation then turned to politics and the railroad.

It was getting rather late when Rachel and Allison finally exited the hotel kitchen, pies in hand. They entered the lobby carrying the pies on potholders. Alex volunteered to accompany the ladies upstairs to open the door for them. He knew that Patrick and Yang would want to remain in the lobby for awhile, conversing with the other men.

On the way to the room, Alex was really tempted by the smell of the pies. He asked Allison and Rachel, "Will there be any o' these pies left over after the judges get through tastin' 'em?"

Allison laughed and said, "Aye, lad, there should be a piece or two at least."

Alex patted his stomach and responded, "Glad ta hear that, Mrs. Mac." Allison and Rachel chuckled, both having a pleased look on their face.

After Allison had closed her door, having wished Alex and Rachel a goodnight, Alex escorted Rachel to her room, opening the door for her. Alex waited at the door while Rachel placed her pie on the wash stand in her room.

Alex asked Rachel, "Would ya' like ta go ta tha stable with me? Ah'm goin' ta check on Storm an' Ginger. Ah'll probably saddle Storm up an' ride 'em a short distance out o' town ta limber 'em up a bit. If you're too tired, Ah can jus' put a halter on Ginger an' lead her behin' Storm."

Rachel responded, "Aye, but I'm not too tired! Sounds like a good way to finish the evening. I wanted to check on the horses as well. Just give me a minute to change into some riding clothes."

Alex said, "Great! Ah'll be waitin' in my room."

In a few minutes, Alex heard Rachel's soft knock at his door. Together, they went to the livery stable and saddled Ginger and Storm. Besides strapping on his handguns, Alex had also brought along his rifle, just to be on the safe side. He now slid it into its sheath tied to Storm's saddle. Lobo joined them in the ride. Alex was glad to have both a horse and a dog, which would help alert him to possible danger, especially with Rachel coming along.

They rode along in silence for awhile, just enjoying the crisp night air and the view of the moon as it hung suspended in the sky, surrounded by the canopy of brilliant stars. The sound of a distant whippoorwill could be heard now and then.

Alex's thoughts were a mixture of sadness and joy. The sadness was brought by the sound of the whippoorwill reminding him of home. A home which seemed so very far away and long ago. The joy was from the sheer pleasure of riding next to the woman he felt was the sweetest and most beautiful in the world.

He wondered at what thoughts might be winding their way through Rachel's mind. He wanted so badly to ask, but was disinclined to do so, ever mindful of his deliberation not to escalate their romantic involvement. It was sheer agony for Alex because his heart felt as if it would burst under the pressure of restraint. It was unnatural to hold back the flood of tender feelings he had for her. It took all the will power he could muster to hold back the torrent of emotions which wanted free rein to express his love for her. He just didn't know how he could continue to fetter his heart in this manner. A thought suddenly occurred to Alex. If Rachel's feelings toward him were equally as strong, he was doing her a *great* injustice by holding back like he was, since he knew it wasn't acceptable for a woman to initiate the verbal expression of love. He thought of how frustrated she must feel.

His eyes drifted toward her as they rode from beneath the shadow of a pine and back into the bright moonlight. Rachel's gaze had been toward the beautiful moonlit sky, but as she became aware of his glance, she shifted her eyes until they met those of Alex. Rachel released a faint, involuntary sigh.

Yes! Alex could see it in those beautiful eyes! He somehow instinctively knew in that instant that their thoughts had indeed both been on the same path. He saw the same recognition of this in her eyes as well. Alex and Rachel saw in each other that same tortured bliss. In that moment, Alex knew in his heart that he undeniably had to open the floodgates of his heart, at least for a few brief moments. He knew he *had* to offer her some solace. He *had* to allow *both* their thirsting souls a drink at love's deep well, even if only for a moment!

Alex reined Storm to a stop and Rachel also halted Ginger. They were close enough that their legs were touching as they sat upon their mounts. Then Rachel looked earnestly at Alex. Her look was a mixture of dread and hope all mixed together, which he read in the expression on her face. Alex knew he *had* to drown the dread and revive the hope within her. How could he have been so insensitive? Even if he *were* to die pursuing the outlaws, Rachel *deserved* to know his heart!

He reached out and took one of her hands, gently embracing it in his. He looked deeply into her eyes. Another faint sigh escaped her lips. Alex began in a warm, soothing tone, "Rachel, Ah feel Ah must speak from my heart. Ah haven't been fair with ya. Do ya remember that mornin' when we put Storm an' Ginger tagether?"

Rachel seemed only able to nod her head in acknowledgment, sensing Alex had something very profound to say. "Wul," Alex continued painfully, "Ah've had a battle ragin' on tha inside o' me since that mornin'. Ya see, Ah'm in a awful dilemma. Ah've been battlin' a certain fear. Tha fear comes from knowin' that one day, in tha near future, Ah'll have ta take up tha trail o' Sanchez an' his men again. Not a fear o' dyin'. That fear was taken care of when Ah was jus' a boy an' came ta know God on a personal basis.

"No, tha fear Ah'm talkin' 'bout is different. It's a fear o' not bein' able ta come back ta ya. Not a fear o' death, but o' tha earthly separation that it causes. If ya feel tha same for me

165

as Ah do for you, then Ah also fear tha *hurt* that would cause ya." Alex paused momentarily, struggling to find the right words.

When he paused, Rachel rather timidly injected a question. "How *do* you feel toward me, Alex?" She seemed to hold her breath in anticipation of the answer.

"Wul." Alex responded, "Ah've known *that* ever since that evening on the porch, after Ah told ya 'bout my family." Alex again paused, and he felt Rachel's hand tighten gently on his own. "After Ah told ya all those things, an' then later . . . we kissed . . ." Alex's heart was pounding as he struggled on, "Actually, Ah knew it before, but it became crystal clear ta me after that kiss . . . Rachel . . . from tha deepest depths of my heart . . . Ah *love* ya!!"

At that, Rachel almost *fell* into his arms. She was trembling. She seemed weak and barely able to speak as she said, "Oh, Alex! And I do <u>love</u> you the *same*. With *all* my heart and soul!" Her voice was quivering and Alex thought she might fall so he held her tightly. They embraced one another for countless wonderful seconds, then Alex put his hand under her chin, which was wet with tears. He gently lifted her face toward his and kissed her tenderly, yet passionately.

Finally, when Alex felt the weakness had left Rachel, he released her and she sat back up in her saddle. She now appeared to sit more erect than before. Alex believed that her posture signified her newfound hope and happiness.

What a glorious and striking silhouette she made against the beautiful moon, hanging directly behind her! Alex could see in the bright moonlight that though tears were still evident on her cheeks, she was smiling her most brilliant smile!

The thought that merely a few words from him could spark such a wonderful transformation in her countenance made Alex feel humbled and very grateful. In fact, he was nonplussed that he could affect such a magnificent woman as Rachel this way.

Here again was a moment in time which Alex wished could last forever. He'd had no plan whatsoever to say the things he had just said. Those words were *contrary* to his plan to stay a bit detached. Yet, having said them, and now experiencing the thrill they had created, he wouldn't have wanted to take those words back for anything!

He could see quite plainly that Rachel had desperately needed to hear that pronouncement and proclamation of his love for her. Alex actually felt a sense of relief and release sweep over him. During the ride back to town, the whippoorwill continued to sound its lonesome call, but the sadness and loneliness it had evoked on their way out of town no longer haunted Alex. Instead, there was a satisfaction of heart and mind for him which brought comfort to his soul. It was quite obvious Rachel was experiencing that same joy.

Alex explained to Rachel his desire to protect her and her family from danger. That this was another reason why he was anxious to get back in pursuit of Sanchez. He told her that there was always the possibility the outlaws may double back to check and make sure their ambush had been successful. This could put them in peril even back at their ranch. He also expounded the fact that Tom Coleman was a former prizefighter, which might lure him and his cronies back to Silver City so Tom could enter the advertised fight. Alex thought that the possibility was remote, but he just didn't want to take any chances. He explained that was the reason he'd brought his weapons with him tonight.

On their way out of town *and* while riding back, they took a look at the markers already staked out for the race. They wanted to familiarize themselves with these markers in preparation for tomorrow. The number of hoof prints on the ground was proof that numerous others had already done the same.

After getting back to town, they unsaddled and groomed Storm and Ginger. They then headed back to the hotel. As they approached, they could hear men arguing loudly. Alex removed the leather thongs from the hammers of his Colts so he could bring them into quick action if necessary. He glanced at Rachel, noticing a concerned look on her face.

22
More Trouble and Prayer

As they walked up the steps of the hotel and neared the lobby entrance, Alex quietly asked Rachel to wait on the veranda while he checked out the commotion inside. He cautiously peered through the front door and saw two of the more unsavory types which had come to town, standing almost nose-to-nose, locked in heated dispute.

Alex entered the door noticing several other people in the lobby watching the pair as they exchanged insults. The onlookers were nervous. They appeared frozen in place, as if afraid any motion on their part would draw attention and possible danger their way. Alex was relieved to see that neither Mr. and Mrs. Mac, nor Yang, were present in the lobby.

Both of the arguing men had a hand on their weapons as if ready to draw, should the other make the first move. Alex, nerves and muscles taut and ready, purposely cleared his throat loudly enough to get the attention of the two. They both looked in his direction. Before entering, Alex had instinctively taken his U.S. Deputy marshal's badge from his shirt pocket, pinning it on his shirt. He had also pulled back his coat, exposing his Colts to view.

Both men noticed the badge, the Colts and the unwavering, dead serious look in Alex's eyes. Though his eyes normally reflected his easygoing manner, he now unknowingly had a definite stern and authoritative appearance. The two ill-natured men who now stared at Alex also recognized distinct danger in his "no nonsense" glare. Both immediately removed their hands from their guns, turning to face Alex, with their arms now carefully rising above waist level, thus signaling their lack of desire for a confrontation with this obviously formidable lawman.

Alex, in a low yet ominous tone of voice, calmly said to the two men, "Ah have no idea what yor beef is with each other, but this is definitely not the place for ya ta settle yor differences. Both o' ya keep yor hands like they are an' head for tha back door. Ah'll be right behin' ya."

Both men carefully turned around and headed toward the kitchen, which everyone knew had the only rear entrance to the hotel. Alex purposefully had them go that way ever mindful that Rachel was on the front veranda. The men passed through the kitchen and out the back door, glancing now and then back over their shoulders at Alex, who was watching their every move.

Once outside, Alex had each man, one at a time, empty their revolvers, allowing them to drop the cartridges into a pants pocket. Alex then said, "Ah don' know if either or both o' ya have a room in tha hotel, but if ya do, Ah want ya ta leave yor weapons at tha front desk, if or when ya come back inside. Ya're jus' too much a risk ta tha other people inside, ta be totin' them hog legs indoors. Have Ah made myself clear?"

Both men nodded in the affirmative and one, swallowing hard, making his Adam's apple bob up and down in his throat said, "Yeah, marshal. Sorry 'bout tha lack o' judgment, gettin' all riled up inside tha hotel."

Alex then said, "Alright then. Ah want one o' ya ta walk off now ta tha left, an' the other one ta tha right."

The men did as instructed, disappearing into the darkness. Alex hurried back through the hotel to the veranda. When Rachel saw him appear through the front door, she gasped a sigh of relief. He took her arm in his and together they went upstairs. Alex paused at Rachel's door after opening it for her. She stepped inside and turned to face Alex as he stood in the hallway.

She spoke softly, "I was doing some serious praying for you while you took care of that problem, my dear Alex. You sure do keep your guardian angels busy."

Alex rubbed his chin in thought for a moment. "Yeah, Ah guess they ain't been gettin' bored lately." Then he added, "Ah jus' don' understan' men like that. Seems like they jus' don' have a lot o' common sense an' don't stop ta consider how their actions can affect an' jeopardize other folk." He noticed Rachel was staring at the badge still pinned on his shirt. He had forgotten he had even put it on. Now feeling a bit chagrined, he took it off and put it back into his pocket.

Alex felt a bit awkward and could sense that Rachel felt the same way. Since the wonderful closeness and bonding of hearts they had shared tonight, it felt like the most natural thing to express his love *again*. He wanted to very much, yet he was hesitant to do so.

Rachel, being the intuitive woman she was, sensed his discomfort and wanted to set him at ease. She grasped his hands and gently said, "Alex, I understand that what you opened your heart and told me tonight was a beautiful moment of truth. Those amazing words brought comfort and warmth to my soul, which I deeply needed. I thank you from the depths of my heart. I also understand you can't repeat those words regularly yet and that you still struggle with fears. I hope and pray that the day will come when we are free to express this love daily, but I understand the time is not yet."

A tear appeared on Rachel's right cheek. She didn't bother to brush it aside, but looked into Alex's eyes and said, "Oh, don't worry. It's a tear of joy from remembering our beautiful moment tonight."

A smile lit up her face. Not the brilliant one, but one of extraordinary warmth and depth. Alex embraced her in a tender hug and kissed her lightly on her beautiful lips, whispering, "Thank ya, my deares' Rachel, for understandin'."

With that, they relinquished their embrace and their hands slid gently apart, as Alex took a step backward. "Wul, tomorrow's tha big day," he said with a warm grin on his face and a sparkle in his eye. "Guess we'd better get some sleep. Goodnight then an' God bless ya. *Y Tú poder se acostar con los ángeles pequeños alrededor de tu cama, Esta noche Querida mia.*" Which in Spanish means, "May you sleep with the little angels all around your bed tonight, my dear."

Rachel replied, "*Y tu también, mi querrero valiente. Dios te bendiga!*" which means, "And you too, my brave warrior. God bless you!"

Alex looked surprised. He said, "Ya never cease ta amaze me, Rachel. Ah had no idea ya speak Spanish as well."

Rachel replied, "Well, our ranch is pretty isolated, but we *do* employ *vaqueros* during roundup you know." She continued, "There's something special I want to do before the race tomorrow."

Alex asked, "What is it?"

Rachel responded, "Oh, it's a surprise."

Alex then said, "Okay then. Goodnight, Rachel."

She said, "Goodnight."

And with that, they retired to their rooms. Once in his room, Alex found that Yang was sound asleep and snoring. He couldn't help but wonder what kind of surprise Rachel had in mind for tomorrow. Lobo found a spot and stretched out on the floor near Alex's bed. When Alex had washed up and completed his ritual of placing newspaper in front of the door and window, he laid on the bed with his arms crossed behind his head. He stared up at the ceiling, pondering the events of the night. He wondered how things would unfold in the near future. His thoughts then turned to the race tomorrow.

Alex knew that Rachel wouldn't want or expect him to hold Storm back, to give Ginger a better chance of winning. He wasn't really concerned, however, about allowing Storm the opportunity to show himself to be the bolt of lightning he was. He was more concerned for everyone's safety, especially Rachel's.

He prayed, therefore, "Lord, Ah know Ya probably don't concern Ya'self much in small things like horse races, but Ah know Ya do want ta protect those who love Ya. Ah know tha McPhersons an' Yang love Ya an' do their bes' ta walk in Yor ways. Ah pray Yu'll keep 'em safe durin' the race tomorrow. Ah thank Ya that Ya helped me ta say tha right things ta Rachel tonight. Ah didn't even know Ya wanted me ta say those things, but Ah thank Ya for Yor Spirit leadin' an' guidin' me, puttin' tha right words in my mouth. Ah feel good an' satisfied 'bout it. Ah ask Ya ta continue givin' me tha wisdom Ah need with all that tha future holds as well. Ah ask Ya ta forgive me my trespasses an' ta answer all these prayers, in the name o' Jesus. Amen."

Alex soon drifted off to sleep, in spite of Yang's snoring.

23
The Race Begins

When Alex awoke, he could hear that a few people had already begun to stir around outside, even though it was still a few minutes before the sun would peek over the horizon. He knew this was due to the excitement that the big day had finally arrived. He got his shirt and pants on and removed the paper from in front of the door. Yang woke up and stretched, as he sat up on the side of his bed.

"Mornin'," Alex said.

"Yang replied, "Morning, Alex. I feel like I could eat a bear."

Alex responded, "Me too. Let's see if Rachel an' her folks are up. We need ta get on downstairs an' grab a bite ta eat 'fore it's all gone. Sounds like mos' folk got up earlier than we did."

Yang agreed, so they roused the McPhersons and headed to the hotel dining room.

When they were finished eating, Rachel said, "I've got something I want to ask all of you to do for me."

"What's that?" asked Patrick.

"Well," countered Rachel, "this being such a special occasion, I want us all to go to the photographers shop down the street and have our picture taken. If, or I should say *when* Alex wins the race, I also want a picture taken of him and Storm with the new saddle strapped on him."

Alex replied with a grin. "But that could be you, or Yang, or who knows whoever else."

Allison chimed in with, "Aye lad, you don't have to be so modest about your ability, or that of Storm."

Yang laughed, as he added, "How about a picture of you, Mrs. Mac, or Rachel, holding the remains of the winning pie and the blue ribbon?"

So, honoring Rachel's request, they left the hotel and went to have the picture taken. They all obeyed the instructions of the photographer and had a group picture taken, which was a close up of them from the waist level up.

After that was accomplished, they all started for the door, except for Rachel. She said, "Wait just a minute please. I want a second one taken." With a lighthearted groan from the men, they returned to the spot they had previously been positioned in. This time however, Rachel asked the photographer to back up so he could get a photo of them head-to-toe. He complied and then told them the photos should be ready in a day or two.

Alex noticed a kind of mischievous expression on Rachel's face, which made him wonder what she was up to and why she had wanted the second photo taken at a distance. But he didn't ask.

Rachel and Allison hurried back to the hotel to get their pies and then headed toward the pie contest areas. Shortly, the judges began their tasting responsibilities, which was clearly a task they enjoyed. Alex sensed their minds were already made up after the first tasting, but they made the excuse that they needed to sample all the pies once more to reach a final conclusion. The truth be told, they just wanted to eat more of the best pies they had ever indulged in.

After whispering quietly and meticulously deliberating among themselves, as if members of some important jury trial, they finally left their huddle. One of the judges then walked in front of the long line of tables where the pies were on display. Each woman stood directly behind her pie. A card bearing her name was in front of it. The judge held the blue ribbon in one hand and held the other up to silence the crowd.

The judge then smiled and turned around, walking directly to where Rachel stood, and with congratulations handed her the blue ribbon. Everyone applauded as Rachel blushed and seemed genuinely surprised at the decision. As she accepted the ribbon, Allison, who stood next to her, gave her a big hug. She was happy for Rachel and beamed with pride, having been able to teach her daughter so well.

After the crowd began to disperse, Alex, Patrick and Yang all came to congratulate Rachel. Of course they each took a piece of pie from both her and Allison.

The race was to start in about two hours, so everyone went to saddle their horses and get ready. All began to assemble at the north outskirts of town. This had been chosen for the starting point so that the street wouldn't hinder everyone from lining up side-by-side because there were about sixty riders competing. The course was laid out around boulders, stands of trees and thickets. It was two miles out and two miles back, forming a semicircle. Posters detailing the rules of the race had been posted all over town, but marshal Clancy explained the rules again before the start of the competition.

One of the rules was that, if a rider fell once, they could get back up and continue the race, but if they went down a second time, they would be disqualified. He reminded the participants that observers had been posted along the course to ensure the rules were followed and that no one took any shortcuts or conducted themselves in an unsportsmanlike fashion.

With that, he made a visual survey of the line of riders to make sure everyone was ready. He then pointed his pistol in the air and fired a shot, signaling the race was on.

The wild yelling of the riders encouraging their mounts to get into a full run coupled with the bugling of the horses was almost deafening. Rachel was positioned next to Alex. Ginger shied a bit at all the noise, as did many other horses, but Rachel quickly steadied her and she charged ahead, beginning to pull out ahead of the rest of the horses.

Alex purposefully held Storm back some, because he knew that the beginning of a race involving so many horses usually had the most potential of danger and mishap right at the starting point. This was because all of the horses and riders were bunched together causing momentary mass confusion for the animals. He wanted to stay behind Rachel at this point so he could see her get off to a safe start.

Just as Ginger was increasing her lead to half a body length, the horse directly to the right of her stumbled and fell against Ginger. She, in turn, stumbled and went down with Rachel tumbling to the ground. She appeared to hit the ground hard, rolling head-over-heels two or three times.

Alex felt a knot of fear in the pit of his stomach as he immediately reined Storm to a halt, leaping from the saddle. In a few quick bounds, he was on his knees beside Rachel.

24

The Heart to Win

Rachel seemed dazed for a moment but with Alex helping her, she sat up just as Ginger was also getting up from the fall. The man whose horse had fallen against Ginger and Rachel was lying on the ground, groaning and holding his right arm. Alex's immediate concern, however, was for Rachel.

Alex asked Rachel, "Are you okay? Do you hurt anywhere?"

Rachel replied, "Yes, I'm okay, except I think I sprained my wrist. I'm going to check out Ginger and lead her back to the livery stable. Please! You go ahead and get back in the race. I'll be fine!"

Alex glanced up and saw that marshal Clancy was checking on the other injured rider. He helped Rachel to her feet and gathered Ginger's reins, giving them to Allison, who had just arrived at the scene out of breath. Together, Rachel and her mother began to walk Ginger back to the stable. At their insistence, Alex had remounted Storm and began to pursue the other riders, who were by this time a good 300 yards out in front of him.

Alex allowed Storm full rein this time. Though the terrain at this part of the course was flat, it seemed to Alex like Storm was a locomotive with a full head of steam and heading downhill. There was a swishing sound as each clump of brush was passed. Storm ate up yards of distance like a hungry bear devouring a small fish. In no time, he was right on the heels of the other horses which were in the rear of the race.

He swept past one horse after another and by the time they were in the part of the course which began to circle back toward town, there were only eight riders still in front of Alex. A couple of riders just ahead of him now had been near Alex and Rachel when the race begun, and Alex knew they had seen Ginger fall and Alex rein Storm to a halt and jump out of the saddle to check on Rachel.

These riders now kept glancing back over their shoulders with amazement on their faces. They spurred their horses furiously but to no avail. In a few more seconds, Storm swept past them.

Alex noticed as he passed by them, that one of the horse's flanks had blood trickling down from the cruel spurs that the owner was using. These were not the more humane blunted spurs used by those who had a love for their animals, but the longer sharp-pointed spurs with rowels which cut into the flesh of the unfortunate horse. This angered Alex. Whenever he saw a man even *wearing* this type of spurs, he automatically knew such a man would also have a cruel hardened heart at least to some degree.

Alex needed no spurs to coax Storm along. Storm's performance was dictated by his love for his master and a heart that naturally desired victory. Even in the midst of the race, this caused Alex to reflect upon what his father had often brought to light in his sermons.

That God is not a cruel taskmaster. That folk who learned of His great love for them by reading His Word with an open heart, didn't have to rely upon painful experiences in life to motivate them into obedient commitment to their Heavenly Father. Their nature is changed by the realization of His merciful love, and they would begin to desire to please God from a thankful heart.

As a person's natural instincts of a corrupt and sinful nature which would normally cause them to be led by their physical

179

senses and desires were replaced by faith in the supernatural love and power of their beloved Master, they could begin to walk by faith and be motivated by love.

Alex thought of how his father would often say that faith operates in love. That through a love relationship with Jesus, the impossible would become possible. That when God's love is perfected in our understanding, we can then overcome fear. The verse of scripture which states that came to Alex's mind. He remembered that first John chapter 4 verse 18, says, "There is no fear in love, but perfect love casts out all fear, because fear hath torment. He that feareth is not made perfect in love."

Such were the thoughts of Alex as he and Storm began to close the gap on the remaining six horsemen, now only a few short yards ahead. The finish line was only a few hundred feet away at this point. Alex was leaning over in the saddle, his head close enough to Storm's ears that he only had to speak gently to Storm as he said, "Ah know ya can do it fella. Now let's go get 'em."

Storm immediately responded to the loving voice of his master and reached down into his great heart, pulling upon the reserve strength which awaited there. Horse and rider were as one. Storm's long, powerful legs reached out in an even longer stride.

In just a few of these great strides, they passed the remaining horses, crossing the finish line a full twenty feet ahead of the rider who had been in the lead.

As Alex slowly reined Storm in, a cloud of dust began to drift in toward town and a crowd of people waiting there began to cheer loudly.

They had witnessed the beginning of the race. They had seen Ginger and the other horse fall. They had watched Alex halt Storm and jump out of the saddle to check on Rachel. They had seen the great distance the main group of riders were already down the trail as Alex remounted and charged off after them.

Not one man, woman or child had believed Storm stood any chance of even catching *up* with the horses at the *rear* of the race, let alone pass them, overtake the *lead* horses and actually *win* the race!

The people were ecstatic! If they hadn't seen this great feat with their own eyes, they would have had great difficulty believing it.

Alex continued to walk Storm, knowing he needed to cool down gradually after a strenuous run. His eyes scanned the crowd to find Rachel. After about five minutes, he saw her mounted on Ginger and approaching him. Evidently Rachel had thoroughly checked her for injuries and had found none.

As Rachel reined Ginger alongside Alex and Storm, her eyes were alight with joy at his victory. When Alex inquired about her wrist, she told him the pain had greatly subsided and there was little swelling. She evidently had not sprained it badly, and Alex was greatly relieved.

Soon, Patrick, Allison and Yang joined them. They were all mounted, although Yang was the only other one of them who had ridden in the race. He was also allowing his horse to cool down.

After the excited chatter from Rachel's mom and dad had abated somewhat, Yang interjected, "I don't know if you noticed me, Alex, considering you were all wrapped up in catching the lead horses, but I was about in 12th place when you and Storm streaked pass me like a bolt of lightning." He continued with great enthusiasm, "I have to tell you I was awestruck and truly amazed at the power and speed of Storm! I *have* never and probably *will* never *again* see another horse like him! The good Lord didn't have an average horse in mind when He put *that* one together! If I had to lose, I'm glad it was to Storm." Yang then reached over and gave Alex a firm pat on the shoulder, stating, "Great job, my friend!"

Alex gleamed with pride in Storm and satisfaction at such a compliment, which came from a man who knew a whole lot about horses. He responded, "Thanks Yang. Understandin' your knowledge o' good horseflesh, Ah consider that a great compliment."

About that time, marshal Clancy approached them, spouting "Great race, Alex! Never seen tha like in my life. Guess ya ought ta head over ta tha booth where that fine saddle an' rifle is waitin' on ya." He paused for a moment, spitting tobacco juice and then continued, "It'll soon be time for the picnickin' an' then tha shootin' contest." He then added, "Oh, an' congrats on tha blue ribbon for yor pie, Miss McPherson. Havin' talked 'em inta lettin' me be one o' tha judges, Ah can tell ya firs' han', it was one o' tha bes' pies Ah've ever tasted. It *was* kin' o' hard to choose 'btween yor pie an' yor mom's though."

Rachel, blushing slightly, replied in her characteristic humility, "Well, I really thought Mom's should have won that ribbon, but thanks."

Then they all headed over to where the saddle and rifle had been on display. A large group of folk were gathered around the booth, and greeted Alex with cheerful admiration, respect and congratulations.

Alex, with some embarrassment, stepped up to the man who was inside the booth. The man seemed quite proud to be the one who had the responsibility of presenting the prizes to Alex.

Once Alex had the fine saddle with matching reins, etc. on one shoulder and the rifle in the other hand, Rachel said, "Please, Alex, let's go have your picture taken now with the trophies of your success."

Alex agreed and after placing the new saddle on Storm, they went down the street to the photographer's shop and had the picture taken.

After this, the McPhersons and Yang accompanied Rachel and Alex back to the hotel, where they got the picnic baskets they had prepared that morning and had left in Patrick and Allison's room. They went back out to where they had tethered their horses.

They took the horses to the livery stable and groomed, watered and fed them. They then rented fresh horses to ride out and find a spot under a pinion tree. There, they spread a cloth on top of a flat rock and placed the baskets on this.

All were feeling famished due to the excitement and activity of the day. During the meal, Patrick asked Alex if he was going to enter the shooting contest. Alex advised he wasn't.

Patrick seemed a bit disappointed, so Alex explained, "Ya see Mr. Mac, Ah have tha personal feelin' that showin' off Storm's ability ta run an endurance race an' showin' off my skills with a gun are two different matters. Ta me, guns are a dead serious business an' Ah feel Ah should only use 'em when practicin' or when they're needed for defense, or tha like. Ah guess Ah'm kind o' gettin' used ta thinkin' of 'em in regards ta enforcin' the law too. But, Ah jus' don' feel comfortable, leas' not now, usin' 'em in a contest o' skill."

Patrick responded, "Now that you put it that way, I completely understand your thoughts and feelings about it, son, and I respect you for that."

When Alex heard Patrick refer to him as "*son*," it struck a deep chord in his soul and inspired a tenderness in his heart. Until now, Alex had not thought about it, but in a way, Rachel's father *was* beginning to fill some of the gap left by his father's death. He pondered this for a while in silence while they continued the picnic and exchanged small talk.

Alex frequently glanced at Patrick during the conversation and was mindful of numerous ways in which Rachel's dad reminded him of his own father. These thoughts and recognitions brought a renewed sense of belonging.

During those moments, Alex noticed that Rachel, ever deeply perceptive, was aware of Alex's glances toward her dad and a sweet smile was on her face. She had seen Alex's initial reaction as her father had called Alex "son." It seemed she could read his thoughts and was pleased.

They lingered at the picnic site long after the meal was finished and past the time when the shooting contest would be over.

It was nearing dusk when Yang suddenly exclaimed, "Oh my goodness! I almost forgot something!"

Everyone looked at him, obviously trying to understand what had brought about this emotional burst from the usually calm Yang.

25
Rachel's Victory

Yang stood up abruptly saying, "I almost forgot about Lily and the dance! I've got to get back and get ready to meet her."

As Yang rushed to his horse, everyone was jesting good-naturedly with him.

They too had forgotten about the dance. They hadn't known that Yang had bolstered his courage and actually asked the sweet waitress to accompany him to the dance.

As Yang was scurrying off, Alex turned to Rachel saying, "Ah almos' forgot 'bout the dance myself. Ah should o' asked already, but will ya do me the honor o' goin' ta tha dance with me, Rachel?"

Rachel playfully countered, "Well, let me see." She paused for a moment and then jokingly said, "Since another man hasn't already asked me, I guess I *could* find the time to go with you." She then grinned mischievously.

Alex said, "Why, Ah'm much obliged, M'am. Shall we mosey on along then?"

The McPhersons chuckled at this and said they were going as well.

As they approached town, they could hear the music of the fiddles, banjos, guitars and washtub bass as the makeshift band was already warming up.

They went to their rooms, bathed and put on clean clothes. When Alex was finished, he waited a few minutes, realizing it took women a bit longer to get ready. He went and knocked lightly on her door.

The sight that met his eyes caught him off guard. Rachel was standing there in a beautiful satin emerald green dress. Her face was aglow and the faint, yet sweet aroma of perfume emanated from her. The green dress made her green eyes seem even greener, and they were sparkling like stars in a clear night sky.

Alex's heart skipped a beat as he stood there dumbfounded for a moment. Finally, he was able to become cognitive enough to offer her his arm. She took it and stepped out into the hallway, pulling the door closed behind her with her dress making a soft, nearly inaudible rustling sound as she moved.

They started off down the hallway and Alex couldn't stop looking at her. He said, "Rachel, ya're by far tha mos' lovely woman Ah ever saw, an' *that's* jus' tha *everyday* beauty. *Tonight*, ya truly do take my breath away!"

Rachel responded by clutching his arm more tightly and saying, "Why Alex, that's the best compliment I've ever had and it makes my heart swell within me! Coming from *you* is what makes it especially meaningful. I made this dress over a year ago and have been saving it for some special occasion. Tonight *certainly* fits that description."

Alex replied, "Rachel, ya make even tha mos' plain *calico* dress look elegant." Rachel's face lit up with one of her brilliant smiles and her cheeks reddened as she blushed. She really *wasn't* at all used to such openhearted and flattering words, and they were coming from the man she loved in the most *profound* way.

The love she felt for Alex was greater than *any* she had *ever* dreamed possible. As they walked down the stairs and outside toward the sound of the music and laughter, she said a silent prayer in her heart. Her heart had been lifted to the heavens last night by Alex's verbal proclamation of his love for her. Her prayer was that God would *protect, guide* and *watch over* Alex.

She didn't even like to think about the inevitability of his resuming the hunt for Sanchez and his men, but she knew that he *must* and that the *time* was drawing near. Despite the great *joy* this night held, she still felt the *dread* of the unknown, transcending the foreseeable realm of her finite understanding. She felt this dread and fear in the pit of her stomach. She, like Alex, had been struggling inwardly with the same temptations of fear.

She finally overcame these fearful emotions as she reminded herself that, though <u>she</u> might not know the future, <u>God</u> *did* and <u>He</u> *was* in control. She felt her prayers would not be in faith and free from unbelief, should she allow the *fearful imaginations* her mind was now being tempted with, to *dominate* her thinking.

She reminded herself of the verses written in 2nd Corinthians, 10:4–5. That the weapons of a Christian's warfare, are not the *natural* weapons of man, but are *spiritual* weapons, provided by God's Spirit. That with *them*, we can pull down strongholds of the enemy. Strongholds which can exist in our <u>imaginations, if</u> they're not committed to God.

She quoted verses 4 and 5 to herself now, "For the weapons of our warfare are not carnal, but mighty through God, to the pulling down of *strongholds*; casting down *imaginations*, and *every* high thing that exalteth itself against the *knowledge* of God, and bringing into captivity *every thought* to the *obedience* of Christ."

Rachel was aware of the Holy Spirit speaking to her heart in that moment. Not with an audible voice that could be heard with the natural ear, but nonetheless she heard His voice clearly with the *spiritual* ears of her heart.

He was encouraging her and reminding her that the *imagination,* which we all have, can be turned from one of fearful *thoughts* and *emotions* to one of purposefully exalting and magnifying God's Word and promises of Divine provision.

She determined in her heart that from now on she would stand in faith *with* and *for* Alex. She determined she would *refuse* images in her mind of Alex being killed or seriously wounded, but instead, she would see him being *protected* and *led* by God's Word and Spirit.

The verse from 2nd Timothy, 1:7, also came to mind, "For God hath <u>not</u> given us the spirit of *fear;* but of *power,* and of *love,* and of a *sound* mind."

Yes! She *would* stand in faith with the man God *Himself* had brought into her life. She understood that God had gifted Alex with natural skills with gun and fists which were certainly good for a lawman to have, *but* that his *real* protection, defense and ultimate victory rested in the *Lord's* Hands, *not* in his own.

At this point Rachel instantly realized that the fear in the pit of her stomach had now been replaced with a peace and assurance that *Almighty God* is in control, as long as we *allow* Him to be. That God is limited <u>only</u> by any unbelief we allow and tolerate in our hearts and minds. He has given us a free will to <u>choose</u> *death* or *life.*

Proverbs 18:21 then came to her thoughts, where it says, "<u>Death</u> and <u>life</u> are in the <u>power</u> of the *tongue:* and they that love it shall eat the fruit thereof."

<u>Whichever</u> one we choose, we will experience the *fruit* of that *choice.* Either good things or bad things are created in our lives according to the words we speak and the thoughts we think.

Rachel knew she didn't want to eat the *fruit* of *doubt* as Eve had in the Garden of Eden. *Instead,* she purposed in her heart to eat the *fruit* of *life* contained in God's Word. He made this available through His promises and the spiritual laws which He had established for the good of those who <u>willed</u> to see with *spiritual* eyes and *hear* with their *heart,* instead of their weak carnal *minds.*

In just those few moments of reflection upon His Word, Rachel had calmed the storm of doubt and fear. Joy now rose up within her to take its place.

As they entered the community building, she sensed the dawning of a new chapter in her life. One which, though possibly fraught with hardships and danger, <u>also</u> held the promise of *love, joy, peace* and *happiness!*

26
Dancing and Reflecting

The community building had evidently been completed recently, in time for the race and all the activities associated with it. The fragrance of freshly hewn Ponderosa pine and Douglas fir greeted Alex and Rachel as they entered the building.

It was quite large and spacious enough to accommodate several hundred people, with elbowroom left over. There were dozens of lanterns on tables and suspended from the rafters. The walls were lined with chairs and bales of hay, which provided extra seating. There were many more chairs scattered around.

A couple of large new washtubs filled with apple cider sat on tables and they were surrounded by many tin cups.

In the middle of the single room structure, there was a large open area of floor reserved for dancing. At the moment, dozens of people were on the dance floor "do-si-doing" their partners in a square dance, passing each other right shoulder to right shoulder and circling each other back to back.

Alex, still embracing Rachel's left arm in his right, made a sweeping gesture with his left arm, inviting her to join him in the square dance. She happily accepted the invitation and they entered the group of dancers, both wearing a happy and carefree grin.

They remained on the dance floor for two dances after the one which they had originally joined. After the third dance, Rachel expressed her desire to sit the next one out.

Alex went to get some apple cider for them. When he returned to where he had left her sitting on the hay bales along the wall, he found she had been joined by her parents. Yang and Lily were still out on the dance floor. They soon joined them and they all enjoyed warm, jovial conversation while sipping their apple cider.

After conversing for about half an hour, the band slowed the music to a country style waltz. Alex looked at Rachel sitting there, radiant in her beautiful green dress and couldn't resist asking her to dance.

Rachel accepted and Alex led her gently by the hand out on the floor. As they danced, their eyes met and their gaze remained focused on each other throughout the entire song.

The musicians appeared to be especially aware of Alex and Rachel, as did all who noticed them dancing. Some folk even stopped dancing just to watch them as they drifted along, completely unaware of the attention many had shifted their way.

Numerous women nudged their husbands or friends in the side, pointing out Rachel and Alex. Even Allison nudged Patrick and said, "Now, that's the look of love, if ever I've seen it."

Patrick, with an understanding grin, nodded his agreement, then replied, "Aye! I don't think we could've handpicked a man better suited for our Rachel, even if we'd had a hundred years and a thousand suitors calling on the lass. I believe the Good Lord arranged this one."

Allison rejoined, "And right you are, Patrick. I feel a sense of destiny at work between them."

As the dance ended and Alex and Rachel headed back to where her parents were seated, they noticed for the first time that there were only three other couples remaining on the dance floor. They also recognized that many folk were looking at them with perceptive smiles on their faces.

Both Rachel and Alex flushed with embarrassment and quickened their pace back to Allison and Patrick, only to discover her folks were both smiling in the same manner. They could tell, however, that Allison and Patrick would glance away, trying not to let their joy of the moment be quite so obvious.

Alex and Rachel were both abashed and felt somewhat awkward. They were soon relieved though, when Yang and Lily walked up and conversation resumed. They noticed that Yang and Lily seemed quite taken with one another and had apparently not noticed the predicament Alex and Rachel had just faced. Both were silently thankful for this.

A bit later in the evening, several ranchers, one by one, approached Alex vocalizing their admiration of Storm and expressing how much they'd love their prize mares to have colts sired by Storm. Alex was very cordial with them, but noncommittal. He realized he'd be getting back on Sanchez's trail soon, and didn't know how long it would be before he returned. He did, however, tell them where the McPherson ranch was and that he'd be gone for a while. He said that maybe in a few months something might be able to be worked out.

Alex and Rachel spent a while in front of the fireplace, which had been constructed at the back of the building in an opposite corner of the room, where the band had set up. They sat on hay bales and basked in the warmth and glow of the fire, listening to the crackling of the logs. They were mostly silent, but would occasionally converse about the day's events and about their mutual enjoyment of the evening.

Rachel voiced her regret that the festivities would soon draw to an end. It had, indeed, been a very special time which neither would ever forget. Especially the night when Alex had let go of his reservations and pent-up emotions. When he had poured out his true feelings for Rachel and had *profoundly* voiced his *deep* love for her, and *she* in turn, had expressed the *same* intensity of love for him.

Unknown to either of them, they were both now during the periods of silence, thinking of those wondrous moments. They were each reliving and savoring each moment as it had transpired. A deep and inseparable bond had been forged between them that night. It was a bond which no circumstance could ever eradicate.

That love had been growing in each of their hearts since they first met, but neither had known where it would lead them until that night. It had been a night of Divine destiny, and each of them saw it in that light as they sat in front of the fireplace.

Both had a definite recognition of the Lord's involvement in their relationship. Both had strong reminiscence of everything which had occurred, beginning with that fateful day Rachel and her father had found Alex lying wounded and unconscious on the trail.

Each of them thought of the day Alex had awakened from his close encounter with death. Both thought of the first time their eyes had met. There had been a spark of recognition from Alex in that moment that there was something *very* special about Rachel. He remembered sensing the strongest feeling of destiny and Divine Providence he'd ever experienced with that first look into those beautiful green eyes.

As for Rachel, she had already experienced that feeling while he was still delirious with fever. Even during all the many hours she had spent at his bedside while his life hung in the balance. At the time, however, she'd not implicitly perceived those inner feelings developing within her. But she *had* been cognitively aware that there *was* indeed something *very* special about Alex.

Yes, it was during those long, tense hours and days while she prayed for him with fervency deeper than she'd ever known that she had begun to experience a strong sense of fate. The seeds of love for Alex had already been sewn in her heart before she ever looked into his eyes or heard his voice.

It was during prayer and those long night vigils that she'd sensed the Lord speaking to her heart that he would somehow become a major part of her life. Now reflecting back, she thought of how God had already used him to save her mother from the rattlesnake. How he had delivered *her* from the clutches of that unsavory man in Silver City. She had a profound sense that Alex would be a part of the rest of her life and was moved with great joy at the thought!

These were the thoughts which occupied their minds during the long moments of comfortable silence as they sat together, hand-in-hand, before the crackling fireplace.

Finally, the band quit playing and folk began to drift slowly out of the building. Alex and Rachel were among the last to leave, neither wanting this night to end.

As they stepped out of the door and into the night, a man approached them.

27
Disturbing News

In the semidarkness of the street, Alex hadn't recognized the man at first. But as the man stuck out his hand and said, "Howdy, frien'," Alex, to his great surprise, perceived that it was U.S. Marshal Tihlman from Las Cruces.

Alex grabbed Tihlman's hand firmly with a broad grin on his face. He said, "How ya doin', marshal?" He was so surprised that it took him a moment to remember his manners and introduce the marshal to Rachel.

Alex beamed with pride as he then said, "Ah'm sorry. Marshal Tihlman, this is Rachel McPherson. Rachel, this is U.S. Marshal Tihlman from Las Cruces."

Tihlman responded, "It's a real pleasure ta meet ya, Miss."

Rachel replied, "Likewise, marshal. Alex has mentioned you numerous times, and quite favorably I might add."

Alex, bewildered, said, "Ah had no idea ya were in town. When did ya get here?"

"Ah jus' got here this afternoon. Ah was really surprised ta fin' out ya were here. Heard all 'bout ya winnin' the race an' 'bout yor other escapades here in Silver City. 'Case ya didn't know it, yo're tha talk o' tha town."

"Well," countered Alex, "guess it jus' goes ta show ya how little they have ta talk about. Why don' we all go ta tha hotel lobby where me an' Rachel's folks are stayin'? An', do Ah ever have a lot ta tell ya!"

"Soun's good ta me, Alex. Miss McPherson?" the marshal queried Rachel, seeing if that was agreeable to her.

"That sounds great, marshal," she agreed. "Please call me Rachel."

They went to the lobby and as they found some empty chairs, Alex said, "Can't believe ya've been here since this afternoon an' Ah ain't bumped inta ya 'till now."

Marshal Tihlman responded, "Oh, Ah was in an' out o' tha community buildin' durin' tha dance some, but ya know *me*. Ah kind o' stay in the shadows. 'Sides, Ah saw ya were occupied an' decided ta wait 'till *after* tha dance ta say howdy."

The marshal said this with the same kind of smile Alex had noticed on many other faces after the waltz he and Rachel had danced together. He then winked at Alex when Rachel turned her head in a moment of disconcertment.

Alex was embarrassed a bit as well, but couldn't help but smile at the marshal's teasing.

Alex queried, "So marshal, what brings ya ta Silver City?"

"Got some business in St. Johns. Ah knew 'bout tha big race, o' course, but my horse ain't no spring chicken an' ain't up ta no racin'. Tell ya tha truth, Ah don' fancy big crowds too much, an' if Ah hadn't heard 'bout ya bein' in town, Ah would o' jus' got a room to rest up a bit. Ah'd a hit tha trail ag'in early in tha mornin' an' wouldn't even o' gone ta tha dance."

The marshal paused a moment and then asked, "So, tell me what ya've been up ta an' why yu're not farther 'long tha Outlaw Trail after tha Sanchez gang."

Alex then began to relate to marshal Tihlman how he'd been ambushed and shot out of the saddle while on their trail. How Storm had gone for help and how Rachel and her folks had brought him back to their ranch and nursed him back to health.

Rachel joined in, giving extra details from time to time. Some of the details of her part in restoring Alex, which she omitted due to her modest nature, Alex embellished upon with ardent praise of Rachel and her mother.

When Alex and Rachel had finished the story, Tihlman remarked, "Ya shor do have somebody up there lookin' out for ya. Also seems certain tha right folks were sent your way, ta help tha Lord with His handiwork."

"Yep," replied Alex, "shor does seem that way, don't it?"

"By tha way," added Tihlman, "there's been some rumor of a couple o' Sanchez's men bein' seen lately in Page, Arizona."

This news caught Alex off guard and started thoughts racing through his mind.

After some more conversation and catching up on events, they all finally retired for the night. In the morning, Alex and Rachel said their goodbyes to marshal Tihlman, wishing him Godspeed.

Once the marshal had ridden down the street and out of sight, Rachel queried. "Why don't we go to the photographer's shop and see if the pictures are ready yet?"

They found that the photos were indeed ready, so they paid for them, and took them back to the hotel to show them to Rachel's parents and Yang. All agreed the photographs had turned out well. Soon, Rachel, with a mischievous grin, excused herself, saying she'd join them all for breakfast in a few minutes. She then hurried from the lobby and headed upstairs toward her room.

The rest went on into the dining area to begin ordering breakfast. Allison ordered for Rachel, knowing what she'd probably want. Lily had taken the morning off and at Yang's invitation, joined them for breakfast. Rachel returned as the food was being served, clutching a small purse in her hand.

Alex was curious about this, as it seemed odd that Rachel would bring a purse to breakfast. He looked at her quizzically, but she just smiled with that mischievous grin.

Patrick called for silence and began the usual prayer of thanks for the meal. He began, saying, "Lord, we thank You for all of Your abundant provision and for Your guidance and wisdom in the way everything has worked out. Thank You that Rachel wasn't seriously injured when Ginger fell. Thank You for the blessing of allowing Alex to win the race and Rachel to win the blue ribbon. We thank You for the good times we've had during this trip and the warm fellowship we shared at the dance last night. Most of all, we thank You for eternal life, which You've so graciously provided through Your Son Jesus. We ask You to bless this food as nourishment for our bodies. We pray these things, in the name of Your Blessed Son, Jesus. Amen." Everyone at the table echoed that amen.

During the meal, Rachel noticed that Alex wasn't as involved in the conversation as he normally would have been and that he seemed preoccupied in deep thought. She knew it had to do with marshal Tihlman's mention last night that some of Sanchez's men had been reportedly seen in Page, which was not far from Silver City.

Patrick and Allison had both noticed Alex's preoccupation as well, and were a bit perplexed by it. Rachel took note of their concerned look and quietly shared with them about the visit they'd had last night with marshal Tihlman and the news of Sanchez's men. She did this while Yang and Lily were talking to Alex about the race and last night's dance.

After a short while, the conversation lulled as everyone sensed that something was up.

28
The Lockets

When the conversation completely stopped, Patrick said, "Alex, Rachel told us about your visit with marshal Tihlman last night and the news about Sanchez's men being spotted in Page. We can tell that there's a lot of thoughts going through your mind this morning. Would you care to share any of it with us? Sometimes it's hard for a man to bear the weight of the world on his shoulders by himself. I just want you to know we'll understand and be 100 percent behind you in any decisions you feel you have to make, son."

Alex was caught a bit off guard, not having realized the others had noticed his preoccupation. He was silent for a few moments, contemplating how to share his thoughts with those around the table. They were looking at him with an obvious mixture of love, concern and anticipation on their faces.

Finally, Alex began by saying, "Well, ta tell ya tha truth, Ah'm a bit concerned that news o' tha race an' who won it might make its way ta Page pretty quickly. If Sanchez or any o' his men get word of it, they jus' might decide ta head back this way an' try ta set up another ambush. My bigges' concern is that you, Mrs. Mac, Rachel an' Yang get back ta tha ranch 'fore any o' that could happen."

Alex paused for a few moments, reflecting on the plan which had evolved in his thinking. He then continued, "Ah think an' feel in my heart that it'd be wise for ya'll ta head back ta tha ranch soon as possible. Ah plan ta stay here in tha Silver

City area for another day o' two, circlin' an' scoutin' tha outskirts o' town ta make sure Ah don' see any sign of 'em showin' up 'round here. If Ah don't see any sign that they've come back sniffin' 'round here, then Ah'm gonna start out for St. Johns and then Page. Ah'll try ta make contac' with marshal Tihlman again ta get tha skinny on any new information he may've gotten 'bout tha gang. Ah plan ta sen' a wire ta St. Johns today, 'case the marshal's still there. Ah also plan ta let marshal Clancy know 'bout it."

Alex paused again, giving the others a moment to digest what he'd just shared with them. He glanced around at them and saw that they were patiently waiting for him to finish speaking his mind.

Alex then concluded by saying, "Ah was prayin' 'bout all this real serious las' night an' feel this is what that Lord told me ta do. Ah also prayed He'd 'specially help ya'll ta stay vigilant on tha trip back ta tha ranch an' that He'd protect ya 'long tha way. Part o' me wants ta be on that trip back home with ya but Ah feel Ah better stick with what tha Lord seems ta be speakin' ta me on the inside."

When Alex had finished speaking his mind, Patrick spoke reassuringly, "Aye lad, I think we all understand the logic in what you've said, and know the Good Lord is giving you wisdom and direction concerning all of this. We'll start back toward the ranch in the morning then. Just know that our prayers will be with you, that He'll direct your every step and help you to accomplish your mission of bringing these men to justice. That He'll also protect you along the way and bring you back safe and sound."

Allison added to this, "We've learned to trust your judgment and your ability to hear the Lord's instruction, Alex. I know in my heart everything will turn out right."

After the conversation ended, Rachel asked Alex to take a walk with her. He gladly accepted her invitation. They wound up in front of the community building and went inside. There was no one else there.

They sat down in front of the fireplace, which now held only ashes. Alex felt a sadness. He knew it was because today and tomorrow would be the last time he'd enjoy Rachel's company for a while. How long a while, he couldn't guess.

As they sat there, Alex glanced over at Rachel and saw a tear glistening on her cheek and knew she was feeling the same sadness. He also saw concern on her face. He reached over and gently wiped the tear away with his hand. Her cheek felt like velvet. He wished he could wipe away the sadness as easily as he could the tear.

They both had known this moment would come, yet neither were prepared for it. Both struggled in their minds to think of the right words to say. Words that would fit the feelings in their hearts, but to both of them, words seemed difficult at this point in time.

Finally, Rachel opened the small purse she had so joyously brought from her room just a short while ago. Gone, however, was the mischievous smile she had worn earlier before Alex had announced his intentions. Alex felt that he had robbed her of the joy she'd had earlier that morning. He felt badly about that and it showed on his face.

Rachel had perceived this and said, "Please, Alex. Don't feel badly about the decisions you had to make. I thank you from my heart for the concern you have for me, my parents and Yang. You're such a wonderfully caring man, and I know you've right in what you've decided."

She then reached into the small purse and pulled two lockets out, giving one of them to him. Alex, a bit perplexed, just held it in his hand looking at it.

Rachel said, "Well, go ahead and open it." Alex did so and found that on the inside was a cutout picture from the photo that had been taken at a distance, making the faces small enough to fit in the locket. It was a picture of Rachel.

Never in his life had Alex received a gift more meaningful or important to him. He saw that Rachel had opened the locket she had kept, and that inside was a picture of *him*.

Rachel then said, "I didn't know the time would come this soon, but knowing that it eventually would, I wanted us to have these pictures to look at. I want us to be able to look at them with faith in our hearts that you'll return safely."

"Rachel," Alex responded, "Ah'm deeply touched an' believe me, Ah'll look at this picture often an' remember tha love in yor heart that put it there. It *will* help my faith an' determination, that Ah'll return safely ta ya an' Ah'll look forward ta that day with all my heart."

Rachel responded, "And so shall I, my dear Alex."

29
A Prayer Brings Hope

The following morning, the McPhersons and Yang had packed all their gear and were ready to start on their trip back to the ranch. The pack animals were lined up behind the other horses.

Alex had helped the others get packed and prepared for the journey. They now all stood in a semicircle holding their horses' reins. The mood was rather somber as Rachel and the others tried to calm the thoughts which tempted them concerning the peril which lay ahead for Alex. Each believed firmly in their hearts that God was able to deliver Alex from danger, yet their natural minds and thinking processes sought to rout that confidence.

They all knew this is a battle every believer has to encounter on a daily basis and overcome through faith in God's Word, His power and His promises. They understood that these battles are not easy, yet they are winnable, when the heart is given precedence over the carnal mind.

Thus was the emotional atmosphere when Patrick asked all to join hands in prayer. Alex had learned long ago from witnessing his father's way of ministry that the joining of hands was symbolic of joining hearts together as a point of contact for releasing and uniting the faith of Christians.

As they stood there, hands and hearts joined, the casual passer-by looked at the group quizzically, not fully understanding why the McPhersons, Yang and Alex were not the least bit embarrassed or self-conscious about praying publicly in this manner. All, by now, had learned a great respect to these God-fearing folk. Therefore, they passed by without the slightest hint of disrespect or contempt on their faces.

Patrick, as usual being the patriarch, led them in a quiet but very sincere prayer. "Our Heavenly Father," he began, "we are tempted to be very concerned for Alex's safety, but we realize that fear is the opposite of faith and works against it. I'm reminded of Your Word, which promises in Psalms 36:7, that Your children can put their trust under the 'shadow of thy wings.' Therefore, we ask that You keep Alex under Your Divine wings of protection. In what better place can we believe Alex to be than *under* Your protection and *in* Your perfect will?"

Patrick paused in a moment of silent meditation before continuing, "We are also reminded in Proverbs 3:5–6, that we are to trust in You with all our hearts, leaning not to our own understanding, and that if we acknowledge You in all our ways, You will direct our paths. We believe that You have given Alex direction by Your Holy Spirit, and that he has committed all his ways into Your Almighty Hands. Therefore, we believe that You are directly involved in showing him each step he should take in pursuing Sanchez and his men. That means that in the future, Alex won't fall into any more traps or ambushes. We thank You in advance, for the answer to these prayers, because Your Holy Scripture also tells us, in Hebrews 11:1, that 'faith is the *substance* of things hoped for, and the *evidence* of things not yet seen.' We ask these things, in the powerful Name of Your Son, Jesus. Amen!"

As Patrick finished his prayer, Alex added, "Father, Ah also thank Ya for watchin' over an' leadin' Mr. an' Mrs. Mac, Rachel an' Yang too. In Your Son's Name. Amen!"

Everyone agreed with a hearty amen and the somber mood was changed to one of hope, confidence and Godly peace. Such was the ability of a heartfelt prayer of faith to lift their spirits and overcome the feelings of dubious apprehension, replacing those negative thoughts with an expectation that the Lord would make good on His promises.

As the departing group began to mount their horses, Alex took Rachel's hand, pulling her aside just a bit, and whispered an affirmation in her ear, "Ah love ya *deeply*, sweet Rachel. Ah'll return ta ya safely."

At that, Rachel responded with her most brilliant smile, saying softly, "And I too, love you deeply, Alex Barrington, and I *know* He *will* indeed bring you home safely."

When Rachel said the word "home," Alex felt a sudden flutter in his stomach and realized that when he returned to the McPherson ranch, he *truly would be* returning "*home*"! This realization brought emotional warmth that blanketed his heart with comfort and a sensation of peace. He could hardly wait for the task before him to be completed, so he could indeed return "*home*" to the ranch and those he loved with all his heart!

Alex helped Rachel to mount Ginger. A smile a mile wide spread across both their faces. In that moment, love and hope were so real and tangible that they both felt they could just reach out and touch it.

Alex had saddled Storm so he could accompany them a few miles out of town. He swung into the saddle and they headed out following the trail which headed toward the McPherson ranch.

Shortly, Allison began to hum "Amazing Grace." Alex remembered the story behind that song. It had been written by a man named John Newton in 1772. He had been the captain of a slave ship. His ship was all but lost in a violent storm. John had prayed for deliverance, a prayer which God had answered. John had given his life to God because of that answered prayer. He later became a pastor.

Before long, Rachel and Patrick joined Allison in humming the tune from that old hymn. It was contagious, and it wasn't long before Alex and Yang joined in. Soon, they all began to sing the words instead of just humming the tune. They sang every verse:

Amazing grace, how sweet the sound,
That saved a wretch like me!
I once was lost, but now am found,
Was blind, but now I see.

'Twas grace that taught my heart to fear,
And grace my fears relieved;
How precious did that grace appear,
The hour I first believed!

Through many dangers, toils and snares,
We have already come;
'Tis grace has brought me safe thus far,
And grace wll lead me home.

The Lord has promised good to me,
His word my hope secures;
He will my shield and portion be,
As long as life endures.

Yes, when this flesh and heart shall fail,
And mortal life shall cease;
I shall possess, within the veil,
A life of joy and peace.

The earth shall soon dissolve like snow,
The sun forbear to shine;
But God, who call'd me here below,
Will be forever mine.

When we've been there ten thousand years,
Bright shining as the sun,
We've no less days to sing God's praise
Than when we'd first begun.

As they sang this hymn, Alex thought how closely the words related to the dangers he faced in his current situation and the hope he felt inside. That *hope* emanated from the same *faith* which had saved John Newton. That *faith* was a *measure* of the same *substance* God used to create the universe.

The melody of the song was Scotch/Irish in origin and Alex had been privileged to hear it played on a bagpipe by a Scottish immigrant.

The insects and birds seemed to join them in the melody. Alex reflected upon the fact that, just a short while ago, before they had joined hands in prayer, their mood had been almost totally opposite of what it was now.

He marveled at the power of change, inherent in turning one's attention from the negative circumstances of life, and instead focusing your thoughts on God and the abundant provision He has made available to His children.

They soon topped a hill and could see to one side a field of prairie grass undulating in the breeze. There were white puffy clouds scattered in the sky. Alex was suddenly reminded of the dream he had experienced not long after he'd begun to recover from the gunshot wound and the subsequent blow to his head, followed by the life-threatening fever. It was like the dream where he and Rachel had been walking hand-in-hand in a field of gently swaying grass much like the field which spread before them now.

There were fields similar to this in various areas surrounding the McPherson ranch. As Alex looked across the distant expanse of waving grass, he could envision a sturdy log home with three large pasture areas enclosed by split rail fences.

He could envision Storm and Ginger running freely in one of those pastures. Running with them were colts, some newly foaled, some yearlings, and some nearing maturity.

In other pastures, he could imagine cattle. In his mind's eye—or was it in his spirit?—he could see a creek with lush tree and shrub growth lining its banks.

He was riding beside Rachel, caught up in this daydream when he was suddenly snapped back to reality as he noticed a group of riders approaching them. They were headed toward them from the opposite direction of the trail.

30

On the Trail Again

The approaching riders were quite a distance away, so it was difficult to determine much about them.

Alex rode out in front of the others as a protective caution. He put Storm into a fast canter, so that he would encounter the riders at a safe distance before they would reach Rachel and the others.

Lobo trotted out in front of Alex and Storm. Alex kept an eye on him to see if he would sense potential hostility from the group of riders. Alex could now tell that there were five riders and that two were women, so some of the tension he had been feeling was eased.

As he got even closer, he could tell that all of the riders were Mexican. They wore the typical clothing of villagers. The concern Alex had felt initially quickly disappeared. As they approached even closer, he could hear them singing a Spanish ballad.

Alex then reined Storm to a walk. When within talking distance, he stopped Storm, saying, *"Hola damas y caballeros. ¿Cómo todo estar se yendo?"*, which means, "Hello Ladies and Gentlemen. How is everything going?"

They all greeted him with broad smiles and one responded, *"Muy bueno mi amigo. ¿Y usted?"*, meaning, "Very well my friend. And you?"

To that Alex replied, *"Bueno. Es un dia muy bonito, ¿no?"*, meaning. "Good. It's a very nice day, isn't it?"

"*Con seguridad y el clima es bueno,*" one of the men remarked, meaning, "For sure and the weather is good."

"*Si,*" said Alex, "*es un día perfecto que uno viajar,*" which means, "Yes, it's a perfect day for one to travel."

One of the women said, "*Lo reconocemos. Usted ganó la competencia, ¿no?*", meaing, "We recognize you. You won the race, right?"

"*Por supuesto,*" replied Alex, "*pero mi caballo fue realmente el que ganó,*" meaning, "Yes, but it was really my horse that won."

The woman responded, "*Sí, y qué magnífico su caballo es!*" meaning, "Yes, and how magnificent your horse is!"

"*Gracias,*" Alex said, and then concluded the conversation with, "*Vaya con Dios,*" meaning, "Thanks. Go with God."

"*Y usted también mi amigo,*" replied the woman, which meant, "And you as well my friend."

With that, the riders passed Alex and the McPhersons and Yang caught up with him.

Alex rode on a couple more miles with his friends and then reined Storm in, saying, "Wul, Ah guess it's time for me ta head on back to'ard town."

He laid a reassuring hand on Rachel's shoulder, looked deep into her eyes and said, "It won't be long 'fore Ah see ya again."

After saying his goodbyes to Rachel's parents and Yang, Alex headed Storm back toward Silver City.

That ride back toward town was the loneliest Alex had felt since he'd left Buck and Tía Anna's ranch those many weeks ago. Yet, Alex encouraged himself with the acknowledgement that God was with him, so that the loneliness was not as acute as it had been after leaving Buck's ranch.

Alex had brought provision enough to last him two or three days so that he could scout around the outskirts of town as he had felt the Lord had directed him to do.

Therefore, when he got within about two miles of Silver City, Alex headed off to the right of the trail, beginning his first circle of the town, never seriously considering someone might be watching him from a distance.

He rode slowly, constantly scanning the horizon in every direction with the naked eye, not bothering to use his telescope. When it was about an hour before dark, he came upon a cluster of boulders surrounded by numerous pine cottonwood and fur trees. He decided to stop there for the night.

After he'd eaten a supper of hardtack and beans, he rolled out his blankets upon a bed of pine straw. The first blanket he laid upon, and the second he covered up with. As he lay there, he pulled out the locket Rachel had given him and looked lovingly at her picture, wishing he didn't have to be apart from her. With emotion pulling at his heart, he put it back into his pocket.

He made no fire so as not to draw attention to his presence. He said a prayer before falling asleep. He, of course, prayed for Rachel and the others. He also asked his Heavenly Father to alert him to any danger and to take control of his dreams.

It wasn't long before he drifted off to sleep. The prayer he'd made committing even his dreams to God paid off in a way he could never have imagined.

31
The Dream

In the wee hours of the morning while all was dark and still, Alex had a dream which would change him forever! Every detail of the dream was so vividly real, that it would be etched into his very soul for the rest of his life!

In this dream, he was a first-hand witness as Jesus was beaten with the "cat-o-nine-tails." This whip he was beaten with had nine strips of leather at the end of which was tied a sharp piece of broken bone, leaden balls, and sharp spikes. Every lash of the vicious whip tore flesh from Jesus' back exposing underlying muscle and small portions of the bones of His ribcage.

After each lash, Jesus would look directly into Alex's eyes. In Jesus' eyes were the emotions of, not only the great physical pain, but a mixture also of wondrous compassion and love.

Each time Jesus looked into Alex's eyes, Alex would start to cry out, "No! No! You must stop this!" But as Jesus heard him, He slowly shook His head looking back again at Alex. Though Jesus never opened His mouth, Alex could hear Him speak directly to his spirit, "No, my son. This is why I came to Earth and took upon myself the form of human flesh. I'm suffering all these things for *you* and for *all* who will believe that I *am* the Son of *man* <u>and</u> the Son of *God*. That I am suffering this to free you from the curse of sin, sickness and *all* manner of affliction *caused* by the curse of sin.

When the beating was finished, Jesus was untied from the whipping post and made to stand upright. A crude, heavy, wooden beam, filled with splinters was forced upon His shoulders. Jesus again looked into Alex's eyes with that same look of compassion and love. Jesus' face was so badly swollen and disfigured from the fists of the Roman soldiers earlier that morning, He was hardly recognizable as human. Yet, looking through swollen eyelids, Jesus' eyes remained clear and focused, always full of the same love and compassion.

The angry crowd thronging Jesus then began to push Him. Jesus stumbled and struggled to remain erect and Alex realized that it was His *great love* which gave Him the strength to begin the walk toward Golgotha upon Mount Calvary. A crown of thorns was thrust cruelly down upon His tortured head. They bowed the knee before Him and mocked Him, saying, "Hail, the King of the Jews."

Shreds of His flesh hung like a torn and tattered garment from His back. His body was a mass of ripped and bloody flesh. Alex was repulsed by what he saw, yet he couldn't take his eyes off His Savior.

As Jesus reached Golgotha, He was thrown to the ground and His hands were nailed at the wrist to the wooden beam He had been forced to carry.

With each blow of the hammer, Jesus continued to look into Alex's eyes. Alex felt *tremendous* guilt and sorrow, understanding that his *own* sins were partly responsible for the great suffering Jesus was enduring for *him!*

Every sin Alex had ever committed flooded back into his mind. Every lie and every moment of ungoldly selfish desire and lust. Every person Alex had ever humiliated with self-righteous criticism. Every self-centered ambition. Every word of gossip. Every unkind or unforgiving attitude and thought against his fellow man.

Alex had always thought he had lived a fairly moral life, but in the presence of the *truly* sinless Savior, *all* his self-righteousness simply melted away and seemed quite adequately described by God's Word, to be as *filthy* rags! Yet, the compassion and understanding in Jesus' eyes, at the same time gave him a sense of hope and an awareness of *total* forgiveness being offered to him *unconditionally!*

Despite the awful sense of guilt and feeling of unworthiness which he understood were rightfully deserved by his carnal flesh, Alex knew intuitively that *all* of his sins *could* and *would* be forgiven if only he *believed in* and *trusted* the Savior he now beheld before him.

If he *only* believed Jesus *was* indeed the Son of God, openly confessed his sins to Him and believed in his heart that the cruelty of the crucifixion he was now witnessing was paying the price *in full* for *all* his sins, then he *would* be wondrously forgiven. He *would* be set free from the bondage and curse of sin which plagued him and *all* mankind! He cried out to Jesus, "Forgive me Lord!" Jesus looked him in the eye again and said, "Your sins *are* forgiven my son!"

Then they nailed Jesus' feet to the cross and raised it to an upright position. As the cross slammed down into the hole which had been dug to accommodate it, Jesus' shoulders, wrists and elbows were *all* pulled out of joint, thus fulfilling Psalms 22:14.

Alex cringed and wanted to look away. He heard a great cry of anguish from some women near the foot of the cross. He recognized this had to be Mary, the mother of Jesus, and Mary Magdalene, the woman who when caught in the act of adultery, was brought to Jesus. The men who were her accusers were demanding she be stoned according to the Law God had given to Moses. Jesus had said, "Let he among you who is without sin, cast the first stone." He had then stooped and written in the sand with His finger. He was probably writing the Ten Commandments. As Mary's accusers saw this, they had all become convicted of sin in their own hearts, and one-by-one they had dropped the stones they held in their hands and left, starting with the eldest and ending with the youngest.

Jesus had then asked her, "Where are those who accuse you?"

Mary had replied, "There *are* none Lord."

Jesus had then said, "Neither do *I* condemn you. Go and sin no more."

From that day on, Mary Magdalene had been one of Jesus' most devoted followers.

Alex understood in that moment that she had *also* looked into Jesus' eyes and had seen that *very same* love, compassion and forgiveness which he was now witnessing from those same eyes of total unconditional love.

Love indeed, is *the great* motivator and brings healing to the soul! Love indeed, covers a *multitude* of sin! For as the Scriptures say, God *IS* Love!

Alex then noticed the two thieves who had been crucified along with Jesus, one on the right side of Jesus and the other on the left. To Alex's *total amazement*, when he looked more closely at the one at Jesus' right side, he saw the man had the face of *Sanchez!*

Sanchez had a look of absolute horror, fear and extreme guilt written *very* plainly on his face. He looked at Jesus and said, "Forgive me Lord!"

Jesus replied, "Your sins *are* forgiven."

Alex then looked at the thief on Jesus' left hand, and saw the face of *another* of Sanchez's men. *This* man had a hard, bitter look on his face and turned his gaze away from Jesus. Jesus looked sorrowfully at this man.

Alex then looked back in the direction of the man on Jesus' right side and to his amazement, he recognized the face of yet *another* of Sanchez's men. This man had the same look of guilt and shame as Sanchez. He *also* asked for forgiveness and was granted his desire by Jesus.

Alex then looked three more times at the men to the right and left side, each time seeing yet *another* of Sanchez's men.

215

The two others on the right asked for and received forgiveness. Only the last remaining man on the left evidenced neither remorse nor hatred and seemed to be weighing all in the balances, as if not yet sure of his feelings.

After this, Alex noticed Roman soldiers near Jesus railing sarcastic remarks at Him and with hardness of heart they were arguing who would keep Jesus' robe, finally deciding to throw dice to decide the matter.

Many folk looked at Jesus hanging upon the cross and spat upon Him and made fun of Him. Jesus still looked with sadness upon these and *all* the others around the scene of the crucifixion. With an audible voice and eyes still full of love and compassion, He looked toward Heaven and said, "Father, forgive them, for they know not what they are doing."

He looked directly at Alex one last time with that same love in His eyes. Then He cried out, "Father, into Your Hands I commend my Spirit." With that, His head fell limp to one side, and Alex realized He had *allowed* death to *temporarily* claim His *earthly* body.

32

Remembrance and Gratitude

Alex awoke with a start and sat bolt upright. He was sweating profusely, though the night air was cold. His heart was racing, as were his thoughts.

The dream had been so vivid and so real that the hair on his neck and arms still stood straight up and chills coursed up and down his spine.

Never, ever had he experienced such a dream! He could still see those wonderful eyes of Jesus filled with such depth of love and compassion. The words of Jesus continued to echo in his heart and mind, "Father, forgive them, for they know not what they do!"

He felt that the dream had been more like a vision imparted to him supernaturally by God Himself! He felt a *very strong* sense of *purpose* had been revealed to him.

His immediate thought was that the Holy Spirit of God had allowed him to not only see and understand the intense love God had for *him*, but for *all* mankind!

He was suddenly aware that it was even *possible* that San-chez, and at least two others of his gang, had the potential of repenting of their evil deeds before facing a bullet or the hangman's noose.

Scripture then began to flow into his memory reinforcing all he had experienced in the dream. He also began to recall teachings his father had so eloquently shared about the things Jesus had suffered during His scourging and crucifixion. These were facts known not only from the things written in the Scriptures themselves, but also very well documented by secular historians, like Josephus, Eusebius, and Jerome. Alex knew that the "cat-o-nine-tails" *was* actually the type of whip used on Jesus by the Roman soldiers. The verse of prophecy in Isaiah 52:13–15, came to mind, regarding Jesus' suffering at the hands of those who beat Him: "The Lord says: My Servant will succeed! He will be given great praise and the highest honors. Many were horrified at what happened to Him. But everyone who saw Him was even more horrified because He suffered until He no loner looked human. My Servant will make nations worthy to worship Me; kings will be silent as they bow in wonder. They will see and think about things they have never seen or thought about before."

He also remembered the words of Isaiah 53:3–12, "He is despised and rejected of men; a man of sorrows, and acquainted with grief; and we hid as it were our faces from Him; He was despised and we esteemed Him not. Surely He has borne our griefs, and carried our sorrows; yet we did esteem Him stricken, smitten of God, and afflicted. But He was wounded for our transgressions. He was bruised for our iniquities; The chastisement of our peace was upon Him; and with His stripes we are healed. All we like sheep have gone astray; we have turned every one to his own way; and the Lord hath laid on Him the iniquity of us all. He was oppressed and He was afflicted, yet He opened not His mouth. He is brought as a lamb to the slaughter, and as a sheep before her shearers is dumb, so He openeth not His mouth. He was taken from prison and from judgment, and who shall declare His generation? For He was cut off out of the land of the living: for the transgression of my people was He stricken, and He made His grave with the wicked, and with the rich in His death; because He had done no violence, neither was any deceit in His mouth. Yet it pleased the Lord to bruise Him; He hath put Him to grief; when Thou shalt make His soul an offering for sin, He shall see His seed, He shall prolong His days and the pleasure of the Lord shall prosper in His hand. He shall see the travail of His soul, and be satisfied: by His knowledge shall My righteous Servant justify many; for He shall bear their iniquities. Therefore will I devide the spoil with the strong; because He hath poured out His soul unto death: and He was numbered with the transgressors; and He bare the sin of many, and made intercession for the transgressors."

Alex had memorized this entire chapter as a young boy and thus could recall it word for word. All these verses of Scripture became more real to Alex than ever before. Tears were streaming down his face. He had memorized many such passages.

He also remembered his father describing how the early Christians were persecuted for their faith in Christ. Many were fed to hungry lions in the Coliseum in Rome before cheering crowds of heathen people. They were impaled on stakes in the middle of the arena and burned alive, yet they sang praise to God even as they were tortured. They, like Christ Himself, had forgiven their torturers.

He understood now how it was possible to forgive even men like Sanchez, for Christ Himself had offered forgiveness for them if they would but repent and turn to Him in faith for forgiveness and mercy. Alex questioned himself thinking, who was *he* to deny *any* man the forgiveness which Jesus had provided at so *great* a cost.

The verse returned to his mind recorded in the gospel of Mark, 11:25, "And when ye stand praying, forgive, if ye have ought against *any* that your Father also which is in Heaven, may forgive *you your* trespasses."

Alex also realized that though his family had suffered great physical and emotional pain and injustice that the moment their spirits left their bodies they were *immediately* with the Lord in Paradise!

Alex had *never* in his wildest imagination *ever* dreamed he would be victorious over the awful darkness of hatred which had engulfed his soul because of what Sanchez and his men had done. But after this *miraculous* dream and the recollection of God's Word that had followed, he felt as though a *tremendous* weight and unbearable burden had been suddenly removed from his shoulders!

He surely didn't *feel* any great love or pity for Sanchez or his men, but that dark ominous cloud of pure *hatred* was now lifted from his soul!

He knew that the Sanchez gang still needed to be brought to justice and that he would play a major role in seeing that accomplished, yet he no longer feared he would just up and shoot the first one of them he came into contact with out of a feeling of pure *hatred* and a *strong* desire for *revenge*.

He now had confidence that he, as a law officer, would only shoot in self-defense or in defense of some innocent by-stander who might happen to get caught up in the situation.

Alex thanked God from the very *depths of his soul* for gifting him with that dream and the Word of God and all else that was brought to his remembrance upon awakening from that dream!

A few minutes later, the dawn began to break. Alex was thinking of starting a small fire to make some coffee. Then he heard a twig snap about 150 to 200 feet away. He looked at Lobo who was lying near Alex. He had his teeth bared and was looking in the direction the noise had come from. Alex also noticed that Storm was twitching his ears and appeared nervous.

Alex quickly unlashed his rain slicker from his saddle which lay near his blankets. He rumpled the slicker up loosely and placed it beneath the top blanket, making it appear that he was still underneath the blanket. He then quickly and silently grabbed his guns and retreated behind a boulder away from the direction of the noise. There, he had a view of his blankets and saddle. Lobo had followed his master, teeth still bared and hackles up.

33
The Visitor

Most men, including Alex, would normally have been very tense in a moment like this, waiting for an unknown man or men to come into view. Alex, however, was quite calm.

It wasn't because he knew the skill he possessed with his handguns, but because of the dream he had just awakened from only minutes ago. Because of the remembrance of the intense love and compassion he'd seen in the eyes of his Savior. Because he knew he'd been given that dream for a purpose and that the scriptures and other things remembered afterward had been inspired by God.

Alex wasn't consciously thinking of these things at the moment. It was an assurance in his heart at a subconscious level which now brought the calm, for Alex knew in his inner being that the dream and the scriptures had been brought to prepare him for days which yet lay ahead.

It all somehow related to how he would deal with each of the men in Sanchez's gang, and even with Sanchez himself.

No, the calm which rested upon Alex now was not a product of himself or his own abilities, rather a product of knowing in his spirit that the Lord was with him and preparing the way before him.

The man that suddenly came into view from behind a nearby tree, however, looked anything *but* calm. He looked as nervous as a deer surrounded by a pack of wolves.

Alex took note that the man had evidently taken his boots off at some point. Probably after he'd stepped on that twig, the slight snapping of which had alerted Alex in the first place. The man had only socks on his feet in an obvious attempt to resume his approach toward Alex's camp unnoticed, hopefully being as quiet as an ant crawling on cotton. Under different circumstances, Alex would certainly have been tempted to laugh out loud at this site. A partial smile did, however, manage to play at the corners of his mouth.

Alex could tell the man was alone because he wasn't glancing back over his shoulder or making any attempt at hand signals, or the like. Alex also knew that if there were other men with him, they would have made at least one mistake themselves by now, giving away *their* positions with the snap of a twig or swish of a branch.

All of these thoughts came instinctively to Alex because of the training he'd received from his Yaqui Indian friend beginning in his early childhood.

Alex didn't move a muscle, but squatted there poised on one knee, as if he were one of the numerous stones or boulders surrounding the area. He held one of his Colt revolvers in each hand.

As the man began to ease closer to where Alex's blankets lay, Alex took notice of the fact that he was tall, wiry, and that besides the gun he had in hand, he had a big Bowie knife sheathed to his left side.

So *this* was the one known as Slim. He continued to creep closer to Alex's blankets. When he was only three or four feet from them, a malicious grin appeared on his face for he evidently thought he'd successfully crept upon Alex unnoticed. He took one more silent step forward, gun pointed at the blankets, and then a puzzled look came over his face. Upon closer inspection, he'd obviously begun to recognize that the bulk beneath the blanket didn't quite appear to be the form of a human body.

Alex decided the moment was right. Being not even thirty feet from the man, he said in a commanding tone of voice, "Alright Slim, drop tha gun!"

Slim froze in place with a look of sheer terror replacing the malicious grin which had been there only a few moments ago. He was all of a sudden certain he was as good as dead. He looked to be in a state of shock and incapable at the moment, of *any* movement whatsoever.

Alex spoke up again, "Ah said drop tha gun!"

Slim evidently regained his senses enough to comply this time and dropped his gun to the ground.

Alex stood up from where he'd been crouched and then said, "Now take that Bowie knife out an' throw it on tha groun' too."

Slim complied with this order as well, carefully taking the knife from its sheaf and tossing it on the ground. He slowly raised both hands above his shoulders and cautiously turned to face Alex.

He began to stammer, "Ah . . . Ah wasn't gonna jus' shoot ya . . . jus' lyin' there like that . . . ur nothin'." He gulped hard and continued, "Ah wus jus' plannin' on kickin' ya awake . . . th . . . then Ah wus gonna make ya lay on yur belly . . . an' then Ah wus gonna jus' shoot both yor han's an' maybe stomp on 'em a bit . . . ta . . . ta break up yor fingers . . . so . . . so's ya cudden use yor guns no more . . . plea . . . please don't shoot me!"

Alex walked closer to the man, saying, "Ah ain't gonna shoot ya, least not yet anyhow." He noticed the man was now shaking like a leaf in a storm. A nervous grin now made its way onto his face, revealing his yellow teeth with the two front top ones missing, just as the wanted poster had described him.

Alex somehow believed what Slim was telling him. He also believed that he would be able to scare more information out of him if he acted mean and tough with him. That's why he'd not totally committed himself verbally as to whether or not he was determined to shoot Slim on the spot.

He therefore eyed Slim up and down with a purposely cynical and mean look in his expression. "Why should Ah believe any o' that bunch o' nonsense ya jus' told me?" he asked in a very threatening manner.

"Ah don' know . . . ma . . . marshal," Slim spouted out, glancing quickly at the badge pinned to Alex's shirt as if he had hopes that maybe Alex being a lawman, might make some difference.

"It wus Ace, what done tha killin' o' yor folks. Ah swear, Ah had nothin' ta do with it. That Ace, he's a bad one alright. Bad as they come. Worse'n any Ah've ever met an' Ah've met some real bad hombres. Even Sanchez is feared of 'em. Sanchez is only leader by name and tha fact he's got smarts. He's tha one plans tha bank robberies and tha like. He's plum bitter at mos' folk 'cause o' tha way his pa an' kin folk treated 'em. But he ain't no natural born killer like that Ace. Shor, he wuz mad up at yor pa fur 'barrassin' 'em in public an' all, an' he wanted ta beat your pa some, but he didn't mean no harm after that. Yessiree, 'twas Ace shot yor pa an' did them awful things ta ya ma an' sister. Truth is marshal, Sanchez wuz real mad 'bout what Ace done ta yor folk, but he dit'en dare try an' stop 'em."

Slim paused, scratching his head with a distant look on his face coupled with what Alex perceived to be genuine remorse. Then he continued, "Yessiree, even Raul Vargas, fas' as he is with a gun, don' dare cross Ace. Truth is, mos' folk think Vargas is tha quickes' with a gun, but Ace kin outdraw an' outshoot Raul any ole day o' tha week. That thar Ace is got tha devil himself *inside* of 'em an' a lookin' out through them eyes o' his. He's tha one ya want marshal, an' he's tha one what's pure danger ta tha core. Don't none o' us know much 'bout 'em, 'cept he bragged once o' killin' his own pa."

Slim then had a distant look as if he was right then looking into Ace's evil eyes. He physically shuddered with the thought.

After a moment, Alex said, "Tell ya what. Ya tell me all there is ta know 'bout all tha rest of 'em, an' Ah might go kind o' lighter on ya than Ah would've."

"Wul," said Slim, "twus Ace what shot ya outta tha saddle on tha trail. Came back braggin' 'bout it. We all thought ya wuz dead, 'till we heard ya won that there race in Silver City. Somebody upstairs shor mus' be lookin' out fur ya. Anyways, Ace hiself an' Vance wanted ta come a gunnin' fur ya, but Sanchez wuz able ta talk 'em outta tha idee. Don' know how he done it, but somehow or 'tuther he got 'em believin' that since he weren't able ta kill ya tha furs' time, that maybe ya was bad luck fur 'em. Me an' Sanchez had us a pow-wow, when Ace an' Vance wasn't listnen' an' 'tween us, we come up with tha idee Ah'd come try an' fin' ya an' cripple up yor han's so's ya cudden use 'em fur gun slingin' no more. Sanchez an' me already felt real bad 'bout yor folks an' all, so we dit'en want ya dead. Jus' dit'en want ya comin' gunnin' fur us is all."

Alex felt inside of him that Slim was telling the truth. He said, "Go on an' tell me tha rest o' what ya know."

"Wul," continued Slim, "Ace an' Vance Smith's always been tha ones what's done all tha killin' durin' tha holdups an' what not. The rest o' us is a bunch o' no count crooks fur shor, but we ain't like Ace an' Vance. Ah think fur shor that if either o' those two thought we was gonna quit on 'em, they'd gun us down in tha back when we wasn't a lookin' jus' outta pure meanness an' ta make shor we dit'en go a tellin' nobody where they wuz, or who they wuz an' tha like. Twurnt fur that, tha rest o' us would o' parted ways with 'em long time ago."

Slim then appeared to hang his head a bit in shame. Alex asked, "So Ah guess they'll be 'spectin' ya back soon an' yu'll be in some hot water with Ace an' Vance if ya can't come back an' tell 'em ya killed me?"

"That there's shor nuff right, marshal."

Alex pondered all of this for a few moments and then asked, "So, where are all of 'em now?"

Slim responded, "They's all camped out west o' St. Johns when Ah left 'em, an' wuz gonna head on down tha trail t'ords Page, once Ah caught back up with 'em. 'Corse, if Ah come back a sayin' Ah hatten seen ya er killed ya, Ah know Ace an' Vance would be a comin' back after ya. If Ah don' come back atall though, they'd mos' likely as not, hit tha trail t'ords Page, thinkin' ya might o' done me in an' wuz a comin' after 'em, maybe with a posse or whutever."

Alex again thought for a moment and then said, "Ah tell ya what, Slim. Let's go an' collect yor boots an' Ah'll take ya on in ta Silver City, ta tha jail there. Ah'll tell tha marshal there an' tha sheriff all o' what ya' told me. Ah'll try an' convince 'em it's all tha truth an' even come back for yor jury trial an' speak up for ya, after Ah've taken care o' tha rest of 'em. Ah give ya my word on it. Ah'll try ta make things a bit easier on ever' body 'cept Ace an' Vance. How's that soun'?"

Slim knew he didn't have a choice about going to jail, but relief flashed across his face when Alex told him he'd come to his trial and speak up for him.

Slim responded, "Don' think Ah'd likely fin' a better deal than that."

Alex then saddled Storm. He'd tied Slim's hands just in case he got a case of "spring fever" and decided to bolt like a rabbit. He had Slim lead the way back to where he'd taken off his boots and then to where he'd left his horse.

With Alex riding behind Slim, they headed toward Silver City.

34
Off to Jail

As they rode into Silver City headed toward the jail, everyone along the street stopped whatever they were doing and stared at Slim and Alex. They noticed that Slim's hands were tied and saw the forlorn look on his face. Knowing that a criminal was being brought to justice, an excited murmur could be heard traversing the crowd of people which began to gather. Some of the men and children began to follow the pair along the street toward the jail.

As they reached the building, Bob Clancy emerged from the jailhouse door to see what all of the hubbub was about. When he saw Slim, his jaw dropped open for a moment, then he turned to Alex, saying, "Mercy me! Ya done caught ya one o' Sanchez's men!"

Alex stepped out of the saddle saying, "Yep. He tried sneakin' up on me this mornin'." Alex then motioned for Slim to get off his horse.

As Alex escorted Slim inside the front door of the jail, marshal Clancy raised his voice, and speaking to the crowd of people now gathered in front of the jail, he said, with some pomp, "Alright. Tha 'citement's over folks. Go on 'bout yor business now."

With a few groans of complaint, the crowd began to disperse. Clancy followed Alex inside the building, grabbed the keys from a drawer in his desk and opened the main door which led back to the cell area. He then opened one of the cells.

Alex untied Slim's hands and Slim entered the cell, collapsing on the bunk as if exhausted. He probably was, after all he'd been through. He not only was emotionally drained, but he'd evidently been warily tracking Alex and had probably stayed awake all night until the break of dawn for sufficient light to begin his approach to Alex's campsite. All of this combined had evidently sapped all the energy out of him.

After Clancy had locked the cell and the outer door, he put the keys back in the desk drawer and sat in the chair behind his desk. Alex took a seat in one of the three remaining chairs in the office.

Clancy asked, "Want some coffee?"

Alex, remembering his last encounter with Clancy's coffee, replied, "No thanks," trying to hide a grimace.

Clancy then pushed his chair back some, propped his feet up on the desk and leaned back, saying, "So tell me how this all come 'bout, Alex."

Alex then related how he'd camped the previous night. How, after awakening, he was thinking of starting a small fire to make coffee when he'd heard a twig snap. He gave the details of watching Slim sneak up toward his blankets as he'd crouched beside a boulder, catching Slim off guard.

Alex also related Slim's account of how Ace, along with Vance, dominated the Sanchez gang and how the two of them were responsible for all the killings attributed to the gang.

When Alex had finished recounting all that Slim had told him, Clancy, looking a bit nonplused, exclaimed, "Wul Ah'll be jiggered. An' ta think ever' body always figured *Sanchez* wuz tha big bad wolf."

"Yeah," replied Alex, "jus' goes ta show ya how rumor can twis' things 'round."

Clancy got up, scratched himself, and walked over to the potbellied stove where the coffee pot was, and poured some more of the strong brew into his cup. He walked back to his desk and set his coffee on it. He hitched up his pants before sitting back down and propping his feet up on the desk again.

He scratched his chin in thought for a moment and then queried, "So watcha plan ta do now?"

"Wul," answered Alex, "Ah sent a wire ta marshal Tihlman yesterday mornin', 'fore Ah left. He was headed ta St. Johns when he left here. Guess Ah'll check with tha telegraph office ta see if he got my message an' maybe sent one back. Since Sanchez's bunch is camped out west o' town there, he probably ain't heard anythin' 'bout 'em. Ah plan on headin' on out t'ords St. Johns soon as Ah stop by the telegraph office an' then get me a bite ta eat at tha hotel Ah was stayin' at. They cook up some tolerable good grub over there. Care ta join me at tha hotel?"

"Wul," replied Clancy, "if my deputy gets himself back here ta tha office soon Ah will. Don't want tha prisoner un-guarded if he don'."

Alex didn't like the apparent air of self-import with which Clancy spoke. He said, "Alright. How long ya think 'fore yor deputy gets back?"

Clancy responded, "He's been gone better part of a hour now, makin' 'rouns'. 'Spect he'll be back right shortly. Gimme 'bout twenty minutes or so, an' if Ah ain't there by then, go on ahead an order ya somethin'. If Ah don' see ya 'fore ya leave town, Ah jus' wanna say 'good luck' on tha trail."

"Thanks, marshal," Alex responded. "Don' wanta soun' smart-alecky or nothin', but Ah got somethin' better'n luck on my side though. Tha Good Lord's always with me. Ya see my pa was a preacher an Ah've learned ta depend on God 'stead o' jus plain luck. No offense, marshal."

Clancy responded by saying, "None taken. Glad ya got that kind o' faith."

Alex could tell by the expression on Clancy's face, however, that he had no real understanding of God or faith. He said a quick prayer in his heart that he'd maybe have a chance to talk to Clancy more someday about the things of God. One thing was for certain. He'd need a lot more time than he had available right now to undertake such a task.

"Alright then, marshal," Alex responded. "If Ah don' see ya today, Ah'll buy ya dinner some other time."

"Soun's good ta me," replied Clancy.

The two then shook hands and Alex headed out the door and down the street toward the telegraph office.

As he walked, he thought about his parting words with Clancy. Alex had never really given it much thought before, but he realized now that he'd always pretty much had first impressions when he'd meet a person. Pondering on this, he knew he'd always had kind of an unconscious sense about whether or not he felt a person had a personal relationship with God. He thought of marshal Tihlman, for example. He realized he'd instinctively felt a kindred spirit with *him*.

It then dawned on him that, from the first time he'd met Tihlman, he had unconsciously and instinctively felt the man knew God on a personal basis. Alex just didn't feel that way about marshal Clancy. As Alex continued to ponder this, he came to the conclusion that the Spirit of God on the inside of *one* person recognized that same Spirit inside of *another* person, *if* the other person were a true Christian.

Alex knew it would be presumptuous to judge people, strictly and solely upon this inner feeling and that in the final analysis, only God Himself *truly* knows the heart of each individual. Yet, Alex was intrigued by this notion.

These thoughts were interrupted when he noticed a young man trotting toward him, an eager look on his face.

35
Telegraphs and Trails

The young man appeared to be about sixteen or seventeen years old and wore the visor hat and black sleeve garters of a telegraph worker. He had a piece of paper in one hand and a grin on his face.

"Marshal," he began as he reached Alex, "saw ya ridin' inta town while ago with tha outlaw ya brought in an' all. Wuz watchin' tha jail ta see when ya'd come out. This here telegraph came for ya yesterday afternoon. Was sent by that U.S. Marshal Tihlman that was here a couple days ago. It came in from St. Johns. Thought ya'd wanna see it pronto."

Alex thanked him and accepted the paper the young man held out.

"Ah 'preciate it frien," Alex said with a smile.

The young man said, "Yor welcome, marshal," and still wearing the grin, he turned and started walking back to the telegraph office.

Alex chuckled to himself about the enthusiasm of the lad. He then turned his attention to the telegraph.

It said, "Caught me just in time before I left town—*stop*—will wait here in St. Johns—*stop*—will wait a day or two—*stop*—wire me when you get this—*stop*—want to go after them with you—*stop*—praying for your safe arrival here—*stop*—marshal Tihlman—*end*."

Alex folded the paper, putting it in his hip pocket. He smiled at the thought of the last line of the message. He couldn't help but reflect on the thoughts he was having just before the young man had brought him the telegraph. He just couldn't imagine Bob Clancy mentioning prayer in a telegraph.

Alex turned and headed toward the hotel pleasured by the thought of a tasty hot meal. He would send a telegraph back to marshal Tihlman as soon as he finished eating. Right now he felt famished after last night's meager fair of hardtack and beans. He felt he could eat the south end of a northbound mule

Alex took a seat in the hotel's restaurant and was glad that it was Lily who came to take his order. She greeted him warmly and said, "I'm so glad to see you got back to town safely. I heard about you bringing an outlaw in to the jail."

They exchanged a few more words before she asked him what he wanted to eat. Alex ordered steak, black beans, potatoes and biscuits. St. Johns was about a two day ride and Alex wanted to eat a big meal to maintain his strength for the trail, and any unexpected events.

He intended to leave as soon as he sent the telegraph to marshal Tihlman. He wanted to get some distance behind him this afternoon and make an early camp to give Storm a chance to get rested up.

Bob Clancy never showed up at the hotel, which was fine with Alex. He didn't enjoy the marshal's company much anyway. He had only invited him to be polite. He simply didn't like the marshal's cocky attitude.

It wasn't long before Lily returned with his food, but Alex's stomach was already growling with anticipation. The smell of the food made him anxious to dig into the meal.

Lily evidently could see how ravenous he was and made herself scarce, except to refill his coffee and bring a glass of water. Once he had finished, however, she sat down with him for a few minutes to hear a brief account of how Alex wound up bringing the outlaw in.

Alex really liked Lily and thought she would be a perfect mate for Yang. He even teasingly mentioned this possibility to her. She blushed slightly, but readily admitted she had indeed, quickly developed deep feelings for Yang. Alex thought to himself that Yang would probably be delighted to hear of her response to his teasing.

Alex left the hotel with his hunger satisfied. He was eager to get the telegraph sent to Tihlman. Once that was accomplished, he went by one of the livery stables and purchased a small bag of oats to take on the trail for Storm. He did this because he wasn't sure how good the grazing would be where he'd make camp that afternoon.

He went to where he'd left Storm tied at a water trough. Lobo was nearby, so Alex and his two tried and true friends headed west of town on the trail to St. Johns.

Alex figured it was about one o'clock in the afternoon and that he could get in four to five hours of riding before making camp.

At the onset, the trail was bordered by elm and cottonwood trees. He passed a copper mine shortly and could see the laborers still hard at work, many of which were Membreño Indians.

He felt sympathy for these handworking indigenous natives who had been sold into slavery decades ago by the Spaniards. Now, many years later, they were no longer slaves, but many still had to eke out a meager existence in the mines. It baffled Alex how one race of people could make slaves of another and still feel they had the moral high ground. Such had been the arrogance of the Conquistadores. They had pillaged South and Central America, Mexico and parts of the U.S.

About the only redeeming factor of their invasion and conquest Alex could think of, were the many missions that had been set up where devout monks and Jesuit priests had taught the basic principles of the Christian faith and the love of God. A lifestyle seemingly not practiced very sincerely by the Conquistadores themselves.

The love of conquest, power, prestige and wealth, seemed to largely be *their* motivation. But the same could also be said of many other Europeans who came to conquer and possess the New Land, including many of the British, French and numerous others. Alex thought that the treachery wrought against the American Indians and the enslavement of blacks was a *horrible* black eye on the face of the fledgling democracy of North America. He felt it would take *many* generations to even *begin* to right some of those *severe* injustices. He understood that only the Lord could bring healing for the *deep* wounds and that the *scars* of these atrocities would probably be *indelible*.

Particularly egregious to Alex as well, was the greed of some of the cattle barons who staked their claims to hundreds of thousands of acres of land *each*. At times they fought and even *killed* lesser ranchers and homesteaders over land disputes.

He certainly didn't want to be in the shoes of these kind of folk when it came time to stand before the judgment seat of Christ, which is referenced in Romans 14:9–13. Alex was not arrogant, judgmental or self-righteous. He simply abhorred the actions of those who brought misery, suffering and poverty to others and he couldn't understand their *unfettered* and *unfathomable* selfishness.

As Alex considered these things, he wondered if he may one day be called of God to be a preacher like his father. If so, he'd certainly have a whole heap of things to say about these issues.

He figured it to be a bit after five o'clock when he came to a shallow valley area, which seemed to have fairly decent grazing for Storm and afforded obscurity from the main trail. This would make him relatively invisible to any passerby. He turned off the trail into this valley and made his camp there.

He removed Storm's saddle and curried him well. There was a stream running through the valley where he allowed Storm to drink his fill. He also allowed Storm to graze for an hour or so. He then tied the bag of oats to Storm's muzzle so he could eat some of that.

He spread out his blankets and before crawling between them, he pulled the little locket out to look at Rachel's picture, wishing again that he was with her.

As dusk turned to dark, he got into his blankets, said his prayers, and soon fell asleep.

It was almost dawn when he was awakened by a slight rustling noise.

36
Thoughts and Scriptures

It was an automatic and instinctual reflex that made Alex grab one of his guns from his holster, which was underneath the edge of his blankets. He discovered it was only a rabbit nibbling at the grass nearby.

Alex glanced at Lobo who was lying nearby, already alerted to the rabbit's presence. Lobo chased the unfortunate creature and was successful at capturing his breakfast. As for Alex, he opened a can of beans, eating that and some biscuits which Lily had wrapped in some paper for him to take on the trail.

Alex felt he was secluded enough to make a small fire with carefully chosen wood, which would produce little smoke. He made a pot of coffee to enjoy with his breakfast. He also opened a can of peaches for dessert.

When he'd put out the small fire and washed his tin plate and cup in the stream, he saddled Storm and lashed his gear in place. He knew he'd have to make good time on the trail today if he wanted to reach St. Johns before dark. Storm was well fed, watered and rested, so this didn't seem to be too daunting a task to accomplish.

Shortly after riding out of the shallow valley and getting back on the trail, Alex, without thinking about it, was humming a tune. After a few minutes, he realized it was "Amazing Grace," the same tune he had shared with Rachel, her folks and Yang on the way out of Silver City two days earlier. This made him miss Rachel even more. He once more pulled out the locket. He opened it, looking at Rachel's picture for a minute or two. When he closed it, he just held it in his hand for a while, staring off into the distance. It was the next best thing to being able to actually hold her hand in his.

In his mind's eye, he imagined riding up to the McPhersons' ranch. He could visualize Rachel opening the front gate of the yard and running excitedly out to meet him. The thoughts and the images it created in his mind brought comfort to Alex's heart.

He came to the realization of how strongly he wanted to complete his mission of apprehending the rest of the Sanchez gang in short order. He silently prayed this would happen soon and that in a matter of days, rather than weeks, he'd be on his way home to the ranch. Yes, *home! Home* at last and for good!

A feeling of nostalgia flooded over Alex, bringing with it a deep yearning to once again hold Rachel in his arms. To kiss those soft lips ever so gently. To then hold her at arm's length and gaze into those magnificent green eyes. To watch her beautiful face light up with that dazzling smile. The smile which made her countenance as radiant as the sun.

Alex already knew in his heart that on that day, or perhaps that night, he *might* just ask her that all-important question. He felt that Rachel's desire to *hear* that question was perhaps as strong as his longing to *ask* it. But *would* he make that decision?

Alex wondered to himself whether most men felt this passionate when they discovered their love for the woman of their dreams. For some reason, Alex believed his emotions exceeded most men's in this respect. Perhaps this was because his heart *and* Rachel's were *both* deeply committed to God and to seeking His *Perfect* will for their lives.

Surely, love must run deeper and have stronger root in the hearts of those who gave the Lord a place in the inner sanctum of their heart and the very core of their being. *Much* deeper than in the hearts of those who simply lived their lives with the main purpose of pleasing *themselves*, blazing their *own* trail in life with little or no thought of what *God's* will may be for them.

Alex felt it difficult to imagine living a life void of belief in and dependence upon a Supreme Being. To live a life which depended solely upon random choices and haphazard decisions just made no sense to him.

By these thoughts, Alex concluded that it was no wonder the world was home to so many miserable and unhappy people. It was thus understandable why so many were desperate enough to turn to a life of crime and debauchery. It also brought some understanding of how folk, such as the Conquistadores he had thought of yesterday, could treat their fellow men with such selfish contempt and hardness of hearts.

Pondering these things truly caused Alex to conclude that the love he and Rachel shared rose above that which was normal to the unbeliever. He was deeply thankful and felt profoundly blessed that he had made a decision at an early age, to entrust his heart and life into the Hands of his Heavenly Father.

He had heard some say that belief in an all-knowing and all-powerful God was a crutch for those who were of a weak mind. Alex knew that the *exact opposite* was true. He knew that *instead*, those who were weak of character and mind were *afraid* to believe in a Supreme Being. If they allowed themselves to *believe* in God as the *Creator*, then they would be responsible to not only *believe* His Word *is Truth*, but also to *obey* His *commandments*.

Alex didn't understand how anyone could actually deny God's existence. It was very simple and easy for *him* to believe because he couldn't argue the simple, yet profound truth in another passage of Scripture he had also memorized as a boy.

That passage was in Romans 1:20–24, "For the invisible things of Him from the creation of the world are clearly seen, being understood by the things that are made, even His eternal power and Godhead; so that they are without excuse; Because that, when they knew God, they glorified Him not as God, neither were thankful; but became vain in their imaginations, and their foolish heart was darkened. Professing themselves to be wise, they became fools. And changed the glory of the incorruptible God into an image made *like* corruptible man, and to birds, and four-footed beasts, and creeping things. Wherefore God also gave them up to uncleanness through the lusts of their own hearts, to dishonor their own bodies between themselves."

To Alex, the *truth* encompassing the *entire* universe, could not be stated more plainly than that. Yes, *creation* itself indeed proved there *had* to be a *Creator*. He had heard of a man named Darwin who proposed the theory that all forms of life had evolved from some kind of primordial slime. This man had published a book detailing his *theory* in 1859. If that were even *remotely* possible, then exactly *where* did the *slime* come from? That, to Alex, was like the proverbial question, "which came first, the chicken or the egg?" Yes, Darwin's thoughts on the matter were *exactly* what they were *called*. They were indeed, *only* a *theory!* Alex knew this man's view was absolutely preposterous.

Another passage came to Alex from Hebrews 11:3, "Through faith we understand that the worlds were framed by the Word of God, so that things which are seen were not made of things which do appear." Again Alex's thoughts returned to the first verse of that same book and chapter, "Now faith is the *substance* of things hoped for, the *evidence* of things not seen."

He knew it was a vital necessity to both know *and* understand God's written Word. That's why King David had written in Psalms 119:11, "Thy word have I hid in mine heart, that I might not sin against thee."

To Alex, even more understanding of the miraculous creation was made clear in John 1:1–5, "In the beginning was the Word, and the Word was *with* God and the Word *was* God. The same was in the beginning with God. All things were *made by Him*; and without Him *was not* anything made that *was* made. In Him was life; and the life was the light of men. And the light shineth in the darkness, and the darkness comprehended it not."

Alex understood, from his father's expository teachings of God's Word, that man was created in the *image* of God and that *even as* God has *three* parts, known as the Trinity, *so* does man. The *three* parts of man are his *body, soul,* and *spirit.* Just as man is *one* being, though having *three parts, so* is God *one* being. The *Father, Son,* and *Holy Spirit* are the equivalent of man's body, soul and spirit.

Thus were the thoughts of Alex, during a large part of the day's journey. He would first think about his relationship with Rachel, then about their mutual relationship with God. Finally, he would consider mankind's relationship *with* God, *or* the *lack* of this God-man relationship, in some folk's case.

The hours passed quickly in this manner and it seemed only a brief period of time until Alex saw St. Johns in the distance.

37

Back to Jail

As soon as Alex rode into town, he began asking around where he might find marshal Tihlman. It wasn't long before he found the marshal in a cantina having dinner.

This reminded him of the first time he'd met Tihlman and gave Alex a sense of déjà vu. He found the marshal, as was his custom, in the back of the cantina with his back to the rear wall.

Tihlman noticed Alex right away and motioned him to join him at his table. Alex was immediately aware of the aroma of refried beans, tortillas and carne asada. The two greeted one another warmly, both sharing the smile of camaraderie.

Alex soon ordered all of the food he'd smelled, plus some cebollas asadas and his usual coffee and water.

As soon as the two finished their meals, they began to discuss the situation concerning the Sanchez outfit. Alex was able to embellish much more on his capture of Slim and the details the outlaw had shared with him.

Together, they began to form a plan to catch the gang unawares, if possible. Their chief concern, of course, was the potential fight which Ace and Vance would likely put up. They also needed to act quickly to lessen the possibility that the gang would leave their campsite, west of town.

An agreement was quickly reached that they would go find the camp that night. Once they spotted the men, Alex would close in from the south of the campsite area and Tihlman would approach from the north side.

If they were successful at getting in close enough without being noticed, Alex, from the cover of darkness, would order the men to throw their weapons out into the dark and away from the campfire light. If they complied with the order, this would make it very difficult for any of the outlaws to change their minds and try to recover their guns.

At about the same time Alex issued his command, Tihlman would bark a similar order from the north side and then quickly and quietly move a short distance west. Changing his voice, he would again yell a command for the men to give up without a fight.

This tactic was designed to make it seem that there were more than two men surrounding the camp. By doing this, the lawmen could possibly gain a psychological advantage over the outlaws.

With this plan fully hatched, the two men set out in search of the outlaw camp, heading in a general westerly direction from town.

Lobo could prove very useful, alerting them with his keen sense of hearing and smell. The two lawmen had agreed in a word of prayer before leaving town. *That* would be their *greatest* tool for a successful mission.

It was a fairly well moonlit night. They had been in the saddle less than half an hour, zigzagging their course, thereby making it more likely they'd locate the campsite. Lobo suddenly stopped with an alerted posture, signaling the location of the camp by the direction of his frozen stance.

He did this long before a fire could be seen by the lawmen and before the voices of the outlaws could be heard by Alex or Tihlman.

The two men dismounted and ground tethered their horses by letting their reins hang to the ground. The horses would wait there, as if physically tied to a hitching post, Alex affectionately patted Lobo, saying softly, "Good boy, Lobo! Good boy!"

They moved on toward the camp on foot. In a few minutes, they could see the campfire nestled among some boulders. They could now hear muffled voices. They motioned to one another and Alex headed toward the south side of the camp and Tihlman toward the north side as planned.

When Alex reached the south side of the camp, he noticed there were only three men at the campfire and only three horses as well. He waited a few more minutes, to make sure Tihlman had enough time to get into position on the north side. Then, with a loud, harsh voice, he yelled, "Put yor han's in tha air, men!"

Immediately, he heard marshal Tihlman yell from the opposite side, "Yu're surrounded! Don' even think 'bout reachin' for a gun!"

The three men around the fire displayed a look of shock and quickly glanced at one another with expressions of disbelief on their faces.

Alex spoke again, "Ah said put yor han's in tha air, an Ah mean do it now!"

He had his rifle to his shoulder and aimed in the direction of the men. He lowered his aim at the feet of one of the three outlaws and squeezed off a shot. Dirt sprayed up from the point in the sand where the bullet had impacted. Immediately, the three men raised their hands skyward.

Then, from what sounded like about thirty feet to the left of where Tihlman had last yelled, a voice rang out. "Tha one o' ya that jus' now almos' los' a foot, slowly pull yor gun out an' toss it out inta tha dark!"

This voice sounded a bit lower, with a more gruff tone, and Alex knew that Tihlman had done a good job of changing both his position and his voice.

The outlaw he'd spoken to did as he was told and slowly lowered his right hand, carefully pulling his gun from its holster and throwing it into the darkness.

Alex spoke next, saying, "Alright. Tha one o' ya sittin' jus' ta tha right o' that man, it's yor turn ta toss yor gun out. Do it nice an' slow, like yor pardner did."

This second man also complied, tossing his gun out of sight.

Then Tihlman spoke again, from his original position and using his normal voice, "Okay, tha one o' ya still got his gun. Ya do tha same as yor frien's did."

This final man followed Tihlman's command, throwing his gun into the darkness. Alex noticed that the gun from the third man was a sawed-off shotgun. This was evidently Tom Coleman.

Alex then barked another order, "Now, all three o' ya, lay down on yor bellies an' put yor han's 'hind yor backs. One o' us is gonna come tie ya up all nice an' neat like."

All three outlaws followed Alex's instruction and when all were on their stomachs with their hands behind their backs, marshal Tihlman stepped out of the darkness. He took a rope off the saddle of one of the outlaws, which was on the ground nearby. He pulled a Buck knife from his pocket, cutting three lengths from the rope. As he began tying the hands of one of the outlaws, Alex queried from the darkness, "Where're yor other two compadres?"

One of the men on the ground responded, with a slight quiver in his voice, "They lef' this mornin'. They's scoutin' tha trail ta Page. They's tha ones yu'll wan'. Them two's tha bad ones."

Judging from the information the one outlaw had volunteered so quickly, Alex figured it must have been Ace and Vance that had left this morning.

Alex then stepped out of the darkness into the light of the campfire. As soon as Tihlman finished tying the hands of the last man, he and Alex helped the outlaws back into a seated position. Upon examining the faces of the outlaws close up, Alex and Tihlman were able to confirm that the three men they'd captured were Raul Vargas, Tom Coleman and, of course, Sanchez himself.

When the outlaws recognized Alex, apprehension and fear appeared on their faces.

Noticing this, Alex said, "Don' worry yorselves. Ah ain't gonna jus' up an shoot ya. Ah captured Slim couple days back, an' he tol' me 'twas Ace that killed my folk an' did all tha turrible things ta my ma an' sister."

Alex paused for a moment then added, "No. Yo're all goin' ta jail alright, but Ah ain't gonna shoot ya."

Relief came over the outlaws' faces once Alex had told them of Slim's account of what had happened that day at the Barrington ranch.

With the three men securely bound, Alex and Tihlman saddled the trio's horses and helped them into their saddles, since that would have been a very difficult feat for a man to accomplish with his hands tied behind his back. They then took the reins of the three horses and led them to where Storm and marshal Tihlman's horse waited.

Once back in St. Johns with the outlaws locked safely in separate cells, Alex told marshal Tihlman he wanted to talk to him alone. They went to a cantina which stayed open late.

After both men ordered coffee, Alex told Tihlman he felt it was important that they interrogated each prisoner separately. He explained that if each outlaw individually collaborated Slim's claim that Ace and Vance had always done the killings attributed to the gang, that it could be reasonably assumed that Slim's story was true.

Marshal Tihlman saw the wisdom in this and agreed it was a good idea. They planned to do the interrogation in the morning. Tihlman advised Alex it would be a good idea to make sure an extra deputy was on duty during the night, to make sure the outlaws weren't allowed to talk to each other. Alex said he'd go back to the jail to see that this was taken care of.

He then thanked marshal Tihlman for helping him capture the outlaws.

Tihlman said, "No thanks necessary, Alex. First o' all, it's my job, an' also, Ah certainly wouldn' o' wanted ya ta go after 'em alone. The county sheriff ain't that dependable, an' ya know tha town marshal here, wouldn' o' had jurisdiction ta help ya out." He paused reflectively, then added, "Tha sheriff's a nice 'nough fellow, but ain't top notch with a gun an' not very capable o' thinkin' on his feet in a situation like we were facin' tanight."

The two shook hands, planning to meet at nine o'clock in the morning in the hotel restaurant where Tihlman was staying. He had advised Alex that there were rooms left at that hotel, so Alex secured one after he'd gone back to the jail to request the extra guard.

It had been a very long, hectic day and Alex was very tired. After washing up and having his customary talk with the Lord, Alex lay on his bed rethinking the day's events.

He was thankful that the Lord had been faithful in helping him and Tihlman to bring in Sanchez, Vargas and Coleman alive and without incident. He was very glad none of the three had made what would have been a stupid mistake by going for their guns. He had not at all desired having to shoot one or more of these *less* evil fugitives.

Once more, Alex pulled out the locket Rachel had so lovingly given to him. As he looked at her picture, he thought of how blessed he was that God had brought him together with such a wonderful, sweet and beautiful woman. A woman that, like himself, put the Lord and His Divine Will first in her life.

Alex realized that on his own and without God making the arrangement, he could never have found a woman that was such a perfect fulfillment of what he had always dreamed of in his heart.

Alex was now able to fully admit to himself that he was head over heels in love with Rachel.

Fatigue caught up with him unexpectedly and he fell asleep with the locket still in his hand.

He woke up shortly after daybreak. Just before nine o'clock, he went down to the hotel restaurant. Marshal Tihlman was seated at a table in one corner, and of course, his back was to the wall. Alex chuckled to himself about the consistency of Tihlman's cautious practice of protecting his back. Alex wondered how long it would be before that too, became a habitual practice which he would adopt. That is, *if* he were to continue to work in law enforcement.

The two friends had a big breakfast. They discussed how they would pull each of the outlaws out one at a time to interrogate them. They had a couple extra cups of coffee as they talked.

Tihlman assured Alex that he'd arrange the details of having Sanchez, Slim, Coleman and Vargas all transported to Las Cruces, New Mexico, where they'd stand trial for the robberies and various other crimes they were wanted for. He said he'd personally handpick a good man or two to help him get them to Las Cruces.

Alex informed the marshal he was planning to go after Ace and Vance while Tihlman began taking care of transporting the others.

Tihlman voiced his concern about Alex going after them alone, but then expressed his faith that the Good Lord would give him wisdom and Divine protection for the task.

Alex agreed with the marshal's conviction about that and reminded Tihlman of how the Lord had saved him from death after he'd been ambushed by Ace and left for dead on the trail near the McPherson's ranch. He said, "Ah know ya understan' that tha same grace o' God that was with me then, will be with me as Ah pursue those two killers. Especially since Ah've better learned, tha need for prayer an' faith concerning such matters. *They're* tha ones that have plenty ta worry 'bout *now*."

Tihlman patted Alex on the shoulder and chuckled, saying, "Right ya are 'bout that my frien'."

Then they went to the jail and interrogated the prisoners one-by-one. The stories of all three were the same. At Alex's request, they had indeed been kept in separate cells, closely watched and not allowed to talk to each other during the night. This had assured they'd had no chance to palaver and agree on telling the same story.

As a result, both Alex and Tihlman were convinced they were telling the truth. That Ace and Vance were indeed the ones responsible for all the killings, which were originally assumed to be the work of most, if not all of the Sanchez gang.

They both agreed that they'd testify to this in court. Alex felt a sense of relief concerning this. He'd already believed in his heart, that Slim had told him the truth.

The circumstantial evidence brought to light by the statements of the four outlaws, including Slim, would almost certainly bring about a lighter sentence for them. At the same time, it would seal the fate of Ace and Vance.

Alex firmly believed that those two would be sentenced to hang. That is, *if* he could bring them in *alive*.

He sincerely prayed the Lord would help him to do just that. He'd never killed a man yet and didn't have any desire to do so now. He'd much rather that this would be taken care of by a judge and jury.

38
Waiting

It was still early morning when Alex rode out of town. He wanted to get to the western side of the outlaw's camp before Ace and Vance got back there and discovered the rest had been captured. He still needed the element of surprise if he were to have a chance at bringing the two back alive.

Alex figured it to be a reasonable assumption that Ace and Vance would think that if the gang was ever caught, the four other gang members would turn on them. That in a court of law they'd be singled out as the killers of the bunch. Therefore, it was pretty certain they'd rather die in a shootout than face the hangman's noose.

With these thoughts in mind, Alex allowed Storm to move at a fast canter. He followed the trail he and Tihlman, along with the three outlaws, had left on their way back to St. Johns last night.

When he reached the outlaw camp, he took advantage of the daylight to spot the exact direction in which Ace and Vance had left the camp the morning before. He followed that trail for about a mile.

At this point, he spotted an escarpment which overlooked the path of hoof prints left by the two outlaws. It had a ledge a few feet wide with a couple of boulders which would make good cover for Alex while awaiting the return of Ace and Vance. It was only about ten feet higher than the trail so it would be easy enough for Alex to jump down, when that became necessary.

Alex checked the direction of the wind and was glad to discover it was coming from a north northwesterly direction. This meant the outlaws' horses wouldn't smell him, Storm or Lobo as they approached. He thanked God for this and said an extra prayer that Storm wouldn't neigh as he smelled the outlaws' approaching horses.

He didn't have much difficulty believing for the answer to this prayer. Storm was very intelligent and seemed to possess a sense about what was going on far beyond that of the average horse. Again, Alex thought back to the night he'd captured Storm, remembering the strong feeling of destiny he'd been aware of then. It was by now quite plain the Lord had indeed sent Storm into his life.

Alex left Storm ground tethered about a hundred feet behind the escarpment. He hadn't physically tied Storm, knowing that when he needed him, he'd only have to whistle and Storm would come to him.

He allowed Lobo to accompany him as he got into position on the escarpment. He sat on a small boulder which was just behind and a bit to the right of a larger one. This larger boulder would afford him the cover he needed as he waited for the return of Ace and Vance.

Lobo sat beside his master and seemed to understand that they were awaiting the return of the men they had been trailing. Lobo too, was a blessing from the Lord. He, like Storm, seemed to possess an uncanny sense regarding events.

Alex knew Lobo would most likely be aware of the approaching outlaws long before he would. Therefore, he could relax a bit and not have to constantly strain his eyes in the direction from which the two men would approach.

He pulled the locket out and looked once more at Rachel's beautiful face. Again Alex marveled at how God had protected him, provided for all of his needs, guided him day by day and provided such a unique and wonderful woman for him to love.

He was awestruck at the depth of that love and the fact that Rachel evidently loved him with that same intensity.

He said in a low voice, "Thank Ya Father for lovin' me, watchin' over me, guidin' me, an' particularly, for providin' me with a new family an' a woman ta share a love with, that's deeper'n any love Ah ever even dreamed of. Yor such a good God an' Ah jus' can't figure why there's so many folk who seem ta jus' not understan' Yor love for 'em, an' so many who don' even seem ta believe in Ya. All they gotta do is look 'roun' 'bout at Yor creation an' know Yu're there an' that Yu're a God o' love. Ah ask Ya ta help me spen' tha rest o' my life tryin' ta help folk understan' all o' this. In Yor Son Jesus' Holy Name Ah pray. Amen!"

Alex sat there waiting and pondering many things as the sun began its descent in the sky. It was late afternoon when he noticed Lobo's head rise and the hackles on his neck go up as well.

39
Takin' 'em Down

At first, Alex couldn't see or hear anything. He waited calmly and soon caught his first glimpse of the two riders, winding their way through the trees and patches of brush and boulders.

As they drew closer, he heard one of them make some remark and the other one laugh in a rather sinister way. Although they weren't quite close enough yet to perceive the remark that had been made, they were close enough for Alex to see that it was Ace who had laughed.

Anger grew inside Alex as he thought of his sister's gleeful and lighthearted laughter, which seemed to echo now in his mind. Hers was a laughter which had been cut short by *far* too many years. Rebecca's pretty young face now came to Alex's mind, followed by the faces of his mother and father.

Now the outlaws were only about thirty feet from Alex. The anger grew red-hot in him until they were only fifteen or twenty feet from the ledge upon which he waited. His anger was very apparent in the tone of his voice, when Alex yelled, "Put yor han's in tha air, ya scoundrels!"

Those words had bellowed out of his mouth with such volume and ferocity, that the two horses the outlaws rode both reared up, hooves clawing at the air. Ace fell to the ground rolling while Vance clung to his saddle horn, trying desperately to stay on his mount.

Alex jumped to the ground below, landing as lightly and sure-footedly as a cat. He immediately had both guns drawn with lightning speed.

Vance then jumped out of his saddle, drawing his gun in the process. The Colt in Alex's right hand roared once and Vance fell to the ground, clutching his left hand in his right. His gun had been knocked several feet away from him as the bullet had passed through the back of his gun hand and then struck his gun.

Ace had, by then, gained his footing and was in the act of drawing one of his two guns.

The Colt .45 in Alex's *left* hand then roared once, hitting the exact mark Alex had aimed at. The bullet caught Ace in his right shoulder, spinning him halfway around.

Ace, ignoring the pain in his right shoulder, attempted to draw his left handgun. Lobo seemingly came out of nowhere and leapt upon Ace, knocking him to the ground. He then opened his huge jaws, enveloping Ace's throat, but he didn't bite down. He just stayed in that position with an ominous growl, daring the outlaw to move a muscle.

Indeed, Ace remained frozen in place, afraid to so much as twitch a finger.

As Lobo held Ace in that position, Alex stepped over to where Vance's gun lay on the ground. He picked it up and threw it behind a clump of bushes. He kept a wary eye on Vance while he stepped over to where Lobo had Ace pinned to the ground. He leaned down and picked up Ace's left handgun, which lay a few inches from his left hand.

Alex tossed it behind some boulders, stood up with his eyes still on Vance and retrieved Ace's remaining gun, which lay a few feet from the outlaw, and tossed it behind the same boulders. He then said to Lobo, "Alright, Lobo. Let 'em up."

Lobo obediently lossened his grip on Ace's throat and appeared reluctant as he retreated a few feet from Ace, a low growl still rumbling in his chest and throat.

Ace then carefully propped himself up on his left elbow and with a face white as a sheet queried, "Ya . . . ya shor he ain't gonna jump me again?"

"Not so long's ya don' give 'em reason ta, an' Ah don't *tell* 'em ta," replied Alex ambiguously, leaving the outlaw to wonder.

Alex then turned his attention fully toward Vance. "You!" he snapped. "Get yor sorry carcass over here an' sit yorself 'bout six feet from yor worthless pardner. If either o' ya move after that, that's *jus'* how deep *under* tha groun' yu'll wind up."

Vance, with fear on his face, did as he was told still holding his left bloody hand in his right.

Alex then spoke to his beloved dog, "Lobo," he said, much more gently than he'd spoken to the outlaws. "Watch 'em, boy."

Lobo positioned himself a few feet in front of the two men, a deep growl rumbling again in his throat. Both men looked like it was a demon instead of a dog watching them.

Alex then rounded up the outlaw's two horses, which evidently were more used to gunfire than a man yelling out almost right overhead. They had only run off a few short yards.

Once he had them in tow, he whistled to Storm who came running up a few seconds later.

Alex had an extra handkerchief he carried with him and got it out of his saddlebags. He then rummaged through the saddlebags on the outlaw's horses, finding some long handled underwear and a bottle of whiskey in one. He also checked them good for any weapons which might be in them and took the outlaw's rifles out of their scabbards, tossing them away. He cut a few lengths from one of their lariats.

He then went over to where the two sat, still fearfully watching Lobo. He ordered Vance, "Stick that wounded han' out here!"

Alex looked at the bullet wound and poured some of the whiskey on it. The blood flow was already starting to clot. He folded the handkerchief and tied it around the hand, pouring some more whiskey on it. He then took one of the lengths of lariat and tied Vance's hands behind his back.

He then told Ace to stand up and take his shirt off. Ace did so, keeping a fearful eye on Lobo, who began to growl again as Ace got to his feet.

Alex calmly said to the dog, "Good boy. Easy now."

Lobo stopped growling, but stayed very alert. It was as if, sensing his master's dislike and distrust for these men, he wanted an excuse to tear flesh with his bared fangs.

He wasn't a mean dog, but very protective of Alex and all he knew to be Alex's friends. His intelligence rivaled that of Storm. In that moment, Alex was very thankful in his heart for such a wise and faithful dog, and silently thanked God for him. This situation would have potentially been much more dangerous had Lobo not been with him. Alex might have had to mortally wound one or both men if this faithful and wise dog hadn't been there to help control and watch them. These men *definitely* would not like the prospect of a hangman's noose, and would have fought to the death had Lobo not presented them with a more imminent danger.

Alex had Ace turn around, so he could see if the bullet had exited the back of his shoulder. He saw that it had and that it hadn't made a larger hole on the rear of Ace's shoulder, than on the front, where it had entered. This was largely due to the fact that no bone had been hit, *and* because Alex didn't notch the tip of his bullets the way a lot of men did. A bullet notched on the tip would spread out upon entry, doing much more damage on its path through the flesh and leaving a hole much larger at the point of exit.

Alex would never use such a bullet, except on a large, carnivorous animal, such as a rogue, man killer bear, which would need to be stopped with the first or second shot, if possible. He felt that to use a bullet like that on a man would be cruel and unnecessary.

From the fact that there wasn't a lot of blood, Alex believed the bullet had passed through only soft flesh, not hitting an artery.

As Ace continued to face away from Alex, he poured whiskey on the long johns, soaking as much as he could with what remained in the bottle. He then told Ace to hold out his right arm. Alex then wrapped the long johns around the man's shoulder, tying them in place.

When he'd accomplished this, he tied Ace's hands behind his back and helped him into the saddle of his horse. Alex then got Vance onto the remaining horse. He tied a longer length of rope to the tail of Ace's horse and secured the other end to the saddle horn of Vance's horse. He tied the feet of each man together beneath their horses, ensuring they couldn't jump from their horses. Not that it would do them any good anyway. He just didn't want any reason for concern on the trip back to St. Johns.

He grabbed the reins of Ace's horse and mounted Storm. The sun was beginning to set as they headed toward town. By the time they got there, it was nearly dusk.

A crowd gathered, gawking at the bloody outlaws and clamoring out their desire to know what had happened. How had Alex single-handedly outdrawn and captured two of the most notorious and dangerous outlaws in the territory, not having to kill either of them? All of the townsfolk knew who the outlaws were because wanted posters with their pictures had been posted throughout the town for a couple of days now.

As he led the pair to the jail, the crowd followed closely, continuing with their questioning. Alex, not desirous of any vain glory, didn't respond either negatively or positively to the people. He merely shook his head, signaling he didn't want to talk about it. He was relieved when he finally arrived in front of the jail.

The town marshal came outside and quickly surmising the situation had his deputies start dispersing the crowd. He saw how weary and emotionally taut Alex was and advised the people they'd get all their answers tomorrow.

He and his deputies helped Alex get Ace and Vance off their horses and into separate jail cells. A doctor was sent for to further treat the men's wounds.

Once inside the jail, Alex realized he needed to give an account to the marshal what had happened. He gave a fairly detailed description of how he'd captured the outlaws. Afterward, he asked if the marshal could spare one of his deputies to assist him in transporting the outlaws to Las Cruces. He offered to pay a reasonable fee to anyone who would volunteer for the task.

The marshal recommended a couple of possible candidates for the job. Alex expressed his desire to speak with these men right away, explaining that if the doctor advised the outlaws would be fit enough for the trip tomorrow, he'd like to go ahead and prepare for the journey in the morning.

The marshal called these two deputies into the office. After speaking with both of them, Alex made an offer of the job to the one he felt appeared to be the most competent. The man seemed to consider the request with some serious thought.

Alex liked the fact that the man didn't merely jump at the opportunity to take part in the transport of two notorious outlaws to a well-known town like Las Cruces. Many would have been motivated by a prideful ambition and would have quickly jumped at the chance to partake in such an adventure, which could possibly bring them some notoriety.

A rapport was quickly established between Alex and this likeable deputy.

The doctor soon came out from inspecting the wounds Ace and Vance had sustained in the fray. It was his opinion that the outlaws were fit enough to begin the journey tomorrow, as long as they had a couple of good meals first and weren't pushed too hard for the first day or two on the trail.

So then, it was settled. Alex, the deputy and the two out-laws would hit the trail tomorrow by midmorning. The affable deputy, seeing how tired Alex was, told him, "Marshal, why don' ya go 'head an' get yorself a meal an' some sleep. Ah'll see ta it that yor horse is taken good care of at tha bes' livery in town, an' Ah'll get one o' tha storekeepers ta get us some grub an' other supplies together. We kin make tha final preparations come mornin'."

Alex responded with a cheerful comment, "Why Ah'm liken' ya better ever' minute frien'."

Alex clapped his newfound friend on the shoulder and said with a grin, "Alright. Ah'll see ya in tha mornin' then, pardner."

When Alex had partaken of a good meal at the hotel restaurant, he put his gear on the floor of the hotel room he'd rented. He pretty much just fell onto the bed. He was really tuckered out. It had been nonstop for him for days now and the intense events of the day had left him physically and emotionally drained.

As he lay there on the bed, he still managed to say a heartfelt prayer. He gave sincere thanks to the Lord for answering all his prayers and intervening in ways that Alex couldn't even have imagined before the events of the day had unfolded the way they did.

The Lord had especially used Lobo to bring the task to a successful conclusion. This thought reminded him that he'd almost forgotten to give Lobo the extra steak he had ordered specifically for his faithful dog. He looked over at Lobo, who was lying patiently on the floor next to the bed.

Alex dragged himself out of bed long enough to grab the steak, which he'd placed on the washstand when he'd first come into the hotel room. As he opened the paper, Lobo's head rose up of off the floor. His tail wagged happily and he got to his feet in eager anticipation.

Alex placed the steak on the floor and patted Lobo gently, as the faithful dog sank his teeth into the big steak. Alex thought to himself that this was a well-deserved reward for a very worthy companion.

He then sank back into bed and was soon fast asleep. He dreamed of Rachel and of riding up toward the McPherson ranch.

When he awoke early in the morning, this was the dream he remembered. It brought joy to his heart and a feeling of contentment, knowing that now the dream would not be long in becoming a reality.

Just a couple hours later, he and the deputy, whose name he'd learned was Earl, were on the trail to Las Cruces with the two outlaws in tow.

Alex had understood the need for a good man to make that trip with him. This was necessary so they could take turns during the night hours, alternately sleeping and guarding the prisoners.

They arrived in Las Cruces a few days later.

Alex had sent a wire to marshal Tihlman the morning they'd left St. Johns. He knew Tihlman would have already begun preparations to get the trial underway as quickly as possible.

Upon their arrival, they were greeted by an eager crowd of expectant onlookers. The town had been abuzz with the anticipation of their arrival for days.

Of course, marshal Tihlman wanted a full account of how Alex had captured Ace and Vance. When Alex had finished filling him in on the details, all the marshal could do was shake his head almost unable to believe what he'd just heard. The most remarkable thing to Tihlman was Alex's account of Lobo's part in the altercation.

After taking a few moments to digest the story, Tihlman *was* finally able to exclaim, "Wul, it's certainly mighty plain tha Good Lord took our prayers very seriously an' answered 'em in a truly remarkable way!"

Alex agreed wholeheartedly, saying, "Yep, He shor plum outdid Himself alright!"

The trial began within two days, with jurors handpicked for their notable honesty, forthrightness and integrity. It lasted only three days, with Alex and Tihlman being key witnesses. Marshal Martin from El Paso had also been sent for as soon as Tihlman had received the wire from Alex the morning he had left St. Johns with Ace and Vance. He gave a valuable account of the incident which had occurred in El Paso, leading to the massacre at the Barrington ranch.

There were numerous other witnesses present as well, who had also been wired concerning the upcoming trial. These were an assortment of bankers, railroad personnel and various other individuals who had been firsthand witnesses to many of the crimes perpetrated by the gang.

The real pivotal point of the trial, however, was the testimony of Sanchez, Raul Vargas, Tom Coleman and Slim. Their stories were collaborated by Alex and Tihlman's confident belief that they told the truth concerning Ace and Vance. Tihlman and Alex's belief was substantiated by the fact that they had interrogated each of the remaining four outlaws individually in St. Johns.

All of this testimony left only one conclusion which could be reasonably assumed. That was, that the only *killers* in the gang were Ace and Vance.

Once all the witnesses had spoken and been cross-examined by the defense, the jury entered their deliberations early the following morning. It took less than two hours for the jurors to return unanimous verdicts.

Sanchez, Vargas, Coleman and Slim, were all found guilty of varying degrees and counts of armed robbery. A couple of these four were also found guilty of minor physical assaults.

As for Ace and Vance, they were both found guilty of numerous murders, as well as robbery and assault charges.

Alex left the courtroom before the sentencing was announced. He already knew that Ace and Vance would hang, yet he *purposed* in his heart to *forgive* them, *a lesson written inedibly upon his heart by the dream God had blessed him with.*

As for the other four outlaws, he had fulfilled his promise to them that he'd speak up for them during their court trial.

He actually felt some sympathy for Sanchez, understanding he'd had a rough childhood. This wasn't an excuse for the outlaw, but at least Alex could understand why he'd been faced with such strong temptation to be embittered and eventually turn to a life of crime.

Alex lingered in town for a couple more hours then went to say a special farewell to his good friend, marshal Tihlman. He felt a special bond with the marshal. It was partly due to the man's character and integrity, but also because he had been a friend of his father.

He made the marshal promise to come and visit him at the McPherson ranch sometime.

Alex was anxious to get *"home"* to the ranch and to Rachel's open arms.

Unable to restrain himself even another hour, Alex packed his gear and hit the trail. He wanted to get as much distance behind him as possible, hoping to reach the McPherson ranch by late afternoon.

40
Going Home

As Alex rode through the familiar coutryside, he thought of the many things he'd have to share with Rachel, her folks and Yang.

He knew that, though they had strong faith in God, they still would have been encountering plenty of temptation to worry about his safety. He looked forward to not only seeing them again, but also being able to set their minds at ease.

Just a few days ago, Alex never imagined that he'd be able to capture the outlaws so quickly, or that he'd have been able to do so without having to mortally wound at least one of them. He had strong recognition of the fact that his Heavenly Father and the Holy Spirit had indeed watched over him and guided him every step of the way.

He also knew that this was made possible, not only by his own prayer and faith, but by that of numerous others. He remembered the promise from so many of those closest to him, that they'd be continuing in prayer for him.

Yes, it was the prayers and faith of Buck and Anna, Rachel, her folks, Yang, and even marshal Tihlman that had made the difference.

Alex knew his own prayers counted, but he seriously doubted that things would have turned out so well or that his task would have been accomplished so quickly without the unrelenting prayers of his friends and loved ones.

For this, Alex was deeply grateful. The words and tune of "Amazing Grace" came to his mind again. He first began to hum the tune and then to sing it, his heart filled with praise to God.

Truly, the Hand of the Almighty had stayed his course, strengthened his heart, guided his way and protected his life. His Heavenly Father had delivered his enemies into his hand and had set a snare for them. With *God* on his side, who *could* be against him?

As Alex rode along singing, he pulled his father's worn Bible from one of his saddlebags, opening it to the passage in Romans 8:31, which says, "What shall we then say to these things? If God be for us, who can be against us?"

He also turned to and read Psalms 27:1, 3, & 6, which says, "The Lord is my light and my salvation; whom shall I fear? Though a host should encamp against me, in this will I be confident. And now shall mine head be lifted up above mine enemies round about me: therefore will I offer in His tabernacle sacrifices of joy; I will sing, yea, I will sing praises unto the Lord."

This is exactly what Alex was doing, singing praise to God. His spirit felt free and joy filled his soul.

He was in this frame of mind when he came to the spot in the trail where he'd been shot out of the saddle. He remembered what had happened here and how the Lord had saved his life, first by Storm rearing up and then by Rachel and her father finding him there and taking him back to the ranch.

Alex indeed had plenty to be thankful for and his exuberance increased as he thought of all the miracles God had performed on his behalf.

Soon Alex was riding up the lane leading to the main McPherson ranch house. Storm caught scent of Ginger and he neighed loudly. Ginger heard him and excitedly trotted toward the part of the fence nearest to their approach. She answered Storm with a loud call of her own.

As Alex was riding toward the house, he saw the front door swing open. Rachel, closely followed by her parents, appeared on the front porch. When she recognized Alex, she let out a shriek of joy and began running toward him.

Alex put Storm into a full canter now, and when he was but a few yards from Rachel, he reined Storm to a halt, leaped from the saddle and ran to meet her.

He grabbed her in a bear hug around the waist and swung her around in a complete circle. He then let her down and the two embraced in a joyful hug.

When at last they let go of each other, Rachel's face was beaming with the most wondrous smile Alex had ever yet seen grace her countenance.

She said excitedly, "Oh, Alex, I'm so very glad you're home *safely!* Our payers have been answered!"

Alex replied jovially, "Why Missy, Ah'm right pleased ta be here my *own* self."

They then both looked at one another more seriously and Alex saw tears of joy streaming down Rachel's cheeks.

He could resist no longer. He embraced her gently and kissed her tenderly, not caring at all that her parents were watching from the porch.

By the time that rapturous kiss ended, Alex felt as if his heart was about to pound right out of his chest. He grabbed Rachel's arm in his and began to walk with her toward the house. Patrick and Allison were waiting on the porch, both rosy-cheeked and smiling broadly.

Storm followed closely behind Alex and Rachel. He pranced a bit more than normal, his head held high as he sensed the festive and joyful atmosphere.

As the pair approached the porch, Mr. and Mrs. Mac came down the steps, each giving Alex a big hug, voicing their joy that the Lord had brought him back safe and sound.

Alex asked, "Where's Yang?"

"Oh, he's out in one of the back pastures mending a weak spot in one of the fences," replied Patrick. "He'll be back within an hour or so. Boy, will he be glad to see you!"

Allison enthusiastically said, "Why don't you all have a seat on the porch and I'll go get dinner started. I'll be able to get along without you this once, Rachel." She concluded by saying, "I know, Alex, that you'll have to tell Rachel and Patrick a bit of what all happened, lad, but please save some of the telling for dinner, so I can hear it as well."

"Ah shor will, Mrs. Mac," Alex replied.

With that, Allison disappeared into the house. Rachel, Alex and Patrick sat in the rockers on the front porch.

Alex started the conversation by saying, "Ah gotta keep my promise ta Mrs. Mac, so Ah'll just say for now that all tha outlaws have been caught, taken ta Las Cruces an' already stood trial. Tha res' Ah'll save for dinner."

Patrick remarked in a surprised manner, "Why lad, it's hard to believe all of that has been done so quickly!"

Alex responded, "Wul, Mr. Mac, tha Lord's tha One caused all that ta be possible an' Ah know yor prayers had lot ta do with it."

After a while of conversing mostly about the faithfulness and goodness of the Lord, Yang came out the front door. He had a very happy and excited expression on his face.

He said, "Alex, my friend. Mrs. Mac just told me you were back. I came in the back door of course from the direction of the barn. I could hardly believe it when I heard you were here!" He gave Alex a big bear hug and then sat in one of the chairs on the porch. He continued, "Mrs. Mac told me you were saving your story 'til dinner. She also said it's about ready."

Rachel then said, "I need to at least go help her set the table." She excused herself, giving Alex's hand a tight squeeze as she left.

They were all soon seated around the dinner table and Patrick did the usual honors of saying grace. He especially thanked God for bringing Alex home safely. Once again, hearing

Patrick associate him with the word *"home"* gave Alex a very pleasant and warm feeling in his heart.

In response to everyone's eager request, Alex shared all the details of how the outlaws were apprehended, beginning with the capture of Slim. He ended with details about the trial in Las Cruces.

All were amazed at the fact that Ace and Vance were the real ringleaders of the gang, and that Sanchez and the others were mainly pawns in the whole situation.

After his account of the capture and trial of the outlaws, Alex told Yang of his conversation with Lily in Silver City. Yang was quite obviously pleased.

When dinner was finished, Alex and Rachel, as usual, did the dishes together and then retired to the front porch with their after dinner coffee.

Yang had insisted on taking Storm to the barn to unsaddle and groom him while Alex and Rachel had been doing the dishes.

Now, they sat together, alone on the porch. The moon had come out to dazzle them with its beauty. Alex felt entirely comfortable and happy.

As he and Rachel sat holding hands, Alex, with a rather mischievous grin, remarked to Rachel, "Ya know, Ah've been thinkin' 'bout goin' on over t'ords El Paso an' hirin' some vaqueros. Thought maybe they could help me ta roun' up my livestock an' herd 'em back this way. Ah've kinda had my eye on a section o' lan' close by, with a nice, grassy grazzin' pasture an' a pretty little spring a flowin' through it. Yu've seen it. We've been out there a time o' two."

"Yes," replied Rachel. "I remember it."

She spoke with the sound of half subdued expectancy and excitement in her voice, which also had a slight quiver. She squeezed Alex's hand a bit more tightly and then added a single word, which left a question lingering at the end of it, "And?" she queried.

"Wul," continued Alex, his own voice slightly quivering now, "Ah was thinkin' that jus' maybe there might be a beautiful woman 'round these parts that might wanna share tha view o' that piece o' lan' with me, an' watch those cattle an' horses a grazzin' on that land. Maybe for a long, long time."

Rachel could stand it no longer. She queried, "Alex, What *are* you trying to say?"

Alex looked deeply and lovingly into Rachel's beautiful eyes and finally got the words out, "Rachel McPherson. Will ya marry me an' spen' tha rest o' yor life with me?"

Rachel, now trembling slightly with the emotion of the moment replied, "Why Alexander Barrington! I thought you'd never get those beautiful words out of your mouth! Yes! Yes I'll marry you, my darling Alex!"

With that, Alex and Rachel's lips met in the sweetest, most breathtaking kiss either had ever experienced!